Praise for
The Guardener's Ta.

"*The Guardener's Tale* is an enchanting read. It has the mind-bending twists and turns of cutting-edge speculative fiction fitted nicely into a lyrical character-driven cautionary novel that always goes where you can't predict."

— Jonathan Maberry, author of *Ghost Road Blues*

"*The Guardener's Tale* ranks as one of my top five books of the past decade."

— Joe McKinney, author of *Quarantined*

"...Aldous Huxley's *Brave New World*, Ayn Rand's *Anthem*, Ira Levin's *This Perfect Day*, or Yevgeny Zamiatin's *We*. These novels are among the pre-eminent classics of dystopian fiction.... *The Guardener's Tale* stands firmly in the same company as the classics mentioned above.... This book certainly belongs as a great anti-authoritarian novel for the ages."

— Anders Monsen, *Prometheus*

"...the sort of story that becomes more significant and powerful in retrospect, as its various ideas seep into the reader. It is a tale of violation and redemption, truth and falsehood. For those who enjoy tales of dystopia, *The Guardener's Tale* is a must-read."

— Jennifer Crow, *Flashquake*

"*The Guardener's Tale* is a smartly crafted, thought-provoking yarn, laced with wry humor and rife with sinister mind-control tech."

— Anthony Bernstein, *Helium*

"Not since Ray Bradbury's *Fahrenheit 451* have I read such a beautifully wrought and realistic cautionary tale of what society might become without our constant vigilance of those who govern us...a visionary work from a writer of fierce conviction and a mighty talent."

— J. L. Comeau, *Creature Feature Reviews*

"The buildings, monuments, streets and homes of his City come to vivid life: slums and glittering towers alike are drawn with subtlety and intensity. Through a lattice of interwoven scenes, the complex nature of the outward world is reflected in a dance of psychology among the book's characters. As a reader I was drawn into this dance with a strength that soon felt like obsession; I could not stop reading, as I became more and more deeply enmeshed in the lives unfolding from page to page."

— Malcolm Deeley, *Gromagon Reviews*

The signed, limited edition of
The Guardener's Tale
was a Bram Stoker Award Finalist
and Prometheus Award Nominee.

THE GUARDENER'S TALE

BRUCE BOSTON

SAM'S DOT PUBLISHING

First Regular Edition
978-0-9828975-9-1

A signed, limited edition of *The Guardener's Tale*
appeared in 2007.

SAM'S DOT PUBLISHING
P.O. Box 782
Cedar Rapids, IA 52406-0782
www.samsdotpublishing.com

The Guardener's Tale

For Maggie, with love,
and thanks for the title

Thanks also to Tyree Campbell,
G. O. Clark, and Malcolm Deeley
for their encouragement

From the personal files of Sol Thatcher,
Guardener, G-21, retired

For ninety percent of our populace primary conditioning creates stable Citizens, individuals capable of expressing their individuality in socially acceptable fashion. Reconditioning accommodates nearly all of the negligent ten percent, eliminating character defects, channeling negative traits to useful social ends. Yet despite the utmost efforts of our Guardeners, the occasional aberrant remains in our midst, at times excelling in our world. Take the case of Richard Thorne, a man whose personality profiles revealed numerous character flaws yet gave no warning of the crimes of which he was capable.

Cybernetic Behavioral Analysis, known as the cyberscan, is the most sophisticated tool we have developed for dealing with deviations from the norm. The scan is capable of mapping the particulars of a life as a holographic matrix. Each life materializes as a multicolored tracery of lines, a flower figure with a narrow stalk and cone-shaped blossom. Lines leading from past to present lie within the stalk. Lines arrayed in the flower figure suggest future alternatives for the individual under examination.

At intersections in the matrix, brighter nodes of light can be detected. The circumference of a node denotes its significance as a behavioral determinant.

In cases of deviance from the norm, the flower figure begins to disintegrate. When aberrant behavior is in the past, the stalk appears shredded and irregular. When future aberrance is forecast, the spokes of the blossom branch in a wider array. The application of advanced conditioning techniques can regroup predictive lines and restore the flower configuration.

Applying the cyberscan to Richard Thorne we encountered a unique projection. His matrix lacked definition and was surrounded by an explosion of lines discontinuous and singular. The relevant nodes were indeterminate. Thorne's projection resembled a malignant cluster of weeds rather than a single flower. His deviance appeared to spring from nothing, without causal linking genetic or environmental. The man's behavior defied rational explanation.

Aberration

After the slum clearance of last spring that was to complete the transition of Delta Sector to a modern controlled environment, a small detritus of twelve blocks remained at the northwest perimeter of the new condominium complexes. This unreclaimed portion of the old city was reminiscent of the squalor that at one time blighted the entire Southside. Richard Thorne often sidetracked on his way to work to pass through this diminutive tangle of dingy streets most Citizens avoided.

Since no land had been set aside for recreation in this area, children could be found playing on the pavement. Unlicensed vendors moved along the narrow byways, hawking their wares from portable carts or packs upon their backs. Unshaved men of assorted ages consorted at random by bar fronts or corner stores. From second and third story apartment windows, women hung laundry on makeshift lines and called back and forth to one another, shouting to be heard over the noise rising from the street below.

Thorne viewed this detour in his morning commute as a trip into the past, a past that in his more imaginative moments he cast in idealized proportions. As his tall angular figure passed down the uneven streets, he saw himself occupying a different slot in history. He envisioned life as it might have been lived before the Gray Years, before the mass migrations, the carnage, and the plagues. The climate had not yet changed and the habitable surface of the Earth was far greater. It was a time when unchanneled individualism could still be considered a virtue.

The drab reality of the slum fell away to be replaced by his own creations. Renowned persons and events from the past mingled in his mind. Taking on the mantle of a life other than his own, Thorne would adventure his way through one fantasy after another. Conquering hero? Philosopher king? Wild-eyed rebel or renowned statesman? Whatever role he assumed on these fanciful journeys, he emerged victorious and revered, leaving his mark upon history.

Then Thorne would find himself at work.

The concrete walls of his office would close about him, followed by the walls of his individual cubicle. His desk and terminal would appear before him. The murmur of subdued conversations and the white noise of electronic cerebration would intrude upon his thoughts. The posters along the walls, their cycling truisms in primary colors and block letters, would remind him:

TEAM SPIRIT MEANS TEAMWORK

THE STATE OF THE CITY IS THE CITY STATE

TOMORROW...THE FUTURE PERFECT

His sense of reality restored, he would take up his appointed task of processing statistics for Delta Standards Control.

Yet there were other times when Richard Thorne chose to enter this unreclaimed portion of the old city. Unknown to his chosenmate, Diana Logan, he would venture forth at night to seek a woman of the streets—for illegal sexual commerce still flourished in this slum remnant and unlicensed prostitutes could be found plying their trade on the streets and in the shabby local bars.

During one of these nighttime wanderings Thorne encountered Josie, whom afterward—after the affair had run its course and the walls of his world had toppled down about him like the walls of a card house—he came to think of as his liberator.

Like many modern chosenmates, Richard and Diana had set aside Tuesday as their night of personal freedom. Given this trend among the mated population, Tuesday has emerged as one of the gayest evenings in the night life of the City, from Alpha Sector to Omega.

As the sun falls and darkness descends, the entertainment districts blossom with light. Soon the glideways are flooded with laughing and talking Citizens. Music fills the streets. Here or there a Guardener in the forest green robes of their profession moves among the more brilliantly attired throngs, restoring order if the need should arise. Trouble is rare. There is so much to do, the entertainments so varied, the feeling of joy so pervasive, dissatisfactions evaporate before they become manifest.

Diana's behavior on Tuesday nights was normal for a woman her age, twenty-nine, occupation, Architect G-15, and social status. She would retreat to the bathroom of their conapt to don her disguise, a dermask that erased her freckles and broadened her features, a short dark blonde wig to conceal her auburn hair. She emerged a different woman. Except for her long legs and the wide full breasts he knew so well, Richard Thorne would never have recognized her as his chosenmate. Diana could now encounter and couple with equally anonymous men without fear of future entanglements.

A few of Diana's more progressive girlfriends had recently shed such disguises, flaunting their identities as a new kind of freedom. Diana was not about to take such chances. She was satisfied with her mating. Their union was City State approved and their careers were progressing steadily. Their eugenic compatibility ranked in the ninetieth percentile, which meant they were eligible for offspring if they chose to have them. Their current conapt, a contemporary two-room with attached microkitchen, was more than adequate. Barring unforeseen demographic shifts, they would soon move to a higher grade complex. Their new home would be more spacious and they would be allowed a wider range of expression in selecting its decor. Whatever adventures befell Diana on Tuesday evening, she planned to leave them well behind by the next morning.

For Richard the freedom of Tuesday posed a different problem. Though slight of build he was not an unattractive man. His blue eyes, in contrast to his dark hair, were his most striking feature. Diana, in the days of their courtship, had once referred to them as "ocean eyes." An aquiline nose and full lips gave his face a distinctive sensitivity many women found appealing. Of course the dermask mitigated all but the eyes and hair, and these were not enough to counter Thorne's other deficiencies.

He lacked self-confidence and social skills. His mind was prone to wander into fantasy. It was not enough to find a woman, spend a few hours with her sharing the City's many entertainments, and couple. For Thorne, the right words had to be spoken, the right moves made. Their encounter needed to involve an idealized romantic scenario he had created in his mind.

The dermask, nearly perfect in its replication of the human face, integral to the anonymity of Tuesday nights, posed another obstacle. Thorne did not mind wearing the mask himself, but being with a woman who wore one prompted endless speculation on his part. From a distance in a crowded street or dancing arena, he would see a face and catch a glance that caused him to respond.

As he drew nearer the illusion held.

Then the encounter would begin and he couldn't help trying to penetrate the disguise of his prospective partner.

What face lay hidden behind this other smiling face?

Was it plainer or more beautiful, the flesh fairer or coarser than the mask that concealed it?

Did he know this woman in everyday life?

The result was an encounter that aborted abruptly, often with an embarrassing retreat on Thorne's part. Or more humiliating, another man would enter the scene, a male with none of the debilitating preoccupations of our subject. Thorne would be left behind, staring into his drink and wondering what to do next.

The freedom of Tuesday provided more frustration for Thorne than satisfaction. Diana's adventures, which she sometimes detailed after returning home, didn't help. Once it became clear a problem existed, being modern chosen-mates, there came a time when Richard and Diana discussed the problem openly and reached the logical conclusion.

In the second year of his mating Richard Thorne began visiting the Halls of Expression. If he had been another man—if lack of confidence, over sensitivity, an unnatural craving for the past, had been his only abnormalities—our story would be over. For in the Halls of Expression every Citizen is offered the opportunity to act out his or her most elaborate fantasies. Here Thorne could find sexual satisfaction and play his games of history, however falsely envisioned. He could lay claim, at least for a time, to the romanticism he so desired.

Tuesday night in early winter. Like any Tuesday night the City was coming to life. That morning a cold front and its associated storm had swept in from the northeast. The Weathermen had diverted the greater part of its force over the Dead Lands. Temperature was above the sixty-five degree minimum set by Standards Control. Barometric pressure was rising and only a thin mist descended through the night air.

Thorne pulled the dermask from his face and brushed back a trailing lock of hair. The drifting droplets felt cool and pleasant on his cheeks. He wore a dark blue slimsuit belted at the waist, a patterned scarf tied loosely about his collar.

He had left the apartment while Diana was still making her preparations for the evening. In sudden apprehension, Thorne imagined she might be watching. Pausing in midstride, glancing over his shoulder and upward, he surveyed the facade of their condominium complex. His vision circled aimlessly, lost amid the multiplicity of windows, uncertain which were theirs.

No matter, all were either dark or presented blank unmoving curtains of light. Thorne wadded the dermask and stuffed it into his pocket.

If Thorne had been attending the Halls of Expression he would have left his mask in place until he passed through the queues and entered his chamber for the evening. Although we strive to live in the present, stigmas of the past survive. Thorne was well aware there was no reason to make his attendance at the Halls common knowledge and a subject for discussion among friends and fellow workers.

15

Tonight, he had a different destination in mind. At the end of the block he turned left, his steps quickening as he moved in the direction of the slum remnant.

Over the past several months his Tuesday night wanderings often carried him to this portion of the City where the unregistered of Delta Sector resided. There he would spend the evening drinking and watching, pretending his life was a different one. Although it was not illegal for Thorne to visit the slum, it ran contrary to the spirit of the code by which all Professionals have sworn to live. With eyes toward the Future Perfect rather than an imperfect past.

Thorne had gone further than mere visits and observation. More than once he'd broken the law by coupling with an unregistered prostitute, none of them exceptional, none as satisfying as the Courtesans of the Halls. Though he was not the only Citizen to be guilty of such a transgression, the fact that he returned and persisted in his offenses provides the first indication his case was one of aberrance.

The transition to the slum was abrupt.

One moment Thorne was walking in a planned and modern environment. On all sides immaculate buildings reached toward the sky, buildings decoratively landscaped with artificial foliage, artistically illuminated by shifting patterns of light. Diana was proud she had played a part in helping to design these complexes. Next moment, in the crossing of a minor thoroughfare, the slum was upon him. Within his imagination, Thorne peeled back the centuries until he could pretend he was walking down a street of the past.

Here the structures were hulking and irregular, with no concept of a unified whole. The impression of entering a different world was enhanced by the insufficient lighting, archaic globe street lamps, many of them broken and unlit. Those still burning were wreathed by the falling mist in halos of light. Dampness darkened the decaying pavements and buildings. Thin streams of water glistened in the gutters, and here or there ancient neon signs, garish and flickering, burned against the night the name of a bar, a restaurant, or the simple command: "EAT."

In terms of vision, the tableau was dream-like, though most Citizens would have considered it nightmarish. For here lay an inheritance from a past we have left behind, a history of disorder and injustice where at heart each individual could be no more than an adversary, both to others and to society.

Couple the other perceptions to vision and any sense of a dream was lost in a reality too sordid to deny. Beneath Thorne's feet the sidewalk was stained and littered. Voices and the squealing of infants leaked from street-side apartments. The light rain, too light to cleanse the air, had raised the odors of the street. The smells of garbage, mildew, cooking food, and a host of less identifiable scents mingled, assaulting his nostrils, spreading to his taste buds and forcing him to grimace in disgust.

The streets were for the most part deserted, but at the end of one block a lone woman stood beneath the shelter of an awning. She wore heels and a cloth coat that fell to her knees. Her legs were thick and without stockings. As Thorne approached, she turned toward him. The falling lamplight revealed her face: hatchet mean, the features craggy yet fleshy, the eyes unfeeling yet inviting. Thorne was drawn by that invitation and unnerved by any thought of accepting it. He didn't understand such impulses within himself. Shuddering inwardly, he moved swiftly past.

Now that he was deep within the slum, many of the buildings he passed were abandoned. On one dark facade, its broken windows crudely boarded over, row upon row of identical City State fliers were plastered, encouraging the unregistered to apply for Citizen status. The denizens of the slum had defaced these fliers with their own slogans, and in turn defaced their own slogans once again, creating a collage of sense overcome by nonsense, reason obliterated by emotion. Personal declarations? Terrorist propaganda? Scatological antisocial outbursts? Who could say? Unreadable or unintelligible, the inscriptions upon the wall seemed to be scrawled in as many different tongues as the number of disturbed individuals who had left them there.

In one small square that had escaped the barrage of fliers and the onslaught of overlapping graffiti, someone had used the accumulated grime of the surface as background and a sharp instrument as a writing tool to inscribe a stanza of doggerel that *was* legible. Thorne paused to read it.

Are the Dead Lands really dead?
Is the City slicker?
When its streets are bathed in red,
Which will make you sicker?

Although the inscription took the form of a childhood nursery rhyme, he knew it was a reference to the Riots of '37, when the streets of many slums if not literally bathed in blood had been thoroughly stained by it. It also incorporated a common slum dweller fantasy, that there were lands beyond the boundaries of the City State that were habitable. In its most elaborate incarnation this fantasy embodied the myth of a fabled nirvana, a land of milk and honey where food grew for the picking and all lived in pastoral harmony.

In a side street, little more than an alley, Thorne found the bar he frequented most often. The establishment was nameless, its only designation an incomplete blue neon proclaiming the word "AVERN"—the missing "T" a burnt-out black tubing, invisible against the night except on close examination. Thorne noticed that in the gutter nearby someone had vomited. He pushed open the heavy door and entered.

Diana's world pulsed with light and color, pleasure and beauty. The stimulant she had taken coursed through her veins. Her favorite girlfriend, Heather, was by her side, their arms intertwined, their hips touching intermittently as the glideway hummed beneath their feet and carried them amid the crowds down the Avenue of the Moon. Bright banners and colored lanterns swayed above their heads. From the theaters and dancing arenas strains of music billowed forth to swirl about them as if the night air had become not only their medium but their very substance.

The rain had stopped and the laughing voices and smiling faces, the human warmth on every side, the drug they had taken, all combined to make the evening seem more lively and special than it already was.

They were playing a game they had played before. Although Diana's figure was fuller than Heather's, both women stood roughly the same height. They had purposely selected their disguises as likenesses of one another. Diana's dark blonde wig and the broad cheeks of her dermask were Heather's own. The trailing auburn strands of Heather's wig and the dusting of freckles upon her dermask were Diana's. Each was one, and each was the other. To complete this sharing of identities, they had swapped blouses and earrings at Heather's apartment before leaving.

Shining marquees shifted past them. They commented on films and shows they had already seen, speculated on others or related what they had heard about them. Diana wanted to see the dancers at The Paladin. Heather was more interested in riding to the end of the Avenue, to the park beyond Severin's Fountain, where the Free City Circus was performing in Founder's Square. Diana didn't argue. She was feeling too perfect for that. She would let the tide of the evening carry her wherever it would.

The two women dismounted at the end of the glideway and saw Severin's Fountain before them. As always, they paused for a moment to stand in awe. This week the outer sides of its pool were lined with bright mosaics depicting the birth of the City State in brilliant primary colors. Diana and Heather circled the fountain slowly until they had viewed all four panels.

First a desolate landscape, with broken cities in the distance and no green showing, the legacy left by the last cycle of wars. In the second panel the landscape changed. Individual cities had begun to rise again and the land about them was dotted with fertile sanctuaries of green. Men and women moved across the plain. In the foreground, others gathered about a table where diagrams were spread. Here were the growth of technology and the great reconstruction drives. In the third scene the cities were larger and flamed with light, the plain increasingly dotted with fertile havens. Men, women and children of every race moved through gardens and past fountains arm in arm, representing the collapse of national boundaries.

The last panel was much the same as the third, except the colors were brighter and the individual cities had fused into one great City, surrounded by a band of green. The positive freedoms of life within the City State were symbolically depicted. A cornucopia in the sky over the plain: the freedom from want. The rising sun beside a daylight moon: the freedom for all to share. And the diverse paths branching through the woods representing the third freedom, the freedom of choice, positive choice the likes of which no civilization of the past had ever known.

More impressive than the mosaics was the fountain itself. Most critics view it as Severin's finest achievement. Sixty meters in height, its water running from one tier to another in patterns too complex for the eye to follow or the mind to grasp, flowing in a multitude of streams, looping and diving and at times appearing to rise toward the sky above rather than falling to the earth below.

As the two women passed around the perimeter of the fountain a spray of random droplets fell against their bare arms. They squealed from the cold and the delight and sprinted into the park beyond. High arc lights made the scene nearly daylight bright.

Trees and grass everywhere. Citizens in groups, couples, and singles, walking freely, playing upon the lawns. Heather and Diana strolled, savoring the natural beauty, watching the other men and women as others watched them, flirting with their eyes and the movements of their bodies. Diana went so far as to brazenly offer her glance to a passing Guardener. He hurried on, seemingly oblivious to her overture.

A basement bar, low-ceilinged and square. Although the hour was still early it was filled with denizens of the slum. Some men, those deemed incapable of employment and supported by the State, spent the entire day here. Having joined in their card games, Richard Thorne knew a few by sight, and they no doubt remembered him. Yet no greetings were exchanged. His clothes, his manner, his speech—all revealed he was from a world these men envied and despised. He could never become a true participant here, only an observer and pretender. An outsider. At the same time his continued visits to the slum increasingly defined him as an outsider in the world where he did belong.

The women present were barmaids or whores, some fulfilling both functions. This was another element out of the past, when establishments such as this abounded in any large city and catered to the leisure occupations of solitary males.

Near the end of the room several men were grouped about a diminutive pool table, its green felt so aged that is was now gray in the overhanging light. A number of card games were in progress and at one table a rowdy game of dice, with much shouting and cursing. Thorne ordered a beer at the bar and retreated to a corner booth to sit by himself.

He sipped from the icy stein, setting it down between swallows. Across the room a passing waitress caught his eye and smiled. He pretended not to notice and slid farther into the shadow of the booth.

He had paid to go upstairs and couple with this woman several weeks earlier. She was younger and more attractive than the streetwalker he had passed, but unlike the Courtesans of the halls she had never bothered to learn the first thing about sexual technique. Thorne managed to complete the act, but the entire episode proved so unsatisfying it had forced him to examine his reasons for coming to the slum at all.

The Halls of Expression seemed to offer all he could desire, the rendering of nearly any illusion he could imagine and describe. For Thorne's aberrant consciousness, this very perfection proved a flaw. In the Halls he could only play at adventure. Except for rare moments of complete involvement in illusion, any sense of real adventure was lacking. If the quality of life and pleasure in the slum was vastly inferior, at the same time there existed uncertainty, risk and perhaps danger. Thorne's disturbed consciousness translated this as genuine experience.

He spun the half-empty beer stein in the moisture of its condensation. Although he had been visiting the slum for several months, except for an overwhelming sense of guilt, his life had not changed. Real adventure continued to elude him. All he found here were prostitutes, petty gambling, the cheap bars and restaurants, the dirty streets, and all about him, the empty lives of an expiring subculture. Even the beer tasted stale and flat once it lost the chill that masked its inferiority.

Thorne downed the remainder. To avoid the waitress, he rose to go to the bar for another.

No one looked at him.

Not even the bartender as he took Thorne's credits and refilled the stein.

Beneath a broad tree, sitting with his back against a bole of its trunk in the natural chair formed by earth and bark, a man was playing a flute. Diana and Heather came closer to listen. He could not play very well, but the tone of the instrument was so beautiful that this alone made his song appealing. The man's dermask was darkly bearded, his wig full and luxuriant, a raven cape flowing across his shoulders. From neck to ankles he wore a silver slimsuit that sparkled like water with each of his movements. After a moment he ceased to play and looked up. His eyes were also dark, the pupils so dilated it was hard to judge the color of the iris.

"Are you flying?" he asked.

"Borealis." Heather provided the name of the drug she and Diana had taken.

"I'm Teatro," He told them. He rolled the "r" as he spoke the name. It was a more interesting fabrication than most.

"I'm Heather," Diana said, "and this is Diana."

Heather giggled softly as she freed herself from Diana's arm.

Teatro stood up. "A pleasure to meet you, ladies." He was a tall, barrel-chested man. Diana noticed a diamond-studded mating band on his wrist. Her own simple gold band was shoddy by comparison.

"It is a lovely night," Teatro went on. He gave a few quick trills upon the flute. "And so are you. The both of you!"

He did a small dance about the two women, playing runs upon the instrument when he wasn't speaking.

"There are two of you...but only one of me."

He was behind them now, and the two women turned their heads to look at him and laugh.

"But I will tell you a secret!" Skipping away and then back. "I have a friend, who in my modest opinion, is a lovely person, too."

He stood before them once again and bowed deeply, sweeping the flute in front of him. "Would you like to go to the circus, ladies? Would you like to meet my friend?"

"Looks like we've already found a clown," Heather whispered to Diana.

"You can take his friend," Diana whispered back. "I don't mind this one. I like him."

Soon the three of them were walking arm in arm down the length of the park. Far ahead, in Founder's Square, they could see the lights of the circus flashing through the trees. The Borealis had yet to peak and Diana could sense its accelerating rise like a series of star bursts showering within. Her arms. Her thighs. Her shoulders. She felt that soon her entire body would be capable of orgasm.

Heather's fingers were twirling through the curls of Teatro's dark wig. The silver flute was sticking out of his back pocket and Diana was running one hand up and down its smooth metal surface, feeling the bumps and depressions. It's all so easy, she thought, so natural. Why does Richard have so much trouble?

Then she remembered this was Tuesday night, her night of personal freedom. She shouldn't be thinking about her chosenmate.

A few hours and many beers.

The drunkenness was rising in him like a tepid wave falling upon his conscious over and again, each time reaching farther up the shore. The bar was thoroughly crowded and the attention of its patrons now centered on the dice game. For these slum dwellers the stakes were high. Piles of crumpled bills littered the table.

The drinking had stopped here some time ago. The press of onlookers stood too thick and solid for the serving of drinks. Thorne had left his booth to stand and watch. A number of men were awaiting their turn at the action, grabbing empty chairs as the losers left the ring of players. Three men—three winners—had remained throughout the entire contest.

Thorne's attention was drawn to one of these, a short dark man, his rugged face aging and lined, small eyes tucked deep beneath his brow. His cheeks and chin were unshaven—there was no beard in progress, only slovenliness. His apparel was colorless, anonymous, the clothes of a common laborer or a man who wore clothes because they were functional, the alternative to going naked.

Intuition tugged at the back of Thorne's mind, telling him that he should recognize this man. There was something about his gestures, the way he turned his head, his voice, lower and softer in the excitement of the game than the rough countenance would indicate.

Through the cloud of his drunkenness, Thorne searched through other nights in the slum, attempting to place this short dark figure and attach some significance to it. He tried to remember the holocasts of the past several months, thinking he'd come upon a criminal wanted by the City State. Could it be he was thinking of someone else who resembled this man? Not a soul he could remember knowing looked anything like this.

The dice game was an ancient one, evolved during the Gray Years from a similar and still more ancient antecedent. Two dice were rolled, each a six-sided cube embossed with colored circles. Red for carnage. Black for plague. Brown for the barren Dead Lands. Blue for water. Green for foliage. Silver for the moon. The object was to roll and repeat certain combinations while avoiding others. It was a simple game for unsophisticated minds in which credits could shift rapidly from hand to hand with chance and a minimal degree of skill as the prime movers.

"Luna...luna...lu-na-tic me," the dark man called out, raising the dice close by his mouth, puffing upon them for luck before he rolled.

The tiny plastic cubes flew through the air and bounced crookedly across the worn table. Two silver disks appeared and a bark of glee exploded from the man's throat. His hands moved forward, raking in bills from all around him.

Thorne stared at the backs of those hands as they entered the cone of light the overhead lamp threw upon the table. They were smooth and pale. Too smooth and pale. Neither the hands nor the voice matched the man's face.

One loser rose, cursing openly, pushing his way through the crowd. Several men jostled for the empty chair. Angry words were exchanged. The tension of the game had spread to the circle of watchers. It looked as if a fight could erupt. Thorne began to back away. Then one man with more bravado than the rest settled his claim on the vacant spot.

Thorne moved in closer as the circle shifted. He was standing next to the table, directly opposite the man he had been watching. The fellow glanced up from his ragged pile of winnings and their eyes met. For a second the man's expression glazed over, numb and sightless. The next second, although the faced remained impassive, the fright in his eyes silently screamed at Thorne.

Blind unreasoning fright!

Thorne recoiled from that glance in confusion. The puzzle he had been playing with was real, not another fantasy. This strange man knew him. And for some incomprehensible reason feared him.

Ignoring the protests of the other players, the short dark man scraped his winnings together, stuffing bills and coins into his pockets wherever they would fit, some spilling to the floor below. The fear had radiated from his eyes. He wouldn't look at Thorne again. His jaw trembled. His pale hands shook as he abandoned his chair.

The jostling for this second empty seat began. Several men fell to their knees, scrabbling after the loose coins and bills that had fallen to the floor. Rather than leaving the circle, the dark man began edging his way along its inner lip toward Thorne.

Thorne realized something different was happening to him at last, a possible adventure looming before him. Only unlike his dreams where his actions were always decisive, his role certain, he didn't have the slightest idea what any of this was about.

Suddenly he wanted to flee, to make himself invisible. The bodies about him were packed too tightly for anything except a slow, steady retreat. Before he could begin, the man was upon him, tugging at the sleeve of his slimsuit. The crowd remained absorbed in the larger drama of the game. Dice were being rolled again.

Thorne turned and tried to pull away.

"No...not yet, don't go...Thatcher, Sol Thatcher, I knew about him...but never you." The man's breath was hot and thick with drink. His words a tumbling melee half lost in the noise of the room. "Don't go. I can explain...everything...make you see...not what you think at all. You...a Guardener...I never suspected...I knew about Thatcher...."

Even once the broken phrases began to cohere into sentences, Thorne could attach no sensible meaning to them.

Thatcher? There was a man in his office by that name. But what did Thatcher have to do with any of this? And the thought of himself as a Guardener! That was the crowning absurdity of the situation.

Thorne's confusion thickened. Clear thought abandoned him and fear like a blast of wind, as blind and irrational as that he had just witnessed, rose through his own being. His imaginary adventures had never involved uncertainty or real danger. He started to force his way back through the crowd.

The dark man would not let go. He clung to Thorne's sleeve, pawed at his shoulder. Though his voice was steadier, the wretched pleading ran on.

"You'll understand. I know you will. I've watched. You're different from the others. Come, come have a drink with me. I can explain everything to you."

The two locked figures emerged as one onto the empty floor beyond the ring of observers. They stumbled over one another's feet in a grotesque dance of pull and tug. It was ludicrous and terrifying and all happening so fast Thorne didn't know whether to laugh or cry. The ocean of beer within his belly rocked in a sickening wave.

"Just one drink! Tell me, what harm can that do?"

The man was small but totally determined. His grip upon Thorne's sleeve would not relax. There was no way he could free himself short of bodily combat. Although he stood a head above his unwanted companion, he had never been a very physical man.

Here was the would-be hero who dreamed of facing fire and storm and returning unscathed while noble ladies tossed garlands of adoration. His hands were sweating. His throat was dry, the blood pulse pounding on his inner ear. Reality had chosen a different coat for him to wear, a truer fit. Without protest, he allowed himself to be led to a booth at the rear of the tavern.

This corner of the room was deserted and poorly lit. The dark man, instead of taking the bench opposite Thorne, wedged in beside him so as to prevent any attempt at escape. At this range the man's face, with its incipient beard, looked so unsavory and dirt-lined that Thorne edged back farther until he was pressed against the wall.

He resigned himself to whatever was about to transpire, though he was by no means looking forward to it. Now that they were both seated his adversary suddenly seemed as dumbstruck as he was. The oddly-shaped head turned this way and that. The mouth grinned painfully. The pale hands tangled and fidgeted with one another.

"A beer...yes, a beer," he said at last.

The man looked around for a barmaid but none was in sight.

Thorne at last found his voice. "I don't know...who you are," he croaked, startling himself with the sudden declaration.

The dark man's motion clicked to a halt. His head turned to face Thorne, jaw dropping, eyes widening. "You haven't been following me? You haven't been spying on me?"

Thorne shook his head vigorously in mute denial, praying that whatever his curiosity had gotten him into, salvation was at hand.

"And you're not a Guardener?"

"No. Never." This time he recognized the words as his own.

A lengthy pause.

Then a bark of glee broke from the small man's throat. Laughter followed. His body rocked back and forth in the narrow confines of the booth. Tears streamed from the corners of his eyes. "It's amazing...truly amazing..." He slapped Thorne upon the knee, pummeled his shoulder. "...amazing the tricks the mind can play on you...truly amazing!"

With one hand the dark man reached up to his hairline and clawed down. The contours of a carefully applied dermask crumpled as he pulled it away from his countenance. "I probably shouldn't have done that," he said, "except I'm a little drunk."

It took several seconds for Thorne to recognize the face before him. Pale, round and innocuous, guileless. It belonged to one of the programmers who worked in his office, several cubicles from his own. A quiet man of whom he'd never taken much notice.

Thorne couldn't remember the man's first name. But his last name was DeLyon.

They were brothers in guilt, brothers in deceit. Circumstances decreed their friendship would be sealed before it began.

They talked, hesitantly at first, awkwardly, after finally getting a barmaid—and a pitcher of beer—with their silences reigning rather than their words. Gradually they opened up to one another. DeLyon the more readily. Then Thorne, surprising himself in his drunkenness by voicing his frustrations and fantasies in ways he never had with Diana.

They became brother confessors, too. It was their similarities they dwelt upon rather than their differences. In truth, the two were nothing alike at all. Only in the initial manifestations of their aberrance did they resemble one another.

As fellow workers put it, Daniel DeLyon was "a strange bird." Forty years old, unmated, still living with his invalid mother, his individuality found its expression in a passion for games, all manner of games, of skill or chance, as participant or spectator. While at work the near-permanent fixture of a white speaker wire ran from his ear to his shirt pocket so he could get the latest fireball or combat scores, or follow some sporting event still in progress. Many who knew him casually thought he was partially deaf, and DeLyon, his smooth oval face impassive, cultivated this misimpression when he didn't feel like speaking.

We have already portrayed the chaos of Thorne's projection: the flower indiscernible, the lines broken and scattered, springing from nothingness and ending in a like vacuum. DeLyon's did not look anything like this. The projection of his psyche was solid and self-contained. Its sole abnormality lay in the fact that from the onset of adolescence it was dual. Two disparate stalks. Two narrow flowers. One growing straight and well within the boundaries of normal behavior. One branching sharply at the age of twelve, the onset of puberty, but then bending once more to define its own straightness and stability, parallel to its twin but mutually exclusive. Daniel DeLyon was a classic example of a dual personality.

He had been born unregistered—his father a slum dweller who had abandoned his family, his invalid mother and his sister still unregistered—and grown up in a slum resembling the one he now frequented. He had been blessed with a keen intelligence and an extraordinary precision of mind, a memory nearly photographic in its accuracy, the latter manifesting itself as a meticulous attention to detail, often in the form of a constant need to correct others regarding insignificant errors.

As a child DeLyon had received no primary conditioning. Yet when he applied for Citizen status at the age of sixteen his personality profiles showed him to be solidly within the normal range. This was his primary persona manifesting itself. Once he was a Citizen, his precision and intelligence carried him through a tertiary degree and eventually to his position as a systems programmer in the Delta Sector.

A former Lector once characterized him: "An adequate student, though never brilliant. A hard worker. A solid fellow, but rather dull." This was the same personality that managed to deceive our tests. This was the man who put in day after day beside other workers who found him only "a bit strange."

During his free hours the second Daniel DeLyon emerged, a man with all the uncivilized traits he had repressed so carefully in order to acquire a registered status. Selfish, petty, compulsive, prone to extreme paranoias. Richard Thorne, in his naiveté and pursuit of something different, was fascinated and taken in completely.

The bar closed past midnight, expelling them onto the dank streets. They decided to meet the next day for lunch, and made a tentative agreement to spend the following Tuesday evening together. Before they parted company at the edge of the slum, DeLyon stopped him.

"There's one thing I don't understand. Why aren't you wearing a dermask?" DeLyon had reapplied his, albeit a bit crookedly, before leaving the bar. "If the Guardeners find out you've been coming here, they'll interrogate you for sure. You know what that means!" His eyes echoed their earlier fright. "If you don't come up with the right answers they can put you on a scanner. They'll empty out your mind. Wash it clean. Every thought. Every action. Every stitch of it! And then they'll put it back together the way they think it should be!" By the time he finished speaking his voice had reduced itself to a fierce whisper.

Thorne had heard rumors about scanners before. He didn't really believe they existed. But when he thought about DeLyon's question, he couldn't come up with an answer. Unless he was asking to be caught, reaching out for some kind of help. And that was ridiculous. He wasn't that desperate or dissatisfied with his life.

Another Tuesday night. Heather had dropped by early to help Diana plan a party for one of their girlfriends. Later they would don their dermasks and go out for the evening. Thorne had decided to stay home. He was trying to find something to watch on the holo. Over a hundred channels to choose from, yet he often claimed he could find nothing worthwhile. Just as he settled on a show that offered a dramatization of the Riots of '37, the last organized resistance against the registration drives, Diana made him turn off the audio so that she and Heather wouldn't have to talk over it. He had identified the hero and the villain, but without sound he was having trouble making sense of the plot.

Three weeks had passed since his first encounter with DeLyon. On the intervening Tuesdays they had met, and as DeLyon put it, "gone whoring together," once in the slum and once at the Halls. Afterward DeLyon insisted on each of them relating their separate experiences in detail. Thorne had to admit this new companionship eased the tensions in his life. His work had improved markedly and his relationship with Diana was settling back into the comfortable pattern that prevailed during the first year of their mating. Nevertheless, there were things about DeLyon that were starting to annoy him.

Diana and Heather were perched on stools at the counter by the microkitchen, their long legs dangling as they leafed through catalogs trying to select a gift and a theme for the party. They agreed on an historical motif, but couldn't settle on the period.

Since Thorne was the purported historian, Heather would periodically slide down from her stool and cross the room to ask his opinion. She would sit on the arm of his chair, hold a page of the catalog open for his inspection, coincidentally touching his arm or nudging his shoulder. Diana appeared unconcerned about Heather's little flirtations. Thorne was increasingly uncomfortable with each of her visits to the apartment.

The door chime sounded and Thorne went to answer.

The man who confronted him was short yet strikingly handsome. So handsome some would call him beautiful. The features of his face were small and perfectly formed. A shock of white-blond hair waved backwards in a high pompadour. Because of the soft hall light it took Thorne several seconds to realize he was looking at a wig and a dermask.

"It's me...DeLyon."

"What are you doing here?" Thorne hissed.

There was no time for an answer. The two women had come to see who was there. With reluctance Thorne ushered his friend into the apartment and made awkward introductions.

"Another of the programmers I work with," he said. It was the truth, though not much of the truth.

"Why are you wearing a dermask?" Heather asked.

"It's new and I wanted to try it out," DeLyon told her.

"It looks fantastic," she assured him.

DeLyon had two tickets to a fireball game in Omicron Sector and was inviting Thorne to go along. Thorne didn't care about fireball and the trip to Omicron, even by tunnel train, was close to an hour. Besides, he wanted to finish the show he was watching.

"Oh, go ahead," Diana told him. "You should get out more rather than sitting around reading and staring at the holo all the time."

DeLyon sidled next to Thorne and held the tickets up for him to see. There weren't tickets at all, but two orange rectangles cut from the cards they used for file dividers at work.

"Come on," he said, "you'll like it. The Stalwarts and the Paragons are playing. This game could decide the league title."

With a sickening rush, Thorne realized he had to get DeLyon out of there before the charade collapsed and Diana's questions began. Muttering his assent, he headed for the closet to find his coat.

"Don't forget your dermask," DeLyon called after him. "You can never tell who we might run into." He gave Heather a lascivious wink, which she returned in kind. "Don't wait up for us," he added.

As they were going out the door Thorne caught one last glimpse of the soundless holo. The actor he had mistaken for the villain had shot the actor he had mistaken for the hero. The heroine, daughter of a Guardener, was running across an open field of windblown grasses to meet his embrace.

A neat trick, Thorne thought, given all the Riots of '37 had taken place in urban areas. Given that less than twenty years ago fields of grass existed only in fertile sanctuaries. Given that the children of Guardeners and other Robed Professions lived in a world apart, with their own schools, their own friends, their exclusive and very private lives.

We have already noted Richard Thorne's lack of confidence and overly active imagination. A third significant character flaw that should be mentioned is his censorious nature, a need at times approaching a compulsion to find fault with everything around him. From the trivial to the significant aspects of life, Thorne was continually carping and cutting, though seldom did his comments involve any positive suggestions.

His work was boring and repetitive. His manager never gave him a chance to do anything interesting. The room was too stuffy. The glideways were too crowded. The shows on the holo were all the same. The Courtesans of the Halls lacked imagination and knew nothing about history. Heather possessed all the intelligence of a paperweight. The chop was underdone and the vegetables overcooked.

At times we want to throw up our hands when dealing with such cases and exclaim that no world, no matter how ideal, could satisfy an individual such as this. Yet the commitment of the City State is clear. We do not bow to nature, even a nature as perverse and contrary as Richard Thorne's. Instead, we attempt to channel it in the service of humanity and civilization.

Yet few individuals can be as tolerant and understanding as a beneficent State. Diana certainly wasn't. In the early months of their mating Thorne voiced his criticisms openly, which soon led to a confrontation and their first argument.

"You're so negative about everything!"

"I can't help it," Thorne shrugged, "that's the way I see things, that's how I feel."

"If that's the way you feel," Diana countered, "you should keep it to yourself...instead of spoiling things for everyone else. If you can't say something nice, it's better not to say anything at all!"

And that was what Thorne had learned to do. Not only with Diana but in the rest of his life as well. Yet in so doing, he had created an ongoing monologue in his head. His negative perceptions didn't cease, they merely became internalized.

Once Thorne met DeLyon his critical nature resurfaced and found its voice again. Soon he would discover another receptive outlet for his constant complaints. He was about to enter a world where his criticisms would be met with acceptance and affirmation, where they would find fertile soil and be encouraged to grow and blossom into flowers of evil.

Thorne waited until the lift whooshed them to street level and deposited them on the sidewalk before he exploded.

"Are you crazy?" he yelled at DeLyon. "Are you trying to ruin everything? Don't ever come here again and do anything like that!" A vein pulsed in Thorne's temple and his hands were tightly clenched. He had seldom lost control like this since his days of primary conditioning.

DeLyon sidestepped a couple paces, skirting the curb. He was already moving in the direction of the slum remnant and Thorne was unconsciously following.

"You won't be sorry you came," the small man said, raising his palms in a gesture aimed both to placate and admonish. "Wait and see. I've got someone special for you to meet. Someone quite remarkable."

Now that Thorne knew who was beneath the dermask, the handsome face looked ridiculous to him. Turning away and wedging his hands in his pockets he began walking rapidly. DeLyon had to skip every two or three steps to keep up.

The man really was annoying, Thorne thought.

DeLyon had a way of manipulating any situation to conform to his perceptions, of turning everyday life into a devious game. His reality consisted of one elaborate charade after another, most of them unnecessary, all of them self-wrought. He created the very conditions that served to fuel the fear he was being followed and spied upon, that a squad of Guardeners was about to pounce from behind the nearest kiosk and whisk him away so they could empty out his brain. Despite such fears, DeLyon was at the same time impressed with his own intelligence and convinced of his superior cunning. He had implied to Thorne more than once that he could out-smart any Guardener.

"You *said* you wanted to meet different kinds of people," DeLyon now told him. "You *said* you wanted to try different things." He shrugged and spread his arms in exasperation. "You *said* you wanted to have adventures."

He was at it again, Thorne thought. Turning the situation around to make it seem as if he was acting selflessly and here he was burdened with an ungrateful friend.

Thorne stared straight ahead and refused to answer.

Wherever they were going, he thought, whatever they were about to do, it would probably be better than watching a soundless holo and feeling embarrassed by Heather's overtures. Little did he know the chain of events that followed was to prove so different from any of his past experience it would etch itself upon his memory with exceptional clarity.

A building of smudged brown brick on a street lined with buildings of smudged brown brick, distinguishable from its counterparts only by a surfeit of broken windows.

DeLyon told Thorne to wait by the front steps as he darted up and within.

On his friend's insistence, Thorne had applied his own dermask. Over the past year he had needed a mask solely for concealing his identity on his way to and from the Halls. This model was less expensive and convincing than the one DeLyon wore. It imparted a blankness to his face, an immobility that mitigated the disgruntled expression he now wore beneath.

Still an unwilling companion on this trip, Thorne was for once perceiving the slum accurately. The full force of its dinginess and decay, its hopelessness, struck home without being colored by romantic notions. He didn't like this perception and wished he were somewhere else.

DeLyon came down from the building, half concealing a tattered plastic bag within his jacket. He handed the package to Thorne, forcing it within the flap of his coat, simultaneously peeling back a bit of the plastic.

Thorne saw a bottle, stoppered crookedly with a crude cork. Amber liquid rose halfway up its neck. Next to the bottle was a small plastic bag, wound upon itself in a tight cylinder.

"Some spirits to lighten the night," DeLyon quipped. "A little smoke to lighten the mind."

The bottle contained an ancient and potent alcoholic beverage known as whiskey. Possession, consumption, or sale of beverages with an alcoholic content higher than five percent is illegal in all sectors of the City State. We have discovered drugs other than alcohol that are more selective in their effects and far less damaging to the body—and these are available for those who need them. The bag contained a natural plant narcotic known as marijuana, ingested by inhaling the fumes of its burning leaves. As an unregistered drug, marijuana was also illegal, a dangerous substance that could severely distort both internal and external realities. Users of the drug exhibit personality shifts and a general indifference to the norms of society. Richard Thorne had appended two more crimes to his name.

They were passing through a residential section of the slum Thorne had never explored. Having questioned DeLyon several times about their destination without receiving a satisfactory answer, he'd given up. DeLyon contended it was "too difficult to explain" and was "supposed to be a surprise." He also repeated several times that Thorne wouldn't be sorry he'd come.

After scouring both sides of the street up and down—DeLyon was constantly doing this—he pulled Thorne into an alleyway.

It was pitch dark. There were no street lamps. The moon shone less than half full and what little radiance it cast was abridged by the shadows of the surrounding buildings.

"Do you have any credits with you?" DeLyon whispered.

Thorne was reticent. Since that first night his new companion had exhibited a penchant for allowing him the expenses when they were together. It was always Thorne's turn to buy the next round.

"I've got my credit chip,"

"No. I mean cash. How much cash do you have?"

"Not much. About twenty," he lied.

A rustling followed and he felt several bills being thrust into his hand. "Here!" DeLyon whispered. "Give her this. And what's in the bag. That should be enough."

"Who?"

DeLyon didn't answer. He had already turned and was headed down the alley.

His eyes acclimating to the darkness, Thorne followed. The curiosity aroused by the intrigue of the escapade was beginning to overcome his annoyance. The narrow passage ran for thirty or forty meters past back doors and refuse cans before it dead-ended at the rear of another structure.

"Watch this," DeLyon said.

There was an empty packing crate abandoned by one side of the building. DeLyon shifted it several feet. Once he made sure it was firmly planted on the crumbling cement, he pulled himself up and clambered on top.

Through the pall of his fascination, Thorne was at last beginning to realize his friend was deranged. He had delivered himself, he thought, into the hands of a maniac.

Standing atop the crate, DeLyon's knees flexed.

Suddenly he jumped. Thorne's gaze shot upward. De-Lyon was hanging from the bottom rungs of a black metal fire escape, barely visible against the sky. Its ladder and several small landings snaked up the side of the building. The flimsy network swayed and shifted with the addition of De-Lyon's weight. He hoisted himself up bodily, one rung after another, and then climbed to the relative safety of the first landing.

"I'm not going up there!" Thorne whisper-shouted at the indistinct figure above him.

"Come on. " DeLyon called down softly. "This is the best way. No one can see us." He pulled a lever and the ladder he had climbed fell downward until it thumped solidly against the top of the crate.

Although it was to evolve radically in the coming months—from passive to aggressive—Thorne's personality remained malleable at this stage of his life. After enough coaxing, DeLyon persuaded him to try the ascent. Once he'd edged his way up three flights to the top floor of the building, trailing DeLyon, haunted by visions of the fire escape collapsing, of irate slum dwellers bellowing forth from their lairs to send him plummeting to the street below, he actually felt proud of himself.

It *was* an adventure, just as his friend had promised.

Once they reached the top landing, DeLyon took a small knife from his pocket and began to pry at the bottom frame of a window. In the faint light thrown from within the building, Thorne could see paint chipped away where the same action had apparently been performed before.

DeLyon raised the window far enough to get a grip, then reached beneath with his fingertips and slowly edged it upward. Once the opening was large enough, he clambered through and Thorne, who could not believe this was happening, let alone that he was taking part, followed. Breaking and entering, he thought, that's what it was called.

They stood in a shabby hallway lined with doors. De-Lyon turned to the first door on their left. Taking a key from his pocket, he fumbled with it in an ancient skeleton lock. They had reached their destination. DeLyon tried to turn the doorknob, then he rattled it. The door had already been open and he had inadvertently locked it.

"She's a careless woman," he mumbled.

"Who?" Thorne asked. Again without result.

Once DeLyon reversed the process, they entered a room wastefully large by contemporary standards. It must have been more than twice the size of an average conapt unit. The ceiling was more than half again as high.

A single light burned: a yellow globe encased by a cylindrical cloth covering and mounted upon a standing fixture. Completely inefficient, it threw a harsh circle of light on the floor in its immediate vicinity while the rest of the room remained in relative shadow. Thorne had never been in a slum residence before. The strangeness of the surroundings impressed themselves upon him immediately, too much strangeness to assimilate all at once.

"Sit down. Sit down," DeLyon encouraged. "Make yourself comfortable."

There was a chair, its back and arms monstrously oversized, covered by a rough and scratchy material worn threadbare in places. Thorne lowered himself into it. The seat was lumpy but soft, surprisingly comfortable.

DeLyon was backing away toward the door.

"Where are you going?" Thorne protested.

"Don't worry," DeLyon said. "Everything's all set." He motioned with both hands for Thorne to remain seated. "She's expecting you. Just wait. And don't forget to give her the bag and the credits. And if she tells you to leave...well...just do it. She can be a real fury if you get her started!"

He was gone, the door clicking shut behind him, before Thorne could say another word.

It was fitting, he concluded, that after rousting him from the security of his home, after dragging him through the night streets and three stories up a wobbling dirt-encrusted ladder with nothing to break his fall except the pavement below, after involving him in the crime of breaking and entering, DeLyon should desert him. And Thorne still didn't have the slightest idea what any of this was about. He was tempted to go back down the fire escape himself, but the room had already captured his awareness.

At last the history lover was within what, in a literal sense, could be termed a room out of the past. There were so many things to look at he had never seen before that his attention became as transitory as that of an unconditioned child. Impressions rushed upon him faster than he could evaluate them.

First, the plants. Real plants sprouting from real soil. Not one or two, but scattered all about the room in pots on shelves, dressers, table tops. Pure soil, untainted by radiation or toxic waste, capable of sustaining normal plant life, has always been considered a premium resource by the City State. As our population continues to grow we must continually explore farther into the Dead Lands for viable agricultural sites. Like many couples, Thorne and Diana had their own box of soil hidden at home. In the early days of their mating they had rubbed some of it over themselves before coupling. Diana developed a rash and had to see a Doctor. But to display soil openly and cultivate plants like a high-ranking robed official, that was a different matter.

Before he could examine any of the plants in detail, Thorne's interest was drawn to the bed. It was the largest object in the room and easily as outsized as the chair. Still more amazing, unlike a normal bed supported by struts or chains and hinged so it could be folded into the wall when not in use, this bed was a permanent fixture of the room. It was braced at each end by two-legged gate-like supports of ornately curling metal. If one wanted to cross that part of the room, it was necessary to walk around the bed. Such a furnishing was an affront to anyone cognizant of the economy of space principles by which City life is regulated.

Thorne rose from his chair. He tested the bed's surface with one hand to make sure it would support him, and then lowered his weight across it. His body sank.

Degenerately soft, the bed began to envelope him.

Then he saw the twisted figure suspended above him and he started. His breath caught within his throat before he realized he was staring at his own dim reflection.

A portion of the ceiling was glass!

Or rather a series of glass panes within a metal framework. Bowing inward, threatening to collapse from age, the panes tilted in non-parallel planes to one another and gave him back his own distorted image.

Thorne remembered reading about such ceilings in Diana's datachips on the history of architecture. They were called skylights. Beyond his reflected image and superimposed upon it, he could perceive the faintly glimmering night sky.

Next, he noticed the books—three long tiers of them running the entire length of one wall. More wasted space! With microchips on every subject one could want to read about, with hand readers available to all individuals registered or not, he couldn't imagine why anyone would want so many books.

He pulled one at random from the second shelf and opened it. The language in which it was printed was not the basic demotic of the City, nor was it a computer language or the technical jargon of one of the Professions, but an archaic foreign tongue of which he could not understand a single word. He tried another, a thick reddish volume with many pages. Its binding was collapsing, the paper yellowed and crumbling around the edges. Yet although some of the words were strangely spelled and the sentences oddly constructed, this book he could read.

> "He walked down slowly and deliberately, feverish but not conscious of it, entirely absorbed in a new overwhelming sensation of life and strength that surged up suddenly within him. This sensation might be compared to that of a man condemned to death who had suddenly been pardoned. Halfway down the staircase he was overtaken by the priest on his way home; Raskolnikov let him pass, exchanging a silent greeting with him."

Thorne looked up from the passage, his mind grappling with its strangeness. It was like nothing he'd read before. If anything, it resembled a kind of holodrama in words. As he was puzzling over it, Josie came through a curtained doorway at the far end of the room and he saw her for the first time.

The second book Thorne had chosen from the shelf was known as a novel, an ancient artistic form that came into being in the seventeenth century, thrived for several hundred years, and declined in popularity after that. As he correctly surmised, novels were a primitive analog to contemporary holodramas and could be viewed as their antecedent. They related a story in the form of a lengthy prose narrative, primarily for the purpose of entertainment.

45

Novels continued to be published through the Gray Years—when they enjoyed a brief surge in popularity due to technological decline and the lack of more sophisticated diversions—and even beyond. The publication of novels was declared a negative freedom and officially banned by the City State more than fifty years ago. As well as their possession, except in the case of certain individuals, such as Guardeners and Historians, where their study was deemed a necessary part of one's Professional duties.

Like holodramas, most novels provided a harmless if innocuous way to pass the time. Some embodied socially positive values or taught simple moral lessons. Yet there was another kind of novel, one that came into being in the late nineteenth century and flourished in the twentieth. This kind of novel exalted the individual at the expense of society, at times romanticizing deviant behavior. This kind of novel, through the sophistic use of words and situations, caused readers to embrace anti-social ideas that influenced their actions and the course of their lives. Such books spoke of things better left unsaid. They bared the kind of emotions that should only be examined in a professional therapeutic setting.

In the months to come, Thorne would read many of the novels he found on Josie's shelves. Their influence on him would be profound and disastrous, filling his already overly-imaginative mind with ideas he would never have thought on his own, emotions he would have never felt, undermining his conditioning and in some instances stripping it away completely. As much as his affair with Josie, as much as the illegal drugs he consumed in her company, it is our surmise that these books were responsible for the events that followed. They may also provide one of the keys to the gross discontinuity in Thorne's holo projection, and the inability of the cyberscan to reconcile or predict his behavior.

Therefore it is more than a coincidence that we have adapted this archaic form for the presentation of this report. We have embarked upon a radical departure from standard psychological practice in the hope of gaining knowledge that lies beyond the sphere of the rational. You must remember we are dealing with a case where traditional methods have failed. It is our firm belief that despite its dangers, its distortions of reality and often misleading metaphoric associations, the novelistic form may also have its virtues. In the right hands, employing the proper restraint and emphasis, the story of Richard Thorne told in the same form that contributed to his degeneration may lead us to an understanding of subtleties in human behavior that have formerly eluded us.

Josie remained standing by the doorway, arms folded in front of her, watching him calmly. She was a small woman, so small and slender he initially took her for a girl. Actually she was thirty-three, four years older than Diana and a year older than Thorne himself.

Her complexion was on the dark side, dark enough to suggest an ethnic mix, but of what elements he couldn't be sure. Her hair was unstyled, a lustrous brown almost black. Cropped short at the neck and fluffed slightly about her head and ears, it added to the girlish appearance. She wore gray cotton pants, a black pullover sweater. The clothes hung loosely from her small frame. The cuffs of the pants were turned up, her feet bare, her ankles thin and delicately boned.

"I'm Josie," she said without preamble.

The voice was clearly that of a grown woman. Surprisingly deep, even husky. Later, in the distortions caused by his infatuation, Thorne would characterize its scratchy tone as "rough velvet."

As soon as she spoke and her eyes moved, he found her beautiful. Beautiful in an unusual way. The eyes were large and brown, alert, animated as if they were appraising and challenging him at the same time. They seemed too large for her narrow face, giving her expression an avian quality that was heightened by the way she tilted her head as she watched him.

"Hello...I'm Richard."

"I already know that," she said.

So DeLyon had told her more about him than he had him about her. At least his name.

"But Richard is rather formal," she went on. "I think I'll call you Rick."

"Rick?"

"Is there something wrong with that?"

"No...it's just that no one ever called me that before."

"Then I'll be the first. If you'd take off that stupid mask, I'd have an actual face to go with the name."

Thorne hesitated a moment, then peeled the mask away, self-consciously brushing his hair into place though it had not been disturbed. Josie approached a few steps closer and surveyed the results.

"Rather nice," she observed, "though somewhat lacking in character."

For a second Thorne thought she was making a joke, but then he realized she was completely serious. He found the woman's manner rude and disarming. Accustomed to dealing with others in polite fashion, expecting the same in return, he didn't know how to respond to such a comment. Josie had never received a primary conditioning in social amenities. She could be honest to a fault—she took a perverse pleasure in it—and her directness would continue to startle Thorne for as long as he knew her.

She moved past him and settled into a chair Thorne had overlooked, though it was no less strange than anything else in the room. A cushionless frame, archaic in styling yet conventional enough to the point where its legs should have ended. Instead, two curved runners were attached to the legs, one at each side of the chair. Through the twenty-first century this had been a common piece of furniture, known as a rocker. Josie drew her legs up to one side so she was curled within the seat. With her hands resting on the arms of the chair, she started to rock back and forth. Thorne stared, fascinated by both the chair and the woman occupying it.

"Did you find something interesting?" she asked, nodding toward the bookcase.

"Oh...uh, no...," he stammered, "I was just curious. It's odd...so many books. Wouldn't it be easier to have them scanned onto datachips and use a reader?"

Josie shook her head. "Sure, scanned and confiscated," she informed him. "That's what they *don't* want you to read."

Thorne had never seen anything on datachips comparable to what he'd come upon in the two volumes he had chosen at random. Yet there couldn't be that many books, he thought, banned by the City State. Not in an age of freedom.

"Why don't you take your coat off and sit down?" Josie suggested, still rocking.

Her back and forth motion, the unabashed staring of her large dark eyes, the oddities of the room—all of it was making Thorne increasingly uncomfortable. As he removed his coat he noticed the plastic bag in his right pocket.

"Here," he said, holding it out awkwardly, "this is for you."

Josie got up from the rocker, which continued to swing back and forth without her. She took the bag from him and peered inside. Her face brightened.

"Ah," she said. "Some spirits to lighten the night. Some smoke to lighten the mind."

Although he had never heard the expression before that evening, Thorne recognized it as the same DeLyon had uttered earlier. He wondered if Josie was quoting DeLyon or he had been quoting her.

"Did Danny give you this?"

He nodded.

Josie smiled. "He does have his ways about him."

"Do you know...Danny...well?" This diminutive of De-Lyon's given name didn't coincide with Thorne's perception of him.

"I ought to," Josie laughed. "Danny's my half-brother."

He hadn't expected that. Except for the diminutive stature there was little family resemblance.

Josie slipped the small plastic bag into her pocket and handed the bottle back to him. She disappeared through the curtained doorway and shortly emerged with two glasses. When she came to stand next to him, holding the glasses in front of her, her head barely reached his chest. Other than her eyes the rest of her features were small and carefully formed, reminding him of DeLyon's beautiful dermask, a travesty of the uninspiring face beneath. Only her face was real, Thorne thought, not a mask.

Once he had the bottle uncorked he filled both glasses nearly to the brim. Josie gave him an odd look as he finished. After handing him one glass, she held hers up and clinked it against the side of his.

"Cheers," she said.

It was an ancient toast, its origins lost in prehistory. Thorne had never heard it before and it took him a few seconds to catch on. He responded with the first thing that came to his mind, the universal toast of the Citizen. "To the Future Perfect," he said.

Josie wrinkled her nose as she turned away and went back to her rocker, where she again curled up. Eyes downcast, she sipped her drink.

Thorne was well aware that many of those unregistered resented the City State despite the benefits it provided them. This wasn't the first expression of that resentment he had seen. Nevertheless, Josie's reaction had caught him off guard. One more impression he didn't have time to evaluate.

He sat down opposite her, in the chair he had first occupied, placing his glass on one of the wide arms. There was a long moment of silence.

"Can I ask you something?" Thorne began

"Ask away." Josie looked up noncommittally.

Thorne took a large swallow of his drink. He realized his mistake immediately. By that time the liquid was searing its way down his throat. He coughed convulsively, spraying the other half onto the carpet.

"Take it easy!"

Josie had come to his side. "That isn't beer." She began slapping him on the back. "Haven't you ever had whiskey before?"

"No...," he managed between gasps, "...never have. Is it supposed to burn like that?"

"Not if you drink it the right way. You're supposed to sip it, not gulp it. Are you all right?"

"Yes...I think so," he said, wiping his eyes with the back of his hand. His voice was hoarse.

"Are you sure?"

Thorne nodded. She was probably more worried, he thought, that he might choke to death *in her apartment* than that he might choke to death.

Josie returned to the chair again, apparently her permanent station. Two lighter bands showed upon the dark weave of the carpet where it had been worn down by the motion of the rocker. Thorne could see that although she was trying not to show it, she was amused by the incident. He felt ridiculous, totally out of place. Perhaps, he thought, he should leave right now.

"Is this how you do it?"

He took another swallow, this time sipping carefully. The whiskey burnt as before, but it was a pleasant burning sensation that soothed the other as it passed down his throat. He could already feel the first swallow spreading a peculiar warmth through his chest.

Josie nodded her approval. "What were you going to ask me?"

Thorne took another careful sip before telling her.

"Why did we have to come up the fire escape?" The hoarseness in his voice was gone.

"Oh, Danny's crazy," Josie said, shaking her head and chuckling. "He thinks the Guardeners have me under surveillance. Actually, they couldn't care less. Tell me, do I look like a threat to you?" She placed the fingertips of one slim hand against her chest.

"Why," he asked with deliberation, "does he think the Guardeners are watching you?"

He had a vision of the building surrounded, of booted City State troopers exploding through windows and doors, riding ropes down from the shattered skylight. Some of De-Lyon's paranoia, he realized, had rubbed off on him.

"Because of my father."

Josie's expression darkened. Her face lost its animated quality and her eyes turned inward. "He was involved in the Revolt of '37," she added quietly. "He was a brilliant man...but he was also a fool. An idealist totally out of touch with reality. He thought you could fight the City State."

Not really a revolt, Thorne thought, merely riots. Yet it seemed a subject not wise to debate at the moment. He took another swallow of whiskey to pass this new uncomfortable silence. He was finding it to his liking now that he knew how to drink it properly.

Thorne remembered the credits DeLyon had given him and pulled them out of his pocket.

"DeLyon...I mean, Danny...said to give this to you."

Josie came back from faraway, brow arching in puzzlement. She eyed the wad of bills indifferently. "Just put it there," she said, nodding toward the table at his side.

"What's it for?" Thorne ventured.

"Just about whatever you want it to be for," Josie told him, "within limits. Though with more of the same...and more of this," she raised her drink, "the limits have been known to change."

"I don't understand," he said. Though he was at last beginning to.

Again Josie's eyes changed expression. He had never seen eyes capable of so many different expressions in so short a time. He was already feeling drunk, as if from too much beer. Only the sensation had come upon him in a rush, faster than it ever had with beer.

"You mean you don't know why you're here?"

"No...," he said, "Danny didn't tell me anything." He was embarrassed about mentioning the "someone special, someone quite remarkable" that DeLyon had told him about.

Josie exploded with laughter from deep in her chest. The rocking chair swung wildly back and forth.

If Richard Thorne had really delved into the past, as is the task of serious students of history, he would have received a far different impression from that which his haphazard dabbling and his imagination had conjured. Here and there he would have found a touch of the color and romanticism after which he hungered, but counterbalancing it manyfold, in any century of recorded history prior to the Reconstruction, he would have found the evidence insurmountable for what a pitiable spectacle humankind's upward journey has been.

Ignorance, disease, poverty, hunger—he would have discovered this and much more. He would have marveled at how millions died in unrelieved and insane warfare: wars for land, for wealth and power, for honor, wars for absurd and long-forgotten religions or ideologies. Wars that increased in intensity and devastation as technological knowledge advanced.

Thorne would have been appalled at society's attitude, its indifference to the happiness and satisfaction of its individual members. He would have puzzled over basic human instincts, sexual and otherwise, unfulfilled and sublimated to destructive ends. He would have balked at the mass frustration, the hatred, the irrationality, at times and in places prevailing as the standing order of the day.

And if, as by some magic not yet invented, Richard Thorne traveled backward through time and his life were transposed to such an earlier era, odds are his lot would have been the common lot, one of ignominy and drudgery rather than glory and adventure. In truth, the high probability exists, given his refined contemporary sensibilities, he would not have survived at all.

Now that he had encountered and was about to become influenced by a mere reflection of that past, the results would be much the same.

Once she brought her laughter under control, Josie stopped rocking. She leaned forward placing both feet upon the floor, elbows on her knees. She pushed back the sleeves of the sweater and steepled her hands beneath her chin. In the circle of light from the standing lamp Thorne could see fine dark hairs on her bare forearms. Once more her eyes challenged him.

"I don't know whether you're terribly naive," Josie began, "or just simple-minded. You...are...here," she enunciated distinctly, "to...get...your...ashes...hauled. Or as your kind might put it, 'To have your system downloaded.'" She drew in a deep breath. "What Danny didn't tell you...is that I'm a working girl...a hooker...a lady of the night...a pro...a woman of easy virtue...a not-so-proud member of the world's oldest profession...an unwilling victim of circumstance and necessity. Sometimes I think there are more words for what I do than there are ways to do it...I'm what's known in not-so-polite company as a whore...but not with a heart of gold, I assure you...I'm what's known in your neat little world as a..." she raised one hand with a turn of her wrist and her voice took on a strange accent for the single word, "...Courtesan!" She leaned back and placed her hands on the arms of the chair. "But don't confuse me with one of those fancy bitches. I may fuck you, but I won't lie to you about it. And if I take money for it, I still pick the ones I take it from. If I don't like you, you're out the door. And if you don't like me...well, you know where the door is!"

Thorne had never heard anyone talk this way before, unless they were delivering a speech in a holodrama. And this was not the sort of topic that actors in holodramas delivered speeches about. If Josie were trying to shock him, she had succeeded in full measure. Though Thorne was as much taken aback by her manner as the words she spoke, half of which he'd barely understood.

And once again she had insulted him.

Though of course she was right. He had been a complete fool. He should have realized from the beginning why De-Lyon had brought him here and given him the whiskey and the credits. Yet there was something in Josie's manner, her bearing, the plain clothes she wore, that made him refuse to see the obvious. On the other hand, he hadn't been a fool at all. When he tried to add things up, none of it made any sense. DeLyon was soliciting for his own sister, yet he was the one paying her fee. And his friend had said nothing about sex.

Now that Thorne understood why he was here, he wasn't sure whether he found the prospect appealing or intimidating. Josie was right about one thing. She was nothing like the Courtesans of the Halls. Although he sometimes talked at length with the Courtesans, they temporarily relinquished their individual identities as part of their roles. They strived to become whatever he wanted them to become, with their conversation as well as their actions. Nor was Josie like any of the illegal prostitutes he had coupled with in the slum. Most of them hardly spoke to him at all.

She was unlike any woman—any person—he'd met before. He supposed that did make her "special," as DeLyon had promised. "Desirable" was another question.

Josie's voice startled him from his reverie. She was again curled in her seat and the rocker had kicked into action.

"And how do you feed yourself and pay your way with whores?"

How much did she expect him to take? Since she already had the credits, was she trying to drive him away?

"I...uh...program computers, like...Danny...for the Regional Government. For Delta Standards Control."

It suddenly sounded absurd to him.

He saw his desk, his terminal. He thought of the years spent hunched before the pair, of the millions of bytes of data that had already passed before his eyes, the millions more to come before he could think about retirement. At that moment, Josie's "profession" made more sense to him.

I should leave, he thought. Whatever DeLyon intended, it wasn't working. Why should he want to couple with a woman who wasn't making the slightest attempt to please him? To be attractive for him? And who was insulting him on top of it?

At the same time, he could feel the whiskey spreading its pleasing warmth through his body. The lumpy oversized chair felt even more comfortable. Given the size of the room, the door appeared to be very far away.

And she hadn't told him to leave.

"So do you want to smoke some weed?" Josie asked, her recent outburst apparently forgotten. She removed something from the small plastic bag that had come with the whiskey and began stuffing it into an object she held in her other hand. "It helps put me in the mood."

Thorne's knowledge of the past came to his aid again. He recognized the object Josie was holding as a pipe, a small cylindrical bowl attached to a long hollow stem. He knew pipes had been used as a means to smoke tobacco, an addictive drug that had at one time been legal, widely used, and responsible for millions of deaths in its heyday. What had DeLyon gotten him into? Again he thought of leaving the apartment. Once more he remained where he was.

"Isn't that bad for you? Isn't tobacco...poisonous?"

Josie laughed at him once again. "You *are* the babe in the woods, aren't you? This isn't tobacco. It's weed. Grass. Mary J. Wanna. Try some and see if you like it."

"But what does it do?" Thorne swallowed hard. He didn't want her to laugh at him again. She had no right to laugh at him. Given where she lived, what she did for a living. She wasn't even a Citizen. Yet there was more to it than that. For some reason he couldn't fathom, he wanted her acceptance and approval.

"Like I said before," she told him, "it lightens the mind. Sometimes it even...enlightens." She crossed the room and sat next to him on one of the wide arms of the chair. Her thigh pressed against his arm. He unconsciously drew away, then consciously placed his arm back next to her. Given the thinness of her frame, she felt surprisingly soft.

"Here, watch me and do what I do."

Thorne looked up. Josie's nearness seemed to encompass him. It felt as if she were towering over him. How could such a small woman intimidate him so?

One-handed, Josie expertly lit a match with a flick of her thumbnail. She applied it to the bowl of the pipe. With the stem of the pipe in her mouth, she used her breath to draw the flame inward. Smoke spiraled up from the bowl as it contents ignited. A sweet acrid odor filled the air. After several seconds, she exhaled sharply.

"Breathe in deeply. Draw the smoke into your lungs and hold it as long as you can. But be careful. If you're not used to it, it's going to burn. Don't take too much at once or you'll start coughing again."

As was his way, Thorne did as he was told.

The smoke burned his throat. He held it for as long as he could stand, then exhaled loudly. In spite of himself he began to cough. He took another drink of whiskey and that helped.

They passed the pipe back and forth several times, repeating the strange ritual in a silence punctuated only by a faint crackling as the drug within it burned, by the deep inhalations of their breath and the sudden exhalations when they could hold it no longer.

Thorne waited for something to happen, for his mind to be lightened and enlightened. Within seconds the reverse occurred. His powers of rational thought and his ability to concentrate were stripped away. His consciousness began to dissociate, to leap at random from one image and impression to another.

He looked around the room.

Its odd furnishings and bizarre objects looked even stranger to him than at first. His eyes were accustomed to the dim illumination and he could see everything clearly. The sagging skylight, the plants sprouting from real soil, the oversized bed, the entire wall of books, the plaster walls badly in need of paint and stained in places. All of it mismatched and out of order. There was no consistent sense of color, shape or arrangement. It violated the principles of interior design he had learned from Diana. Yet it still seemed to hold together to create a kind of coherent whole.

As the drug continued to corrupt his perceptions, the room appeared intensely *real* to him—there was no other word for it—somehow more real than any room he'd ever seen. A perverted analogy flashed through his mind. His own conapt with its efficient storage units, its coordinated colors and planned spatial dimensions, its collapsible space-saving furniture and shifting walls, was like a dermask, concealing the reality of life beneath. This room was how one should actually live, surrounded by the objects of one's everyday existence.

Josie was still perched by his side on the arm of the chair. Her presence, her nearness, suddenly struck Thorne as overwhelmingly erotic, and he realized he was aroused. He tried to slip his arm around her waist, to pull her toward him, but before he could complete the action she rose from the arm of the chair and slid out of his grasp.

A battered chip player lay partially hidden amid the plants atop the bookcase. Josie crossed to it, selected a chip and inserted it in the play slot. Thorne found himself watching the movements of her hips beneath the thin cotton pants.

Then the music began...quietly at first, almost impercep-tible. Soon rising to a crescendo...then sweeping forward in a progression of well-defined passages. Non-cybernetic, non-electronic, composed on the outmoded twelve-tone scale, like everything else in the room it was from another era. Thorne had never listened to music like this before. There was an appeal in its pure simplicity. His mind took a new direction.

"That's nice. What is it?"

Josie appeared pleased by his reaction and smiled.

"It's a symphony, *The New World Symphony* by Dvorak. Another of life's little ironies. The music is beautiful, and here we are in our own new world and it's not the least bit like that. There's nothing beautiful about it at all." She made a sweeping gesture to indicate the world beyond the room.

Thorne wasn't sure whether she was referring to the slum or the entire City. In any case, it was now thirst that claimed his transitory attention. He refilled his empty glass and raised it toward her.

"Cheers?" he said questioningly.

This was his first concession that while they were to-gether they would inhabit her world instead of his, her val-ues and not the values he had lived by all his life. It was the first of many concessions to follow, to corrupt him with their outmoded ideas.

Josie smiled again. That smile ignited something in Thorne that rose from within his chest and radiated through his body. Or was it only the whiskey and the weed having their way with him?

"Yes," Josie agreed, raising her own glass. "Cheers."

Apparently he had passed some sort of test and would not be leaving after all.

Consumed at illegal levels alcohol can disrupt the chemistry of the brain's recording system in radical fashion, failing to store impressions or storing them in different areas than memory can access. By this time the alcohol in Thorne's bloodstream had reached a critical level. The marijuana completed the debilitation of his mental processes. When he later tried to recall the events that followed, they came back to him piecemeal, in flashes sometimes vivid, mostly hazy, all in all as discontinuous an array as his own cyberscan.

In this instance our most sophisticated techniques have done little better in reconstructing an accurate account of the next hour. Although Josie was more inured to the effects of the drugs they had ingested, she was also intoxicated, and her impressions stand in such marked contrast to Thorne's that we cannot trust the memories of either participant. Rather than offering an inaccurate account of what transpired—fragmented perceptions, words that may never have been spoken, actions that never took place except to a distorted consciousness—all we can provide is a summary.

Enough to say they talked more of the same nonsense. Their lopsided conversation continued with Josie baiting her customer—for customer he was—and Thorne taking the hook over and again. Enough to observe they listened to more of the ancient music and despite Thorne's protestations that he didn't know how, Josie convinced him to dance. Standing more than a head above her he moved haltingly, bent forward to watch his own feet and following her every move. Significant to note that although Josie had affected indifference when Thorne deposited the credits upon the table, she pocketed them and left the room briefly. When she returned the dark pullover and baggy pants were gone. She wore nothing but a robe that barely reached her knees and an excess of cheap fragrance.

The mists that had disrupted his perceptions slowly dissipated. The walls were no longer spinning. The music had ceased and the room was unnaturally quiet. Josie sat in her rocker, humming to herself at a level that reached audibility only on certain notes. The empty whiskey bottle stood by Thorne's side. He had no idea what time it was and he didn't care.

"Can I try your chair?" he asked.

Josie's eyes opened, and although she looked tired she looked lovelier to him than ever.

Although he didn't remember her changing clothes, she wore a robe of cream colored satin, sashed at the waist, short enough to leave her legs bare. He did remember the robe falling open during their dancing, giving him a brief glimpse of her dark slender body beneath.

She stood up and moved to one side of the rocker. Bending slightly, with the flourish of one hand, she offered it to him as if it were a gift.

Thorne approached with care and lowered himself into its seat. His weight carried him back. The arc of the runners carried him forward. Josie moved behind the chair and began to rock him, slowly at first. The room shifted forward and back. Faster. The room flowed forward and back. Faster still. Though the air in the room was still, a breeze blew against his heated cheeks.

"Stop," he yelled, laughing, trying to stand. "Stop! I'm getting dizzy!"

Josie let go of him and his feet clapped against the floor.

She came around the chair and Thorne, still sitting, wrapped his arms about her waist, let his head fall against her body. She held him momentarily, running one hand through his hair. Then she pushed him away and opened her robe. She was naked beneath as he already knew. The lamplight that had seemed harsh so long ago was soft upon her flesh. She came close to him and he pressed his lips, his cheeks, against her belly, reached within the robe to encircle her with his arms, his mouth moving lower against the wiry forest of hair. Her body was taut, her head thrown back.

"Let's make love now," she whispered.

Thorne had never heard the act of coupling described this way except when it referred to chosenmates. He also knew both from his studies of history and his primary conditioning that this was one of the greatest errors of past societies: the repeated confusion of love with the sexual act. At that moment he had no interest in arguing the point.

Josie turned out the light and they went toward the bed together. Thorne fell across it and she slipped her robe off and climbed on top of him while he ran his hands up and down her body. With her help he made it out of his clothes. Then they were beneath the covers, bare flesh sliding on bare flesh. The desire within him called forth what energy remained and found new reserves. They were kissing. Josie was clawing and biting him. With no concern for technique or one another's pleasure, they became a frenzy of tongues, teeth, fingers, and intertwining limbs. He couldn't wait. He was on top of her and she was pulling him within. The ancient bed rocked and creaked beneath them. Their bodies beat against one another. Without subtlety, only with thoughtless passion, cries real or feigned—he didn't know, didn't care, though she had said she would not lie to him—springing from Josie's throat, driving him on until he exploded from deep within in a fury of sound and motion.

The harshness of their breathing faded gradually. Thorne rolled off her and onto his back. Through the skylight he could see the stars in the darkness above. They looked very close, as if they were pasted upon the glass. He was going to reach up and touch one...but before he could raise his arm, exhaustion overcame him and he fell asleep.

If it hadn't been for that skylight, he might have slept through the morning. A minor disaster might have struck his life and he would have been spared the far greater disasters that were to follow. As it was, the first strands of gray streaked the sky, the sun nosed above the horizon pushing a white dawn before it, and light falling through the ceiling brought him to wakefulness.

He was due at work in less than an hour! What would he tell Diana? It was not unheard of for chosenmates to spend Tuesday night apart as well as the evening. Diana had done it on several occasions, but this would be the first time for Thorne.

Pushing back the sheets and blankets, he forced himself into action. Slices of pain divided his skull into throbbing segments that left little room for thought. His mouth and tongue felt as if they had been packed with sand. The room was cold and pale. At one edge of the large bed Josie's curled and tucked body was no more than another rumple amid the bunched covers.

He staggered naked through the curtained doorway, down the length of a narrow dingy hall to the bathroom. The primitive fixtures confounded him, as they had the night before, but he managed to relieve himself and splash cold water on his face. When he had first passed down this same hallway for the same reason the night before, he had opened the wrong door.

Given the layout of the apartment, the room he had come upon must have been intended as a large closet. He had quickly shut the door and turned away, but what he had seen in the light from the hall, what he had pushed from his mind at the time, now returned to haunt him.

On his way back down the hall, Thorne paused before the door and opened it a second time.

No, he hadn't hallucinated.

Although he hoped it wouldn't be the case, his drunken perception proved true.

Books lined the walls of the small room from floor to ceiling, as many books as in the living room. But that wasn't what caused a chill to run up and down his back. A chill that had nothing to do with his nakedness or the cold apartment.

In one corner of the room, atop an L-shaped corner desk, sat a computer terminal with a small printer attached. It was an older model, similar to a system they had phased out at work nearly ten years ago because of its tendency to slip into unexplained wait states. This model looked to be of that vintage. The keyboard had seen so much use the designations on several keys were worn away. Yet regardless of the quality or condition of the unit, it had no business being in a slum residence.

Those who do not learn from history are condemned to relive it. One thing we *have learned*—the philosophical bedrock upon which the laws of the City State are based—is that there are positive freedoms and negative freedoms. Certain societies of the past have attempted to grant their citizens a nearly unlicensed freedom. The ideal may be admirable in theory, but until the human species is perfected, any such system is doomed to failure. There are technologies so powerful in the modern world their misuse by one aberrant member of society can generate catastrophe for all. This is why the possession of personal computer terminals, except for high-ranking members of the robed professions, has been deemed a negative freedom and banned by the City State since its inception.

Josie's other violations of City State law—her books and plants, her prostitution, the consumption of unregistered drugs and of beverages with a prohibited alcoholic content—

were minor infringements compared to this. Thorne had now come upon a serious crime, entailing severe penalties.

His duty as a Citizen was to report the existence of this illegal unit to the local Guardener Station. His primary conditioning should have made this report a mandatory response. But as the thought occurred to him, as it became a nagging compulsion within his mind, Thorne knew he would resist its demands and report nothing.

If he went in person to the Guardener Station, he'd have to explain what he had been doing in a slum residence. If he reported the crime anonymously, it would still involve a betrayal of DeLyon and Josie, a betrayal he realized he was not prepared to make. Inexplicably, the personal loyalty he felt toward two individuals he barely knew was proving stronger than his conditioned loyalty to the City State. One more puzzle concerning the behavior of Richard Thorne for which we have no reasonable explanation.

Stumbling into his slimsuit, checking his pockets, Thorne came upon a roll of bills, his own cash. He peeled off several and placed them on the table by the chair, noticing for the first time the other credits had already been removed.

He was supporting her, he thought, rather than reporting her. Supporting...reporting. The stupid rhyme set off a new wave of pain coursing through his skull.

He needed some coffee. Or at least some water.

Back in the hallway he tried another door and found a kitchen, again wastefully large by contemporary standards. There was a can labeled coffee in one of the cupboards, but how to prepare it in Josie's kitchen without modern conveniences was beyond him. Instead he ran a glass of water from the tap.

Staring out the window, beyond the dismal blocky buildings of the slum, Thorne could see the towers of the City beyond. It must have been a trick of the morning light, a peculiar way the sun was rising, but for the barest second he could not perceive the order of those towers.

He saw them as chaos, abstract cubes and cones and vertical slabs trespassing on the sanctity of the sky. He didn't want to go home. He didn't want to go to work. He didn't want to return to the reality of the present.

Thorne looked down. The water glass was broken and his hand was bleeding.

The door of the apartment closing woke her briefly. It took her several seconds to remember who was closing it. Then she gave an internal shrug. She should have never let Danny talk her into it in the first place, she thought. The man was nothing like what she'd expected...and Danny's plans for him made no sense.

Josie snuggled more deeply into the bed, pulling the covers over her head to block out the light from above. She drifted back to sleep for several hours and did not rise until late morning. She never rose until late morning or early afternoon. In the coming months she would tell Thorne this more than once, bragging about it as if she were proud of her sloth. "I'm a creature of the night. I don't really come alive until the sun goes down."

When Josie did get up the apartment was still chilly. The building once had central air but it had long ago ceased to function. The only warmth came from the oven in the kitchen. Josie sat in a straight-backed kitchen chair, sipping her morning coffee, hunched in front of the oven, its door canted open at an angle so the heat flowed into the room.

It was just one more of Danny's schemes, she concluded, ill-conceived and ill thought-out.

"You have to seduce not only his body," Danny had told her, "but his mind as well. Then his heart will follow."

"But why? What do I want with his heart?"

"Because we can use him. Believe me, he's primed to be taken."

"Taken for what? Use him how?"

"Plan number one," Danny had announced, raising a finger by the side of his head. "He's your ticket out of here. He falls in love with you and asks you to mate with him. You can have all the rights of a Citizen without having to pass any tests or take a conditioning. It could mean security for the rest of your life."

"I thought he was already mated."

"Matings can be dissolved. It happens every day."

"But suppose I don't want to mate with him. Suppose I don't like him. Suppose I don't want to live like a Citizen."

"Do you want to spend the rest of your life living here?"

"It's not so bad. At least I've got the freedom to move around. I'm not crammed into some cracker box hive with six hundred Citizen workers."

"Yeah," Danny chided. "you've got freedom to move around, all right. Freedom to freeze every winter and swelter in the summer, freedom to be afraid to go out in the street after dark. To worry about how you're going to spend every credit. To wonder when some lunatic is going to come breaking in to rape and kill you. To worry about what will happen and where you are going to go when they clear the slum and tear this place down. Which *is* going to happen someday. You know it will."

Josie sighed from deep in her chest. "I suppose there's a plan number two."

There was always a plan number two with Danny. Like his personality, the man's very thought processes were bipartite. As if there were two answers for every question, two answers that could be contradictory yet equally valid.

"Plan number two," Danny announced as she knew he would. Grinning at her, enchanted with his own cleverness, he raised two fingers as if he were giving a victory sign. He simultaneously opened the palm of his other hand to reveal a micro recording device. "We make records of your encounters with him and threaten to show them to his chosenmate unless he pays us. You can probably get him to complain about his chosenmate, say things he would never want her to hear him say."

"You mean blackmail him. I don't think I could do that. It isn't right."

"But he's a Professional. I thought you hated Professionals." The fact DeLyon himself was a Professional had apparently slipped his mind. The fact that if Josie hated Professionals she'd be unlikely to want to mate with one had clearly been ignored in the formulation of the first plan.

"I do," Josie said. "I hate everything they stand for. I hate the inhuman code they live by, the way they kowtow to the City State as if it were some sort of ultimate religion. How they pretend to care for the welfare of others when all they care about is themselves, all of them trying to get ahead and not really...."

"That's enough," Danny cut her off.

"What do you mean?"

"That's your father talking, not you."

"And what if it is? That doesn't mean it isn't right."

"Right or wrong, it doesn't matter. This isn't the revolution. There is no revolution. There is never going to be a revolution. So what's the point of revolutionary rhetoric? I've heard enough of that nonsense to last a lifetime and more. Remember, I was raised by the man, too. What we have to concern ourselves with is the here and now. And if you hate Professionals, then it shouldn't bother you to take advantage of one."

She had at last given in, as she often did to Danny's persistence. "All right, all right, I'll meet the man. But I'm not promising anything."

"And one more thing," Danny looked around the room at her scattered clothes and books, the unmade bed. "Straighten this place up before he comes."

So she'd straightened the place up. She had concealed the recorder in the upper branches of a split-leaf rhododendron and made sure it was running before the man arrived. But the man turned out to be nothing like what she had expected. He was naive and gentle, not cold and hard like her image of a City State Professional. Like her, he was more a product of circumstance than calculation. And now none of it made the slightest bit of sense. She'd have to tell Danny the whole thing was off. She had no intention of blackmailing him. And as far as mating went, she'd no doubt scared the man half to death with her talk. Rather than seducing his mind, she'd blown it completely away. Odds were she would never see him again. He'd had his taste of danger, his little adventure. Now he could go back to his safe life and his chosenmate, his weekly Courtesan at the Halls. And she'd go back to....

The oven door swung open, its spring hinges long since shot, banging and shaking the entire fixture, startling her out of her reverie and causing her to spill what remained of the coffee on her robe.

"Damn!" she said out loud. There were days when everything around her seemed to be falling apart.

Josie's cyberscan presents a case of classic aberrance. The stalk of her flower is shredded and irregular. The blossom is widely flattened and several lines angle sharply toward the edge of the cube. Like many aberrants her nodes shine brightly and are clearly defined, yet lack any socially positive elements.

The overriding factor in her personality was a negative one, a constant and pointless rebellion against authority that she had inherited from her father. Unlike her half-brother, there was no way she could dissemble and pass the standard personality tests to achieve Citizen status. She had once taken the tests at Danny's insistence, and with Danny's coaching, and had failed miserably. She would need a complete conditioning if she hoped to become a Citizen.

Josie was trapped in what the ancients referred to as "Catch-22," a term derived from the title of a popular novel of the twentieth century, a book filled with unbelievable characters and preposterous events. Yet the term was accurate when applied to Josie. The deviance that possessed her, her refusal to accept authority of any kind, kept her from accepting the conditioning that could have cured her of that very deviance.

Back in the living room, Josie removed the recording device from its hiding place. She popped out the chip, bent it back and forth several times, and then snapped it between her fingers, congratulating herself on her integrity. If she had little else, she thought, at least she had that.

But her action really had nothing to do with integrity. It represented one more minor rebellion against authority. This time it was the authority of her older brother.

The concourse that fronts the Delta Government Complex is one of the widest and most beautiful of its kind in the entire Sector. The lawns of dichondra and clover, the hedges of barberry, box and privot, all are maintained green and well-trimmed the year round. Life-sized statues honoring the various trades and Professions adorn the gardens. Numerous fountains, decoratively placed and feeding small running streams, foster the illusion of a natural setting. In spring, real flowers bloom in abundance: roses, lilies, marigolds, geraniums. The colors are magnificent and the scents intermingle to turn the air fragrant with their blossoms.

Clearly the concourse is not a recreation area. The grounds beyond the pathways are set off by a high iron grillwork and remain inviolate. The Guardeners make sure of that. Still, the legal paths are well situated and lined with benches for the pleasure and relaxation of all Citizens.

Here, during the weekday noon hour, Richard Thorne could be found taking his lunch along with hundreds of other government workers. In recent weeks, his new friend Daniel DeLyon could usually be found by his side, a chessboard set up between the two programmers as they passed the lunch hour together. The day after his first encounter with Josie was no exception.

Thorne moved through the morning like a man in a trance, a simulation of his normal self, the figures on the screen blurring before his eyes. After leaving Josie's apartment he had tried to call Diana, but there was interference on the line and he couldn't get a connection.

At the office, his hangover continued to dog him. His mind teemed with a rush of confusing thoughts and images, nearly all of them involving Josie in one way or another. As soon as he found DeLyon in the concourse he could contain himself no longer.

"I want to see her again," he announced.

"Not now! Be quiet! It's your move."

DeLyon had finished setting up the board. He'd taken the white pieces for himself without asking and already advanced his king's pawn. Now his eyes rolled warningly in the direction of the building. Thorne shoved a pawn forward at random before looking up.

Across a flower bed and a short stretch of lawn, Sol Thatcher was seated by himself on a bench, eating his lunch from a plastic sack.

Thatcher was a large paunchy man, middle-aged, florid and balding. Although Thatcher was a Supervisor, G-16, Thorne had always viewed him as a pathetic figure. He wasn't sure what the man's function was in their unit, exactly what he did supervise. Most of the time he wasn't even in his office. But Thorne didn't think for a minute Thatcher could be a Guardener. And if he were, how could DeLyon possibly know about it?

Then he remembered the terminal at Josie's.

The moment that thought and its subsequent realization occurred to him, the implications were staggering.

The terminal wasn't Josie's...it belonged to DeLyon!

His friend had somehow smuggled it from the office piece by piece and reassembled it at Josie's. And now DeLyon was tapping into the City Net to read government files...perhaps even to change them! That was the only way he could know that Thatcher was a Guardener. It also meant—Thorne's heart plummeted—that Josie's apartment could very well be under surveillance. To his own blank astonishment, it made no difference to him.

"I want to see her again," he repeated, lowering his voice. "Next Tuesday night."

"I told you, you wouldn't be sorry," DeLyon clucked reprovingly. "But we can't talk about it here. Not now!" He shook his head back and forth, briefly, less than half an inch in each direction. "Let's just play. Pay attention to the game. It's your move again."

DeLyon sometimes spent ten minutes in rapt concentration before touching a piece. Regardless, he was always pressuring his opponent to move. Or rattling on incessantly about something else during his opponent's turn. The one time Thorne called him on this, DeLyon merely shrugged. He said he considered it a legitimate strategy of the game. He launched into a lecture on the subject, noting that the complete rules of most games, including their strategies, were not to be found in rule books.

Despite DeLyon's assorted ploys, Thorne had discovered if he concentrated totally, committing all of his logic and creative energy to the game, he could overcome DeLyon in the first twenty moves and provoke a petulant resignation on his friend's part. When he failed to do this, when he allowed his mind to wander from the intricate and immutable patterns of the board, his position eventually became hopeless. DeLyon, slow and methodical, lacking strategic genius yet without tactical error, would finish him off minute by dulling minute. Their longest trials would resolve in tedious endgame pawn battles. No matter how many times and ways Thorne counted the squares, he would always come up one short of the magical queening incarnation.

"Next Tuesday night," Thorne persisted. "Sooner if possible. I need to see her again." He could hear a note of pleading in his voice. He pushed another pawn forward.

"All right! All right!" DeLyon hissed. "I'll see what I can do. She may be busy, you know. She *does* have other commitments. And *you're* the one that's going to have to pay for her from now on."

Thorne felt as if he had been dashed with ice water.

Although he already knew it, although it was a given with prostitutes, the actual thought of Josie with other men—her smile, her voice, the touch of her hands—filled him with a sudden rage. So vivid a rage that for a moment it gave him a sense of power. Anything was possible, he thought. If he wanted Josie badly enough, if he wanted her all to himself, he would find a way to have her.

For once DeLyon moved swiftly, sweeping his white queen along a black diagonal to the right side of the board.

"Fool's mate," he proclaimed, grinning enormously, rocking back and forth, clapping his hands together several times in self-congratulatory applause.

Thorne stared down at the classic text position.

His sense of power evaporated as quickly as it had seized him. His head ached and his vision shimmered. His stomach felt as if it were trying to find a way into his chest and making certain progress. At the back of his skull, as it had on and off all morning, a tiny insistent voice kept repeating its mental itch like an infernal metronome: "Report the illegal terminal...report the illegal terminal... terminal... terminal... terminal...."

"Are you up for another game?" DeLyon asked. "We still have time. I get white again since I won."

Without waiting for an answer, his friend returned the pieces to their original squares. Thatcher strolled by them, without so much as a glance or nod of recognition. He deposited his empty lunch sack in a nearby receptacle.

"Excuse me," Thorne said. "I think I'm going to be sick."

That evening he had to confront Diana. In a brief morning call to her office he had put her off, claiming it was all too complicated and desperately thinking of what he might say.

When the time came, with his back to the wall, Thorne astonished himself once again—and experienced a brief resurgence of the sense of power he'd felt earlier in the day—by concocting an elaborate tale about a woman he and DeLyon met on the tunnel train returning from the fireball game. She had been so aggressive she refused to leave him alone until he promised to come home with her. He explained the cut on his hand as a bite the woman had given him.

"She was more than passionate," Thorne elaborated, "she was like some kind of maniac." He thought about Josie. He couldn't stop thinking about Josie. "Believe me," he lied, "I'm sorry the whole thing ever happened."

Diana was angry at first...but she did believe him! She had girlfriends like that. They saw what they wanted and they went after it. And after all, there was no reason for her not to believe him. What could her chosenmate have to hide? She did make him promise to call her sooner if anything like that ever happened again. So she wouldn't worry.

Thorne was so tired he went to bed after dinner. He felt ready to sleep the sleep of the dead. Instead he was haunted by dreams, or rather a single elaborate dream—the first in a series of nocturnal fantasies that were to imprint themselves forcefully on his consciousness and plague his waking hours in the months to come.

In the dream he was playing chess upon an enormous board. Not actually playing it so much as involved with it, waiting for the game to begin. This was no normal game. All the pieces were alive and they kept having conversations with one another, wandering about the board with no concern for the squares they were supposed to occupy. It was Thorne's responsibility to enforce the rules of the game, yet each time he consulted the rule book the print blurred and shifted before his eyes. Or it was written in a language he had never seen before. At the same time, he knew if he were able to decipher the rules, every last syllable and punctuation mark, it wouldn't make any difference. The real rules were not in the book and he would never be able to understand them completely.

Diana, emerald-eyed and imperious, was the white queen. Josie, amber-eyed and brazen, almond-eyed and vulnerable, was the black queen. DeLyon materialized as a kind of hyper-knight who could leap anywhere on the board, who could disappear and reappear at will, always with a computer terminal under one arm, forever grinning and winking. Heather drifted in at one point, thoroughly drunk, wearing a creamy white robe that left her legs bare. Beautiful legs, everyone agreed, but it was unclear to which army her allegiance belonged. Sol Thatcher, sporting the tall miter of a bishop, led her away in tears.

In the opening moves the two queens' pawns advanced across the board to confront one another. Thorne found himself inhabiting the bodies of both pawns simultaneously. Wearing a visored helmet, gripping a short dirk-like sword, he stood rigidly at attention in the center of the battlefield, facing his own white double, facing his own black double.

Obsession

On his second visit to Josie's apartment, Thorne discovered who she really was. He considered going up the fire escape as he had with DeLyon, then decided it was nonsense. Instead he took the front steps of the building, an aged brownstone in an advanced state of decay.

Thorne paused in the poorly lit entranceway. At one time the door to the building had been reinforced with a metal plate, now buckled and pried loose in several places. When he tried the knob the door rattled loosely in its frame but remained securely locked. On the side wall of the alcove there was a row of numbered buzzers. He peered at them in the dim light. Most had no names mounted next to them. Of the few that did, none of them read "DeLyon." He knew Josie's apartment was on the top floor, but he couldn't remember seeing any number on its door.

He looked again at the buzzers. It had to be one of the higher numbers. Most likely the highest since her apartment was at the end of the hall. Then he saw it. It *was* the highest number—sixteen—and there *was* a name attached to it. Only it was not "DeLyon." The small white card in its tarnished brass rectangle read "J. Jimson." Josie Jimson. She didn't have the same surname as DeLyon because they were only half brother and sister. Instead she had her father's last name. And Thorne realized who she was. Josie had told him her father had been involved in the Riots of '37, but not that he had instigated those riots. Not that he was the chief spokesman for an illegal organization popularly know as SDL, an acronym for Self-Determination League.

Thorne had never seen a holograph of Stuart Jimson, though he had seen him portrayed in numerous holodramas. Usually the same actor played Jimson, a ponderous bear of a man who sported unkempt hair and a straggly beard. A wild-eyed fanatic and terrorist who made unreasonable demands and bellowed unproved accusations against the City State in classic demagogic fashion.

Jimson had vanished during the course of the riots. The official explanation was that the man's followers had turned against him. They assassinated their leader and disposed of his body, which was never identified in the chaos that ensued. Thorne sensed that if he pressed her, Josie would have a different tale to tell. Though there was no way to be sure which he should believe.

Now he understood why DeLyon was worried his sister could be under Guardener surveillance. Thorne reconsidered the fire escape, but it was too late for that. If the entrance to the building was being watched, or monitored by a holocam, he had already been seen.

Thorne pushed the button next to Josie's name and waited several seconds for her to buzz him in. There was no response. He pushed it again with the same result.

He was wondering what to do next when the door of the building opened and she stood before him.

"The release doesn't work," she said, nodding at the door. "It's never worked for as long as I've lived here." Then she smiled. She was pleased to see him. Thorne felt his spirits rising and he smiled back.

Josie was again barefoot and wearing an outfit similar to the one he had seen her in before: baggy pants, a dark shapeless sweater. As he slipped in beside her, Thorne was struck again by how small and sleight she was.

The holodramas must have it wrong, he concluded. It wouldn't be the first time. There was no way Stuart Jimson could have looked like the ponderous giant who portrayed him. Not if he was this woman's natural father.

The disintegration of normality in Thorne's life, his growing alienation, his affair with Josie, all kept pace with one another over the weeks that followed. The pace was a rapid one that continued to accelerate beyond his control. Like his friend DeLyon, Thorne became a man divided. DeLyon had lived such a life for decades. The transformation from the conservative City State programmer Thorne knew by day to the garrulous trickster he knew by night had become second nature to DeLyon. For Thorne it was not so simple. He felt as if his consciousness were split in half, something like a man navigating the currents of a treacherous river, leaping back and forth between two boats and trying to pilot each one. Yet Thorne was not a split personality and he would not maintain this dual existence for long. Extending his own analogy, he was in the process of moving from the security of a safe and comfortable craft to the dangers of a makeshift raft that was destined to capsize, from the sane and ordered life of Richard Thorne to the compulsive and haphazard existence of a man known as "Rick."

It was no longer a hypothetical past our subject fastened upon in his moments of fantasy, but a real present existing a few blocks away from his home and office. He wanted to be alone with Josie, talk with Josie, make love to Josie. He continued to see her every Tuesday night when Diana assumed he was attending the Halls of Expression. Also any other time he could manage it, using DeLyon's friendship and their bogus attendance at chess tourneys, fireball games and other sporting events as a cover.

Of all humanity's past foibles and misconceptions, one of the gravest on the personal level has been that of infatuation, also known as "romantic love." We now realize such "love" is founded on illusion, the projection of individual desires and needs in the form of an ideal mate upon another individual who in reality may bear little resemblance to that idealization. Once such "love" is consummated it must confront reality. It is inevitably transitory and can often leave no residual affection in its wake. If feelings do survive, they are sometimes more negative than positive, the projection of one's own disappointment and lack of judgment onto the former object of desire.

Thorne learned all of this in primary school. He had been warned against the dangers of romantic love and its attendant illusions. He had received the standard conditioning against infatuation and the irrational behavior it entailed. Yet once again, inexplicably, his conditioning failed to take in any lasting way.

Thorne's obsession with Josie continued to exalt him in the first weeks of their affair. All of his perceptions, channeled through the distorting lens of his ardor, were heightened. His thoughts and ideas took on the ring of inarguable and what he perceived as revelatory truths. At the same time, again not unlike DeLyon, he was plagued by fears of exposure. Now that his illegal excursions were more than an occasional pastime, rather a steady passion involving one woman, Thorne knew a single misstep could send him plummeting. He sensed a pit opening before him and its fall appeared limitless. Then he became convinced the pit was within him, there was a limit to its fall, and there he would discover the bedrock of his being, his true self.

One night when he was leaving her apartment, as if it were an afterthought, Josie said to him. "Here, why don't you take this?" She handed him a key to her building. "That way I won't have to come down to let you in."

Thorne took it from her as if it were a talisman. All the way home he held it tightly in his fist. And from that moment on, it seldom left his side.

Diana Logan would have noticed the changes taking place in her chosenmate if she had not been coping with unexpected changes of her own. Not long after Thorne's first encounter with Josie, Diana returned to her cubicle from morning break to find the mail light on her terminal blinking. When she called up the message she was at first startled...then pleased and excited.

DIRECTOR WILLEM COOPERSMITH
requests your presence
for a luncheon
in his office
at 1200 hours.

Diana's career had progressed at a steady pace, rapid by most standards yet never fast enough to satisfy her ambition. At last her dedication appeared as if it were about to pay off in some substantial way. Lunch in the Director's office had to mean a promotion, or at least a commendation.

Coopersmith was the ultimate authority for all architectural projects in Delta Sector, a living legend in his field. His name could be found frequently in the texts Diana had studied in graduate school. While still a young man, he had been involved in the design and construction of some of the most famous buildings and monuments in the City State. Severin's Fountain. The circular Museum of Unnatural History where humanity's errors through the ages were depicted in cycling holographic tableaus. The blocky though nonetheless soaring tower of Delta Conditioning Center, where model Citizens were forged from the aberrant and maladjusted. Coopersmith had realized the dream of every serious Professional by crossing what is often—though never publicly—referred to as "the Royal Barrier."

Since genetic superiority tends to breed true, most of the robed professions are occupied by the sons and daughters of those already robed. Yet Coopersmith had overcome his common origins. He had graduated from the ranks of architects, achieved a cardinal rating, and now wore the blue robes of the City Planner.

Diana had seen the Director speak on numerous occasions—building dedications, professional social functions, the yearly promotional banquet—yet she'd never formally met the man or exchanged so much as a "good morning" with him. As far as she knew, Coopersmith was unaware of her existence. She was merely one of the scores of anonymous designers who worked far beneath him. At least until now.

She speculated on what other luminaries would be at the luncheon. Directors from other sectors? Famous architects? Probably not many since it was being held in Coopersmith's office rather than a conference room. Odds were that she'd get a chance to speak to the Director, a chance to score more points than she was already in line for. She began planning what she would say.

Diana spent what remained of the morning at the mirror in the rest room, redoing her hair and make-up. She thought about painting her nails but decided there wasn't time. She did abandon her everyday work shoes for a pair of higher heels she kept in her desk for special occasions.

Diana was nervous. At the same time she felt very sure of herself. Unlike her chosenmate, self-confidence had never been a problem for her. She'd always had enough for the both of them.

Inspired by Josie's illegal books, which he'd taken to reading while his paramour slept by his side, Thorne began to write a "book" of his own. Actually no more than a diary, filled with random jottings of his new experiences and observations. These jottings, over time, would reach modest book-length proportions. To reproduce this disturbed and ill-conceived compendium of illusions and misconceptions in its entirety would be pointless. Thorne's actions would soon speak louder than his words. However, certain passages are worth noting. His first entries were fragmentary and personal.

> "There are vapors rising from deep within me. As I confront them, they take form: the need to love and be loved, the need for unrestricted freedom, to assert my self, my individuality, even if it is aberrant by the standards of the age. What good is a society if it locks the most basic part of our beings within us?

> "Why I record these thoughts I am not sure. Unless perhaps to clarify them within my own mind and bring some order to the confusion that overcomes me."

Later his voice would adopt the tone of a would-be political philosopher. As his alienation continued to grow, as his conditioning was stripped away, he would become expansive and visionary.

> "Bureaucracy and its endless rules, what many societies of the past saw as a necessary structural evil, has become our way of life. In our world nearly all diseases have been cured or controlled. War has become a thing of the past and likewise famine. Yet in many ways our species has reduced itself to a state of existence akin to that of its once-distant insect brothers."

More trite speculations to cover the tracks of an anguished psyche. Any qualified Guardener of the lowest grade would have been able to see this diary was one more secretive outlet for Thorne, another way he could rebel without repercussions. Increasingly close-minded and subjective about his own actions, having forsaken his objectivity training, Thorne failed to grasp this. He had already passed beyond a point from which he would never be able to confront himself objectively again.

The top floors of the building were a sanctum that ordinary workers seldom entered. They were not listed on the building's directory and one had to change lifts and pass a sentry station to reach them. In this day and age, when peace and harmony reign throughout the City State, it was an unnecessary precaution, a holdover from days when acts of terrorism remained rampant.

The guard at the sentry station checked Diana's name off a list. He gave her a thorough once-over before handing her a small plastic card.

"Just follow the beeps," he told her. "Don't go anywhere else or it will set off an alarm."

The illumination on the top floor emanated from large panels mounted on the ceilings and walls. There were no shadows anywhere. The light had a pervasive quality that revealed every object clearly yet was soft and diffuse at the same time. The pile of the carpet was so deep it clutched at Diana's heels with every step.

The first thing she saw upon emerging from the lift into a broad foyer was a holographic model of Delta Sector. As she passed around the exhibit she marveled at its detail. Everything was up to date. Buildings under construction appeared to be under construction. Glideways moved and lights shone from office windows. Diana realized this was not a recording that cycled through a repeating pattern, but a real-time holograph. As clouds passed outside the windows she could see their shadows passing on the model before her.

Beyond the exhibit, large planters with living plants were spaced along a wide hallway. A lesser woman might have been intimidated by such luxuriant surroundings, but Diana immediately felt at home here. In her heart of hearts, she knew this was where she belonged.

The hallway branched several times, but with the softly beeping card in hand there was no problem finding Coopersmith's office. In a large and sumptuously furnished anteroom she was greeted by the Director's personal assistant, a stocky woman with flaming red hair whose cool efficiency and cooler glance sent a chill up her spine. Diana gave it back in kind with her own icy stare. After all, even if the woman occupied an office five times the size of her own cubicle, she was nothing more than an exalted secretary.

Once she was ushered into Coopersmith's inner sanctum, Diana was surprised for the second time that day. The room was large enough to accommodate several luncheons...and several conference rooms! Groupings of expensive furniture were scattered across the floor. Oversized holos of exceptional clarity—not slogans but natural scenes—slowly evolved upon walls paneled with real wood. Yet it was not only the room that surprised her, but the fact that there was no table with luncheon settings. And besides the Director and herself, no one else was present.

Coopersmith stood with his back to her, looking out a window that covered an entire wall from floor to ceiling. He left her fidgeting for several seconds before turning to face her.

"Sit down, my dear."

He was a tall, barrel-chested man who looked to be in his early fifties. Diana knew he was more than a decade older. What little hair he had left was gray-white and cropped close to the skull. A high forehead and prominent nose gave his countenance a striking if somewhat ominous appearance. Coopersmith wore a light blue robe stitched with intricate geometric designs. A darker blue sash, cinched at his waste, shimmered with gold tassels.

Diana was about to select one of the chairs that faced Coopersmith's desk—a long oblong, its surface fashioned from a single slab of dark cherry-colored wood—but the Director had already emerged from behind the desk and was gesturing toward a couch at one side of the room. As she crossed to the couch Diana realized the carpets here were even thicker than in the hall. The heels had been a mistake. She felt herself wobbling slightly. She sensed or imagined she could sense Coopersmith's eyes on her back.

The Director approached and stood looking down at her. He gazed at her expectantly for several seconds before speaking.

"You don't recognize me, do you?"

"Why of course I do. You're Senior Director Coopersmith." Diana was about to go on, to deliver the speech she'd rehearsed earlier. She wanted to tell the Director how much she admired his designs, how she had looked forward to meeting him, but the way the man was staring made her hesitate.

"That's not what I mean, my dear." Coopersmith smiled and reached within the folds of his robe. He drew forth a small silver flute, placed it between his lips, and proceeded to play a few halting notes.

"Teatro?" Diana exclaimed with alarm.

Richard Thorne's conversations with Diana were limited in topic and scope. Every time they talked about something serious, they snagged on the same cusp: Thorne's overly critical nature.

In contrast, Josie encouraged this nature. Rick and Josie discussed everything and anything, from the trivial to the sublime. The seduction of his body accomplished, the seduction and abduction of his mind continued apace. Whether she knew it or not Josie was a master at sophistry, at making the most outrageous conclusions seem sensible. Echoing the revolutionary claptrap of her father, she would draw Rick into conversations that supposedly showed all the errors of the City State.

"How long was the work week when you were a kid? How many hours did you father and mother work?"

"A standard week." Thorne shrugged. "About forty hours, I guess."

"And how long is it now?"

"It's supposed to be forty, but it's usually longer. There's always so much to do."

"But haven't we made technological advances over the last twenty years? Labor-saving devices? Machines and computerized assembly lines that allow a few people to accomplish the work of hundreds? Shouldn't the work week be shorter rather than longer? Shouldn't you have more free time than your parents had?"

"But our goals are different," Thorne explained. "We're trying to accomplish more than we did then. To continue to raise the standard of living. To ensure the Near Future and strive to create a Future Perfect." He realized he sounded like the posters that lined the walls of his office. Despite his own dissatisfactions with the City State, when confronting Josie he often found himself defending it.

"So what's the point of technology if all it does is create more work? I thought it was supposed to free us from drudgery."

Neither Richard nor Rick had an answer for that. He was no match for Josie when it came to argument. Her rhetoric could tie him in knots and then untie him to her own advantage.

And another time:

"Has it ever occurred to you that most of the work you do is meaningless? What do they do with all those statistics anyway?"

"They get published in reports."

"Reports for what? Reports to whom? They just want to keep everyone busy so they don't spend too much time thinking. And when you're not working, they try to fill your life up with nonsense. Meaningless sports rivalries, vapid entertainments, the latest styles to wear and the newest fads to embrace. It's a soft and easy slavery but you are still in chains. The real choices lie beyond your reach."

This contention is so absurd it hardly warrants a response. Josie no doubt thought it would be better if our Citizens spent their time engaged in illegal sexual couplings, reading censored books, consuming deleterious drugs, sleeping until noon and failing to contribute in any way to the general welfare.

"What you don't realize," she went on, her eyes hard and piercing Rick's faltering gaze, "is that the City State is your enemy. It represents special interests, and unless you are part of those interests, it only wants to use you. Under the guise of freedom it fosters a kind of stifling paternalism. It decides what's good for us and what isn't. I'd rather make my own decisions and mistakes."

And another time still. It wasn't enough that he paid her handsomely for their time together, she had to keep pounding away at him, hammering her thoughts into his.

"And what about the destruct incidents? How does your perfect City State explain those?"

Josie was referring to those rare occasions when certain individuals seem to inexplicably snap and go on a suicidal rampage of one kind or another, killing and injuring other Citizens and eventually committing suicide themselves.

For once Richard's study of history came to his advantage. "It's because we're not perfect yet," he told her. "Nearly all societies have spawned destructive fanatics of one kind or another. It's a behavioral anomaly that's yet to be resolved. Besides, it doesn't happen very often."

"More often than you think," Josie nodded knowingly, with no knowledge except unsubstantiated slum rumor. "They hide it whenever they can."

Not long after such conversations, Josie's extreme notions would find their way into Thorne's diary, transformed and warmed over but their origins clear to all except the man who was writing them down, who imagined he was uncovering profound insights.

Spurred on by horror stories from Heather, Diana harbored an ongoing fear that one of her Tuesday night couplings would pursue her into everyday life and disrupt her mating and career. Men could be so ridiculously passionate and obsessive about things, particularly sex. Now her fear had become a reality. Yet this was no ordinary man pursuing her. Coopersmith was not only robed, he was one of the leading members of her profession, a man who could make or break her career. There was danger here, yet there were also possibilities. And surely some way she could play them to her advantage.

"How did you find me? How did you know who I was?"

Coopersmith grinned. "The dermask can hide the freckles on your face, my dear," he said with relish as he sat down next to her on the couch. "But not on your arms. Not on your legs. Freckles have distinct patterns."

"I take it you like freckles."

Up close, in the pervasive light of the sixtieth floor, Diana could see the Director was wearing make-up. As he leaned toward her, his face revealed its full six decades and more. He was practically an old man. Easily old enough to be her father, perhaps her grandfather.

"Do I like them?" Coopersmith asked rhetorically. "Why, I love them. I adore them. I am a connoisseur of freckles...a gourmet and a gourmand of freckles. And I can assure you, my dear, yours are exceptionally delicious." The smile that split the Director's face was obscene and slightly crazed. He was now sitting next to her on the couch and had placed one hand on her bare forearm. Clearly what he had in mind for lunch involved neither soup nor salad, fish nor fowl.

Diana recalled her encounter with "Teatro" with unpleasant clarity. She remembered when he removed his silver slimsuit he had also unfastened a girdle that revealed, even in the relative dark of the mating chamber, the rolls of fat around his waist. She remembered how he had drooled over every inch of her flesh. How their actual coupling was, thankfully, almost over before it had begun. And how afterward she hurried home to take a shower that was long and hot.

Like many of her Tuesday night encounters, Diana had merely tolerated the sex. It was not the sexual freedom of Tuesday night that appealed to her as much as all that preceded it—the varied entertainments, the music, the dining and dancing, the flirtations and the idle conversation—the air of a carefree romantic interlude that pervaded the atmosphere of the evening. She enjoyed both the pretense she was a free woman and the ongoing confirmation she was a desirable one.

Coopersmith was running his hand up and down her arm. He was breathing heavily and his eyes were glazed. Diana again noticed the expensive mating band on his wrist. She reached out and lifted Coopersmith's hand away, taking it in both of hers.

"Does your chosenmate," she asked, "have freckles?"

"My chosenmate!" Snapping out of his trance. "What does *she* have to do with anything?"

"If not," Diana went on, ignoring the Director's question, "I'm sure you can find plenty of freckles at the Halls of Expression. Freckles that could please the most demanding gourmet. More freckles than the most dedicated gourmand could consume in a lifetime."

Coopersmith may have been a member of the robed professions, she thought, a legend in his own time, the ultimate authority for all architectural projects in Delta Sector...still he was a man, and she had seldom encountered a member of that species she couldn't run in circles. She had once joked to Heather that she kept her chosenmate on spin cycle more than half the time.

Gracefully as the morass of the carpet would allow, Diana rose and strolled across the room to the window. She could see beyond Delta Sector and into Gamma to the south.

As far as her eyes traveled there was City stretching to the horizon. She knew there would always be more City to build, more buildings to design, ample opportunities to prove herself...if she were given a chance.

Rick and Josie discussed anything and everything. From the mundane to the fantastic. Even the rhyme Thorne had seen scrawled upon the wall of the abandoned building came up.

"Maybe we should run off to the Dead Lands together," Josie joked.

"Sure, if we want to die of radiation poisoning."

"How do we know the Dead Lands would kill us? They lie about so many other things, why not that? If the Dead Lands are so dangerous, how come the City keeps growing?"

"The new lands have been decontaminated."

"What? From radiation? Most atomic radiation has a half life of centuries." She nodded toward the bookcase. "Look it up if you don't believe me. It seeps into the rocks, the subsoil, the water tables. How can they decontaminate that?"

Thorne didn't know what a half life was and had only a vague idea of a water table. He realized, not for the first time in their dialogues, that Josie's reading had given her knowledge to which he had no access. What he didn't realize was that most of this knowledge was useless, much of it in error.

"If they can change the weather, they can decontaminate the land."

"Sure," Josie said, nodding toward the rain-streaked glass. "Sure they can." Clear skies had been forecast.

As every child is taught in primary school, only death lies beyond the sanctum of the City. The rad count rises swiftly to fatal levels. And in those areas where radiation is not a hazard, there is nothing but a wilderness where no Citizen could possibly survive for long.

Turning back to the room, Diana rested against the window glass with her hands behind her, hips forward. Coopersmith stood in front of her. His eyes moved up and down her body. His arms were folded across his chest.

"I've looked over your file, my dear," the Director said, "and I'm quite impressed. You could go far in the department. With the right...sponsor...there could even be a robe in your future someday. I have a project that's starting up...a personal project that could use a talented young architect like yourself. It's something that requires special attention...a special commitment. The hours can be long and irregular, but the rewards are there for a person with the right attitude."

"It sounds...interesting," Diana said, maintaining the charade that Coopersmith was discussing an actual project. And perhaps he was, she thought. Perhaps she could play the old man to her advantage before letting him down. "I'm flattered you should consider me. I'm sure I wouldn't disappoint you and I'm very interested...in rewards." She rocked back and forth against the window. "But could you tell me more about it, what it would entail? Give me more details and time to think it over...and I'll get back to you as soon as I decide."

As she delivered her coy recital Diana saw the Director's features cloud over. She suddenly realized she had misjudged both the situation and the man. The real Coopersmith retained none of the affability and charm of the false Teatro. His stare was now openly hostile. This was clearly not the response he had expected to hear and he was not pleased with it.

"Think quickly, my dear!" Coopersmith stabbed the air in her direction, moving his hand up and down as he spoke. "I can make sure you stay a G-15 for as long as you're in this District. I can have you designing bathrooms for fireball stadiums for the next ten years. Think quickly! I'm not going to ask you again!"

Rick and Josie discussed anything and everything. From the books they read together to the drugs they took. From the stars and other worlds that might circle the Earth to the Riots/Revolt of '37. From Severin's Fountain to the vendors in the streets to Daniel DeLyon. From the meaninglessness of existence to the meaning one could define.

Everything except for Diana. And Josie's other clients.

For when Thorne entered Josie's domain he left the reality of life behind. And she did also. He came to her as if he had no chosenmate and home to return to. As if this slum apartment with its books and drugs and ready sex were his true habitat and they were the true couple. As if only the moment existed and there was no tomorrow.

Diana glanced around the room. The thick carpets, the plants, the perfect lighting, the exquisite furniture and the oversized holographs slowly cycling on the wood-paneled walls. She may have felt at home in this environment, but when it came to the power that resided here, she was not even a worthy interloper. Whatever circles she could run Coopersmith in were bound to be of limited circumference and duration...and only serve to irritate him further. She considered her options and concluded that she had no real options at all.

Steeling herself with a deep breath, which she expelled as a sigh, Diana moved away from the window and sat on the edge of Coopersmith's desk. Once a decision was made she had never been one for halfhearted measures. She crossed her legs and leaned back, supporting her weight with the palms of her hands, letting the already short skirt ride farther up her thighs.

"Did you know," she said, meeting the Director's eyes head on, "if you come close enough, you can see freckles right through my stockings?"

Coopersmith moved toward her, undoing the sash of his robe. "Now that, my dear, is what I call the right attitude."

Ten minutes later Diana found herself in the lift being whooshed downward. She was starving and had to be back at her desk in less than a half hour. She headed for the cafeteria on the ground floor. Yet once she filled her tray with the usual fodder, she discovered her appetite was gone. What she craved more than food was a long, hot shower.

Thorne was having to work late more often to maintain the pace of his assigned duties and make up for time lost by his ever wandering mind. One night among many such, as he plodded on through the dinner hour and his co-workers went off to homes and families and evening entertainments, he found himself alone on the floor, immersed in the emptiness of the deserted chairs and desks. The faint buzzing of the overhead fluorescents was the only salve against complete silence.

In this tomb-like atmosphere, his forgotten powers of concentration shook off the corrosion of disuse. His mind, for once free of its carnal preoccupations, shifted into the abstract realm of number, symbol and logic. He became a blithe skier upon such pure white slopes, and each ride down was invigorating enough to call him up for the next. Once, when he was younger and his life simpler, it had often been like this. If he'd been able to summon a similar intensity for a fraction of his normal working day, he would have been ripe for a promotion rather than an upbraiding.

After he finished his work, shutting up his desk and turning off the lights behind, Thorne entered the central processing room. A few lights glowed upon control panels.

Other than that it was dark, but the many machines were still functioning without need for illumination. The steady hum of their thinking was everywhere. It fled to the porous ceiling and floors to seep back out at a lower frequency that could be felt in the bones and teeth if one stood motionless. It rose all around him from shapes not hulking in the dark, but clear black squares and rectangles against the speckled tiles of sound proofing that lined the walls. There had been a time when Thorne's consciousness sensed itself as attuned to the harmonics of that humming, when he saw his work as a complement to his life. Now it had become a contrary vibration within his chest, a multi-tonal heaviness linked to what he increasingly perceived as a worthless existence.

He moved amidst the shapes and wondered not for the first time about the degree of their sentience. He ran his hands across the dry, lightly grained plastic surfaces, which from a distance gave the appearance of metal. He resented that duplicity because the illusion had once fooled him.

Later that night he wrote in his diary:

"We live in a world of plastic simulated to a million different forms, wearing as many masks as there once existed true variety in the world. The floors beneath our feet are plastic. The walls, the table, my clothes, my pen, and a good part of the paper in which I write are plastic. It is all the same, dreadfully, horribly the same."

His twisted mind would not stop its endless dissection. It had taken another blessing of the world in which we live and cast it as a curse.

Diana Logan could have rejected Willem Coopersmith's advances and accused him of violating the Sexual Code. Coopersmith's robed status gave him extraordinary privileges yet no right to threaten her career. As we ultimately learned, Diana was not the only woman who suffered as a result of the Director's excesses. If the man's criminal behavior had come to light during his life he could have been tried, convicted, and reconditioned. Or more likely, given his age and status, forced into an early retirement.

Yet Diana's conclusion that she had no choice but to give in to Coopersmith was not without its logic. Facing an unsubstantiated accusation from a G-15, Coopersmith would not have been required to submit to a cyberscan. The best Diana could have hoped for was a transfer to another sector, a longer commute, and a questionable mark upon her record that could hinder future advancement. A like mark on Coopersmith's record, one that would have no effect on his career, offered her little incentive to level charges against the Director.

Yet Diana not only submitted to Coopersmith's demands, once she made her decision she committed to it fully. In the first months of their involvement she exhibited no outward reluctance, attempting to please the Director in any way she could.

In many ways Coopersmith and Diana spoke the same language. They saw the world in terms of those who ruled and those who did not. That the Director would offer her advancement in return for sexual favors made perfect sense to Diana. If Coopersmith had been functioning rationally, they could have both profited from their illegal relationship. However, it was not only Diana's freckles that drew Coopersmith to her, but the disturbed need to exercise control over another individual's life.

As their relationship progressed, the Director's demands grew more extreme. On one occasion he recited a series of dirty jokes, making Diana touch parts of his anatomy and hers as they were referred to in each vile narrative. More than once he made her don a garish dermask that was more heavily freckled than her own complexion. Diana tolerated all of it, awaiting the rewards she'd been promised. She smiled seductively. She moved the way she was told to move. Though she sometimes felt like crying out in disgust when she rubbed the sparse bristles of the Director's balding scalp, the only sounds that escaped her throat mimicked sighs of pleasure.

Yet each time Diana raised the question of rewards, Coopersmith told her to be patient. He was waiting for the right project before reassigning her. He couldn't be too obvious about it. There was already a surfeit of G-16s, too many supervisory promotions in the last year. Though she'd done everything she could to please the old man, Diana began to realize there would be no rewards, no new projects or promotions. Only further demands.

For Coopersmith, any concession to Diana would have been an admission that she held a degree of power in their relationship. For a man who had come to understand little else than power, that was not acceptable.

It is no longer possible to scan Willem Coopersmith and view his matrix, though it is possible to make an educated guess as to its nature. A strait and narrow stalk with few striations, a clearly defined blossom well within the accepted range, at first glance varying from complete normalcy only in its narrowness and the excessive brilliance of certain nodes. One would have had to look carefully to see the faint aberrant strand, a Death Path that split radically from the defined limits of Coopersmith's life, branching from the node where his personal aspirations and sexual obsessions collided and intertwined.

Diana had always had enough confidence for the both of them, yet Richard Thorne—or Rick, as he thought of himself when he was with his slum lover—was beginning to develop a confidence of his own. One with no basis in reality. Ever since meeting Josie he'd experienced the same transitory illusions of power he'd felt while playing chess with DeLyon the following day. During one of these brief megalomaniacal episodes, Thorne found the courage to bring up Josie's other clients.

They had already coupled and were lying in bed together reading. Josie was rereading one of her favorite books, an impossible fantasy called *Don Quixote*. Thorne was struggling through a twentieth-century novel titled *Gravity's Rainbow*. It made little sense to him. Nor has it to our finest scholars. Yet the more Thorne read, the more it seemed to communicate a warped kind of meaning. Only he could not be sure whether it was the meaning the author had intended or one he had created in his own mind.

Thorne stopped reading and shut the book.

"I want you to stop seeing other men," he stated.

Josie glanced up. For the first time in their relationship he'd taken *her* aback. She was silent for a moment before she laughed awkwardly.

"Why?" she said. "What difference does that make?"

"I just want you to myself."

He could have said he was falling in love with her, that he was in love with her already, but his courage didn't extend that far. And if it *were* only infatuation, he knew the feeling would have its day and pass.

"How am I supposed to support myself?"

"Can't you get a stipend from the State?"

"I already tried that. They told me to get a conditioning first. Then I could apply for Citizen status. They only support the ones they can't condition."

"Would that be so bad...to get a conditioning?"

Josie's eyes flared. "I don't want anyone messing around with my mind." Her voice was angry. "I like it they way it is and I thought you did, too. I'm not seeing that many men anyway. Only a few regulars. I'm not a street walker, in case you haven't noticed."

"I don't care how many there are. I want you to stop seeing them. All of them. We'll work out something." The sound of his own voice surprised Thorne. The sudden depth and weight of it.

"I'll think about," Josie said, her own voice trailing into the "rough velvet" Thorne was so taken with. "Let me think about it."

Daniel DeLyon was trying to watch a fireball game on the holo—a classic rivalry, the Stalwarts versus the Paragons—while his mother paced the small room in smaller circles, shredding a tissue and periodically blocking the screen. De-Lyon had bet on the Stalwarts. Not much but enough to make it count. They were leading by a single goal. The ball was barely glowing. Any mitt could pick it up and score.

"Sit down, Mother," DeLyon said.

There was no obvious response, but after several more circuits of the room, the old woman sat next to him on the couch and looked at him expectantly.

"Where's your father? Shouldn't he be home by now? I know he's usually home by this time."

DeLyon had long since given up telling her Stuart Jimson was *not his father* and that the man had been dead for twenty years. Clearly the woman belonged in a Senior Center where she could receive the care and attention her condition warranted. Each generation as it comes of age must live its own life without being hindered by those whose lives are nearly over. That is why there are senior facilities for those who can no longer function. DeLyon's mother had refused relocation and the treatment she needed. She chose to remain with her son, a detriment to his life. Out of a misplaced sense of loyalty, DeLyon acquiesced to her wishes.

"Would you like your medicine now, Mother?"

The old woman's eyes brightened. She was used to non sequiturs. Most of her own conversation was composed of them. She stopped shredding the tissue and lit up like Severin's Fountain.

"Yes, that would be so nice!"

DeLyon knew how to handle his mother. It was Josie who was the problem. She had failed to follow through on either of his plans: to seduce Thorne away from Diana or blackmail him with threats of exposure. Yet DeLyon had not abandoned the first plan completely. There might be ways to realize it even without Josie's cooperation.

As he returned with his mother's whiskey, toting a healthy dose of the illegal brew for himself, a sudden roar erupted from the holo. The fireball had exploded, spattering blood across the playing ground and knocking several members of the Paragons senseless. There were only minutes left in the game.

DeLyon's pale face broke into a grin. "I've done it again," he said aloud to himself. Though he was used to winning, nothing gave him greater satisfaction.

"Your glass is bigger than mine," his mother carped. "Let me have some of yours."

Thorne was more exhausted with each passing day. Dreams unwanted and bizarre continued to disturb his sleep. During the time he spent with Josie he rarely slept at all. When he did he would sometimes dream about Diana. When he was with Diana he would invariably dream about Josie.

In one frequently recurring nightmare he and Josie were lost in a City sector neither had ever seen. They were trying to find their way back to the slum and her apartment. The glideways had malfunctioned. They walked along a lone street, circuitous and in disrepair. Chunks of asphalt and mounds of construction debris hindered their passage. The street ran without intersections for what must have been miles, winding past deserted concourses and anonymous buildings. Tier upon tier of windows towered above them. The thin band of sky revealed beyond their steep concrete ascent was clotted with dark clouds.

Sometimes the street would begin to fill with scattered pedestrians, as lost as they were. Solo and in pairs. They would encounter strangers who in the context of the dream were strangers no longer. Though Thorne had never seen any of these people in real life, they seemed to know him and he now recognized them. Perhaps from some other dream incarnation. Most of them also knew Josie and took it for granted the two of them should be together. Yet when he asked these familiar strangers how to find the slum, most of them would merely shrug as if they had never heard of such a place. On occasion one would begin pointing and gesticulating, launching into a series of directions so lengthy and complex they were impossible to follow let alone commit to memory. Josie had a scrap of paper in her pocket but no one had anything to write with. Or she would have a pen and no paper. Sometimes a subplot of the dream, tediously nightmarish in its own right, would involve the search for a pen or paper so they could write down directions.

"We're going in circles," Josie would declare. "We've been down this way before."

And that would be the cue for Stuart Jimson's arrival. He would come stumbling toward them from what would have been the end of the block if the street had blocks. In one version he came floating and swimming toward them, as if he was a fish and the air was water. Not the ponderous and hirsute Jimson of the holodramas, but a compact dark-complexioned man no older than themselves. He resembled Josie so closely he could have been her male clone.

"You...have to...go now," Jimson would tell them, forcing the words from between small white teeth, pointing back in the direction he had come. Though there was no visible sign of an injury, the man acted as if he were in pain. "You...have...to...run!"

In the direction of Jimson's outstretched arm, Thorne suddenly saw a phalanx of Guardeners marching down the street. Row upon row in battle armor like the assembled pawns from a hundred endgames. Marching forward with blind determination.

Beyond their massed ranks the City was burning. A high wall of flames scalded the sky and illuminated the smoke from its own conflagration.

At that point, Thorne always woke covered with sweat and convinced he had cried out. Yet his chosenmate remained unconscious by his side. Though there were times when Diana was whimpering from deep within her throat. Times when she grasped the sheets with hands clenched as if she had somehow tapped into his terror.

"It's your move," DeLyon announced.

"Sorry," Thorne muttered.

As usual, his mind was wandering from the game.

Along the promenade a group of young women with sparkling gold-and-silver-sheeted legs were passing. Thorne had fastened upon one whose sheer black blouse was undersized enough to accentuate her breasts, while its short sleeves pressed against the pale flesh of her arms. In his fantasy he had removed the blouse, skirt and silver stockings, centered her upon a bed, and stood dazzled by the expanse of her whiteness.

Despite the fact he was sleeping with two women on a regular basis, or perhaps because of it, he was more sexually aware than ever. This was one more side effect of the drugs he was taking with Josie. He was becoming an addict both to chemical stimulation and his own carnal desires.

With no clear plan of attack, Thorne shifted his king to a safer position.

DeLyon laughed out loud at the move.

"I think you should stop seeing Josie for a while. Things are getting far too serious between you," he suddenly announced.

"It was your idea I should see her in the first place."

"I just wanted you to meet her. To see her once and a while. I thought it might be a way for her to make some extra credits. I didn't know it was going to turn into a steady thing. Instead of making more money, she's making less. She's cut back on seeing other clients. You're giving her—."

"All of them?" Thorne broke in.

DeLyon waved the question away. "Some of them? All of them? How should I know? She doesn't tell me everything. The point is you're giving her hopes that can never be realized. And I'm having to give her even more credits so she can get by."

"What kind of hopes?" Thorne asked.

"She thinks you're going to leave Diana and mate with her instead."

DeLyon's argument made no sense to him. He had never promised Josie anything. Not because the thought hadn't occurred to him, but because he was afraid she would laugh in his face. Though they acted like lovers in the time they spent together, their relationship remained that of Courtesan and client, or whore and john as Josie would have crudely put it.

He continued to pay her for each of his visits, and although she took his credits without comment, as if they were incidental, she took them nonetheless. He sensed what was bothering DeLyon was jealousy. He no longer had Thorne's companionship to himself, seldom had it at all for that matter, and he was no longer the main person in his sister's life.

A shadow fell across the board, across the sun. A man was standing by their bench, his face in shade, the light shining through the fringe of hair that crowned his head. It was Sol Thatcher.

DeLyon knocked over the piece he was about to move.

"Hello," Thorne said. "Do you play chess?"

Thatcher rubbed his hand along his jaw, and his cheek wrinkled as if it were made of paper. "Used to play. Not anymore. Don't have time for games. Not chess anyway. Was pretty good once. In my day." The man's speech was as clipped as the grass beyond the iron fences.

"Got any advice for me?" Thorne nodded toward the board.

Thatcher took another step forward.

"Hmmnn...." He scratched his jaw again and tugged on one ear. "Use your queen. But not in the way you might think."

"Thanks," Thorne answered, though he didn't have a clue what the man was talking about.

DeLyon hadn't said a word. Thorne could see his friend's hand trembling as he righted the piece he had upset.

Thatcher glanced at the building behind them. "Well...back to it. Back to it again."

As soon as he was out of earshot, DeLyon hissed, "He suspects something. He's on to us."

"What could he possibly know? He was only making conversation. The Guardeners are after terrorists and criminals, not people like you and me. They don't have time for the likes of us." Thorne was deluding himself once again. Despite his numerous crimes, he still considered himself a normal Citizen.

"My stepfather was a terrorist," DeLyon reminded him. "You don't think there's a tag on my file? You don't think they've got their eyes on me, waiting for me to slip up?" DeLyon paused and all at once shifted course. "You and Josie need to stop seeing each other. At least for a while. It's too dangerous right now. You've got nothing to offer her anyway. You'll never leave Diana."

Thorne looked at him a moment before replying. He couldn't see the connection between Thatcher's interest in them, if it existed, and his own involvement with Josie.

"It's not up to you whether we continue to see each other or not. That's between Josie and me. I'll see her whenever I want, as long as she wants to see me. And I'll give her whatever credits she needs. If you're really worried about your sister you should get that computer terminal out of there before someone besides me finds it!" Thorne looked down at the board. "It's your move."

"Half-sister," DeLyon corrected him. "Josie's only my half sister." He advanced a pawn. "And she promised she would keep that door locked."

All at once Thorne saw what Thatcher had been talking about. The combination was so obvious he didn't know how he could have missed it. He moved his queen to the last row, sacrificing it in trade for a knight. It didn't matter whether DeLyon took the trade or not.

"Mate in three," Thorne observed. "You can't win playing half the board."

That evening, lying abed with his inamorata, deranged by the drugs they had taken, staring at the smear of stars beyond the warped skylight, Thorne decided to test DeLyon's claims. He hinted at a future for them together.

"Who knows? Maybe we'll become chosenmates someday."

As he feared, Josie laughed, not exactly at him but laughter nonetheless. "Don't be ridiculous. I could never live in your world." She turned away. "What would I do? Become a Courtesan at the Halls?"

"You could become an actress," Thorne said, fastening on the first thought that came to his mind.

Josie laughed again. "What? In some computer-generated propaganda play proclaiming the glory of the State? Denouncing my own father? I'd rather be dead."

Tuesday night in late winter.

Earlier in the day a cold front and its associated storm had defied all computer models and swept in from the northeast. The Weathermen had been caught off guard and meteorological barriers breached. Last minute holding actions had been to no avail. The storm released its full force against the City. Temperatures plummeted into the low thirties and the winds were unmerciful. Barometric pressure continued to fall. Standards Control was in an uproar. By the following afternoon, as the rain continued unabated, angry words would be exchanged between the two bureaus and careers would be damaged.

An icy sleet beat down through the night air, obscuring visibility, slicking streets and glideways, filling the gutters with a dirty slush. Thorne hunched into the wet chill as he made his way to Josie's loft. It was the kind of weather that could dampen the brightest mood, yet as the thunder rumbled and the lightning cracked and the cold droplets beat against his face, Thorne felt exhilarated. The force of the weather, its raw unleashed energy, matched his mood.

Within minutes he would be at Josie's side and her arms would be around him.

The streets of the slum were deserted in the downpour. There were no vendors or prostitutes out tonight.

Then a dark figure loomed out of the rain from the opposite direction, staggering toward him, straightening as it came abreast. Suddenly Thorne found himself shoved swiftly back into an alleyway, against the wall of a building.

"Your credits or your life, friend," a guttural growl informed him.

"What?"

"Your credits or your life. Hand them over, Citizen!"

The man spit the last word with contempt. He was wearing a knit cap pulled down over his forehead, a dirty shapeless jacket. A rank animal odor emanated from his damp clothes. He shoved Thorne harder against the wall. The rain continued to stream down all around them.

"Now, Citizen! And I'll take that timepiece, too."

The man was holding up something dark and pointed.

The personal possession of firearms is of course prohibited in the City State. The only guns Thorne had ever seen firsthand were those holstered in the belts of Guardeners. Yet he'd seen enough on the holo to recognize one when it was thrust in his face.

Conditioned to avoid violence, a normal Citizen would have acquiesced immediately and reported the incident to the nearest Guardener Station. Thorne's reaction was abnormal in the extreme. If he gave up his credits, he instantly reasoned, there would be nothing to give Josie. Without further thought he reached out and grabbed the man's wrist, forcing him bodily backward at the same instant.

There was a sharp explosion and a flash of blue-white light as the gun discharged and fell to the pavement. The man leaped away from him

"You crazy son of a bitch!" he shouted. "Are you trying to get someone killed?"

The gun was lying at Thorne's feet. He bent down and picked it up.

The man continued to back away from him, waving his arms wildly about his head. "It's not supposed to be like that. I'm supposed to show you the gun and you're supposed to give me your credits. That's how it works! Don't you know anything?"

Thorne raised the gun to take a closer look. It was so small it fit comfortably into his palm. Yet it was capable of taking a human life. He held death in the palm of his hand.

"You're crazy!" the crazy man screamed at him as he ran off into the night. "You're completely insane!"

Thorne pocketed the gun but remained standing in the alleyway for several minutes, indifferent to the falling rain, astounded by the incident and his own response. He was trembling, but it was from excitement rather than fear.

When he reached Josie's apartment he found her waiting for him with a large bath towel. "You're soaking wet," she said. "Get out of those clothes. I'm going to dry you off."

Then she saw the expression on his face and dropping the towel she came to his side.

"What's wrong?"

"On the way here...there was a man...he wanted me to give him my credits."

Josie shrugged. "What do you expect? This is the slum. That kind of thing happens all the time. Are you okay? How much did he get?"

"He didn't get anything." Thorne showed her the gun. "I took this away from him."

Josie's eyes widened. "Good for you!" she said excitedly. Ignoring the wet clothes, she put her arms around him and hugged him. "I didn't think you had it in you! Tell me all about it!"

It was the first time she had openly praised him.

Praise for violence. For emotions beyond reason.

A flash of lightning illuminated the skylight and thunder sounded nearby. The entire building shook from the impact. The lights flickered off and on. Then off again.

Rick would save his story until later.

Immersed in darkness, he lifted his lover and carried her to their bed.

Diana was surprised when Thorne had donned his dermask and announced his intention to venture into the storm. Although it was Tuesday, she expected him to stay home on a night such as this. He always had in the past.

Thorne was equally puzzled when Diana said she was also going out. Between Thorne's supposed evenings with DeLyon and Diana having to "work late on a new project," the two were spending less and less time together. Each suspected something was amiss with the other yet neither seemed to have the time or inclination to explore it further.

Thus far Diana had told only Heather about her dilemma. After all, she never expected anything from her chosenmate besides companionship and compliance. Even if Richard had been a more forceful man, there was nothing he could do. She didn't expect much from Heather either, except some sympathy. Yet Heather proved incapable of grasping her problem.

"You're coupling with an actual Director!" her friend exclaimed. "I should be so lucky. Who wouldn't want to couple with a Director?"

Diana liked Heather well enough. Though there were times she had to admit that Richard was right. The woman could be a complete idiot.

By the time she reached the address Coopersmith had given her, Diana was drenched to the skin. Until now the Director's demands had been limited to their "luncheons" together and an occasional evening tryst in the confines of his office. Sometimes a week would go by without her hearing a word from him. Then he would decide to see her for several days running. Although their actual couplings remained short, no more than a few seconds, the preludes were often long and involved, increasingly bizarre and often humiliating.

Coopersmith had never demanded to see her outside the office before. Diana didn't know what to expect but dreaded it nonetheless. When she arrived at the address she had been given, she found herself confronting an ordinary apartment building, somewhat shabby, in an older section of the City. Once Coopersmith buzzed her in she had to trudge up two flights of stairs—there were no lifts—dripping water all the way.

The inside of the apartment proved no less shabby than the building that housed it. The Director was sitting on a couch with a drink in one hand. He was not alone. His stocky personal assistant with the flaming red hair was by his side, already partially undressed. She had far more freckles than Diana, who after her first visit to Coopersmith's office had guessed the form much of her "personal assistance" took. The woman glared at her as always, icy and hostile. Diana was feeling too depressed to return the frigid glance. For the first time in her life, the world was taking a direction completely beyond her control.

"Diana, this is Connie. You two have already met," Coopersmith said, "but I thought all of us could get to know one another other a little better. For starters, I want both of you naked."

As he was flipping through his diary, admiring his own en-tries, a shadow fell across the page. Thorne started back, nearly tipping over his chair. It was after work and he thought he was alone in the office.

Sol Thatcher was standing over his desk, looking down at him. He had approached without a sound.

"Burning the midnight oil?" Thatcher asked in his usual clipped fashion.

"Someone's got to do it," Thorne managed.

In the fluorescent lights Thatcher's florid complexion was cast in a dirty pallor. His eyes were like two shiny beads lodged in the fat of his face, impenetrable, so dark that Thorne could not distinguish the iris from the pupil. Yet for a second, as he met the man's gaze, he sensed something be-yond those eyes, as if a curtain had lifted to reveal a room filled with strangers engaged in incomprehensible acts. Then the curtain fell back into place.

He felt an overpowering urge to close the notebook. Could Thatcher read his writing upside down? His hands were frozen in place.

"Strange bird, that DeLyon," Thatcher announced apro-pos of nothing.

Thorne nodded.

"Could go far. Get behind the ball. Push like the rest of us. Not really a team player though. Heard that he gambles."

"Well...," Thorne hedged, "he does like games." He didn't like the direction the conversation was going.

"Dangerous habit. Build up debt. Can't pay it off." Thatcher shook his head and frowned. "There a problem there?"

"I really don't know," Thorne answered. "I don't think so." Actually he did know. DeLyon always seemed to win far more than he lost. The bets were for relatively small amounts, but they must have accumulated over time. He suspected DeLyon's illegal computer terminal was in some way the source of his good fortune.

"Do me a favor," Thatcher said. It sounded more like a command than a request.

"A favor?"

"Keep an eye on him. Any trouble. Let me know. Nip it in the bud. Before it gets out of hand."

Thorne nodded dumbly. "Sure," he said, "I'd be glad to do that."

"Well. Let you get back to it." Thatcher nodded toward the open book on the desk. "Like you said. Someone has to do it."

It was only later, on his way home, that Thorne realized the incongruity of the phrase Thatcher had used when he approached his desk. "Burning the midnight oil" was an anachronism, an idiom that had fallen into disuse centuries ago. Thorne had first encountered it in one of Josie's books and she had explained it to him. It referred to a time before electricity when people used oil lamps to light their homes. How could Thatcher know about such a thing unless he was a student of history? And why had he used it in a conversation with him?

Another bizarre dream that night. Prompted no doubt by Thatcher's visit. Thorne was playing game after game of chess with the man. Losing game after game. Each time Thatcher won his physical stature would increase. He became so huge that when he reached to make a move his hand covered the entire board. And when that hand withdrew, although he could not be certain, Thorne swore that more than one piece had shifted squares. Yet what could he say? Thatcher was a supervisor. He couldn't accuse him of cheating.

Just before he woke, Josie and DeLyon appeared. They each stood on one of Thatcher's shoulders, no larger than chess pieces themselves relative to the size of the man. Chains were attached from their necks to Thatcher's immense ears. They both stared at Thorne accusingly.

With one forearm Thorne suddenly swept the pieces from the board. They drifted off as if they were feathers. Several clung to the sleeve of his slimsuit. Suddenly he was as large as his adversary. Thatcher leaned forward, reaching out for him with both hands, shaking his head and frowning. Josie and DeLyon swung back and forth like long dangly earrings.

"What's the matter?" Diana mumbled.

"Nothing," Thorne mumbled back. "Just a dream."

"You cried out. Something about roses and lions."

"It was nothing. Just a bad dream. Go back to sleep."

Diana spotted Connie sitting by herself in one corner of the cafeteria. On a sudden impulse, she carried her own tray to the table and sat down opposite her.

The woman looked up, gave Diana one of her absolute zero stares, and returned to her food without a word. Although they'd been intimate with one another days before, albeit not by choice, they might as well have been strangers.

"Why do you hate me?" Diana asked.

"I don't hate you," Connie answered, "I just have no use for you." The woman was in her late thirties, yet there was no mating band on her wrist. She was plain and overweight and there was nothing remarkable about her whatsoever except for her bright red hair and the freckles that densely covered her flesh like a flaming brand.

"Have you ever thought about doing something about it?"

"About what?" Connie asked. She took another mouthful of string beans and chewed them thoroughly.

"About him. About what he's doing to us. If we stuck together, if we talked to the right authorities, if we backed one another up...."

Connie interrupted before she could finish. "The Director is a great man. He can't be judged by ordinary standards. He deserves special privileges...special liberties." It sounded to Diana as if Coopersmith was speaking rather than Connie. "Besides, don't worry, he'll get tired of you soon enough. I've seen your kind come and go before. I'm the only one that stays."

"And what about his chosenmate?" Diana said.

"His chosenmate! What does she have to do with anything?" Connie picked up her unfinished tray and moved several tables away without a backward glance.

The next day when Diana was summoned to Coopersmith's for "lunch," she discovered the woman had reported their conversation to the Director.

"I understand you've been making plans behind my back," Coopersmith began before she was halfway across the room.

Diana paused in mid-stride. Coopersmith was sitting at his desk with papers spread before him. It was the first time Diana had seen him working on anything. She improvised desperately and quickly, nodding toward the outer office. "I don't trust that woman. I was testing her loyalty to you."

"Connie has always been loyal to me. You're the one who wants to betray me."

"No!" Diana lied as sincerely as she had ever lied about anything. "No. I'm telling you the truth. I was testing her. Maybe only because I'm jealous. She gets to spend every day with you."

"I'm afraid not, my dear." It was Coopersmith's turn to lie. "I was about to approve your promotion to G-16 and assign you to your own project. But you can forget that now." He leaned to one side and began digging in a bottom drawer of the desk. "You've been a very bad girl. And you are going to have to be taught a lesson."

As Coopersmith's hand emerged from behind the desk and Diana saw what he was holding, she took a step backward.

"No!" she cried out. "You can't!"

Coopersmith laughed. A bark of a laugh that contained more malice than humor. He flipped on the voice line to his outer office. "Connie," he said, "will you come in here for a minute. I've got something I want you to help me with."

Afterward, after she had been taught her lesson, once she admitted she had been "a bad girl" and begged the Director's forgiveness with tears running down her cheeks, Diana spent what remained of the lunch hour regaining her composure in the private bathroom adjoining Coopersmith's office. It was the largest and most sumptuous bathroom she'd ever seen. Walls of black marble veined with gray-white swirls. Fixtures that were real gold. A tub that could accommodate a trio and more. She hated everything about it. She hated it because it belonged to Coopersmith. She had never hated anyone so much in her life, never grasped the true meaning of the word before. Or the word "fear" for that matter. For she feared the Director more than she hated him. No man had ever made her cry before...for any reason.

And she cried again that night, uncontrollably, when with nowhere else to turn she at last told her chosenmate everything. At least her version of it.

Utter disbelief. Followed by blinding rage. Leading to a deadly inner calm and a compelling sense of purpose. These were the emotions Thorne experienced one atop another as Diana's story unfolded by fits and starts, as he held her in his arms and he brushed away her tears only to see them fall again.

Diana's tale of her travails as related to Thorne omitted her own involvement, her attempt to ply rewards from the Director. Instead it dealt only with Coopersmith's threats and actions against her. She had become an innocent victim in this scenario, and to a large extent in her own mind.

Thorne had never seen his chosenmate behave like this before, and it was hard for him to envision her in this role. Diana had never exhibited vulnerability in any way except as a ruse during the brief courtship that had preceded their mating. Once their vows had been taken and their mating bands sealed, Thorne soon realized that any helplessness on her part had been an act. Diana had taken charge of both the details and the direction of their lives. She had always been the dominant one, the more forceful, when it came to making decisions. Thorne had come to rely on her strength while at the same time resenting it. Seeing her like this—her face pale, eyes red, the expression in those eyes bruised and haunted—the tenderness he had felt in the early years of their relationship was reawakened.

Rather than being put at a loss, he now embraced the role of hero and protector as if he had been waiting in the wings for his entrance. Like an understudy who might never get a chance at such a meaty role again, he was all at once prepared to play his part to the hilt. No clues to the source of his newfound determination can be traced in the disarray of Thorne's projection. Perhaps the fantasies he had imbibed from Josie's books influenced his behavior. In some of these absurd tales lone individuals not only took on the impossible and accomplished it, but overthrew entire governments single-handedly.

"You're not going to see him any more," Thorne told his chosenmate. "That man is never going to touch you or hurt you again!"

"But I have to see him!" Diana said. "He can destroy my career. Don't you understand, that's why I can't report him? No one would take my word over his!"

"He's not going to destroy anything. Don't worry. I'll take care of it."

"No!" Diana insisted. "Believe me. You can't do anything. He's one of the most powerful men in the Sector. He can ruin both of our lives. All I can do is apply for a transfer and hope he doesn't block it. You can put in for a transfer, too. We'll move to a different sector and leave all of this behind us. We can make a new start."

This was the Diana he knew. Forlorn as she appeared to be, she was once again planning the course of their lives. She hadn't confessed to him because she expected him to help her in any way. Only because he was essential to a decision she'd already made.

"I said I'd take care of it," he repeated.

"But there's nothing you can do!"

Given that he no longer loved her, that from his current perspective he had never loved her in terms of what he now thought of as love, Thorne felt that he owed her this much. His twisted mind had fastened on a plan that would not only solve Diana's problem but lead to the solution of his own. If he freed her from Coopersmith, he reasoned that would make them even. He could then leave her without internal recriminations. All that remained would be for him to convince Josie they could have a life together.

Conveniently forgetting the extent of his own crimes against the City State, Thorne was appalled that Coopersmith's crimes could go unpunished. He had probably seen the man before, at some social-business function he'd attended with Diana, though he had no memory of what he looked like. Though now he could see him vividly in his mind's eye. A thousand and one scenarios of revenge tore through his imagination. Coopersmith battered and bloodied. Coopersmith with a lance impaled through his heart. Coopersmith consumed by flames in the deepest pits of Hell. Coopersmith's head upon a block while an immense steel blade descended from the sky and the populace cheered wildly.

"Stop it," Diana cried, pulling away from him, "you're hurting me!"

As fantasies of the Director's death played through his mind, he had been gripping her arms more and more tightly.

"I want you to go to bed now and get some rest. Take a sleeping tablet if you have to. I'll be back later."

"No! Where do you think you're going?"

Thorne was rummaging in the closet on his side of the bed. Diana had never seen him like this before. Waves of feeling rushed through his eyes. His voice sounded different, deeper and suddenly commanding, possessed of a resonance that had always been lacking in the past. He was showing her a side of himself he had thus far revealed only to his slum lover, a side that had been primed and fueled by that lover.

Thorne took something from the closet and shoved it into a pocket of his slimsuit. Diana couldn't tell what it was. He was already slipping on his jacket and heading for the door.

"Get some rest," he told her over his shoulder. "I want you to stay home from work tomorrow. And don't worry. Willem Coopersmith will never come near you again."

"No!" Diana cried. "Come back here! You're only going to make things worse!"

But she was talking to the empty air.

She fell back on the bed and consoled herself with another fit of tears. She didn't deserve this. Hadn't she always been a hard worker and a satisfactory mate? Hadn't she sacrificed more than once to make Richard happy? Now he was acting like so many other men, trying to order her around just like the Director. There was no way she deserved this. Not any of it.

Later, as she waited in vain for Thorne to return, Diana not only took a sleep tab, she took two. For the barest instant she toyed with the idea of swallowing the entire bottle.

Thorne was looking at Josie as an old woman. An old and sick woman...and also a little crazy. She stood in the doorway, blocking his passage. Her face was anxious.

"Do you have a message from Stuart?" she asked. "Did Stuart send you?"

Then DeLyon appeared behind her.

"No, Mother, he doesn't know Stuart. This is a friend of mine from work." He gently took her by the shoulders and turned her back toward the room. "It's almost time for your program. Why don't you get ready to watch?"

As his mother wandered back into the room, DeLyon now blocked Thorne's passage. "What are you doing here? What do you want?"

"I need some information."

"What kind of information?"

"Let me in and I'll tell you."

His friend backed reluctantly away from the door and Thorne moved past him.

"You caught me...us...at a bad time," DeLyon said. "It's usually not like this."

Although DeLyon's conapt was only a few blocks from Thorne's, he had never visited his friend at home before. There were papers, clothes, dirty dishes, scattered everywhere. As meticulous as he was at work, DeLyon was the opposite at home. His split personality became manifest, the Citizen and the incurable slum dweller existing side by side in the same body, the same mind. Thorne was so obsessed with his own concerns he barely noticed.

DeLyon took him by the arm and led him to one corner of the small room. "Now what's this all about?"

"Willem Coopersmith. I need to know everything you can find out about him. Where he lives. How he spends his time."

DeLyon's mother was sitting on the couch flipping though the holo channels. A montage of unrelated images flew past. A fireball game. An announcer reporting on a destruct incident. A child in tears. Dancers daubed with blue paint. A scenic waterfall vista that existed only as a computer simulation. Another fireball game. The sound was a barrage of scissored music and sentence fragments.

"It's on thirty-four," DeLyon shouted to her. "Press the three first and then the four. And turn it down!"

The sound vanished completely but the images continued to flow. A man harnessed to a strange machine. A silently laughing audience. A cartoon bear being chased by a cartoon mouse.

"Why do you need to know about Coopersmith?" De-Lyon asked. "And what makes you think I can help?"

"It doesn't matter why. And you think I don't know what you use that terminal for?" He grabbed DeLyon by his shirt and shoved him against the wall. Just as the would-be thief in the alley had once done to him. "You can find out and you're going to!"

"Let go of me!" DeLyon yelled, struggling in his grasp. "What are you doing? Have you lost your mind?"

"Now don't fight, boys," DeLyon's mother called from the couch without looking around. "If you fight, you can't play together anymore."

Throne released his grip and took a step back.

"It's all right, Mother," DeLyon said.

"I'm sorry," Thorne told him. Yet he remained close by, towering over the smaller man.

"What's come over you?" DeLyon was smoothing his shirt front and trying his best to put on an injured expression. "You're not acting like yourself."

"I may be more myself than ever before." Thorne felt as if his existence, all of his perceptions, were accelerating in a single direction. He'd felt this way ever since Diana's confession. "Are you going to help me or not?"

"Why should I?"

"Because we're friends," Thorne told him, "and I'm asking you to."

That gave DeLyon pause.

"All right," he said. "I can help you. But you have to tell me something first."

"I need the information," Thorne improvised, "to help Diana at work. To help her get a promotion. There's no time to explain it all, but I have to find Coopersmith tonight!"

"Not that. I don't care about that."

"Then what?"

DeLyon drew himself up to his full height. "I want to know what your intentions are regarding my sister. Are they honorable?"

Despite the situation, Thorne almost laughed out loud. DeLyon sounded like a character from one of the centuries-old novels he'd read at Josie's. The fact that she was a prostitute made the question even more absurd. Perhaps DeLyon had read the same books. Though it was hard to imagine him reading anything that didn't have to do with work or games.

"Maybe it doesn't make any sense to you," DeLyon went on. "You grew up in a City State crèche. You barely knew your parents. But I care about my family and what happens to them. I want to make sure—"

Thorne interrupted before he could finish. "I love your sister. My intentions are to make her my chosenmate. If she'll have me."

He realized his declaration also sounded like a speech from an ancient book. Along with the fact that he was announcing his intentions to his prospective mate's brother rather than to her. But there it was. He'd said it at last. This was both the direction in which he was accelerating and his destination.

"What?" DeLyon asked.

"You heard me. Now let's get out of here and get to your terminal."

"Have you told Diana you plan to leave her?"

"Not yet. But don't worry. When the time is right, I will."

DeLyon nodded slowly. "I get it. First you make sure Diana gets her promotion. Then it's okay to tell her good-by."

"That's right," Thorne agreed. "You figured it out. Now let's go!"

"No." DeLyon gestured toward his mother. "I can't leave her by herself. Every time there's a show on about the Riots she insists on watching it. Then she gets terribly upset. Someone has to stay with her. I'll go. You stay and keep an eye on her. Just switch the channel and get her to watch something else when Jimson comes on. That's what always sets her off."

His coming confrontation with Coopersmith consuming his thoughts, his perverted sense of purpose intact, Thorne sat down on the couch next to DeLyon's mother, found the right channel, turned the sound on, and tried to watch one more holoplay about the Riots of '37. This one was called "A Triumph for Tomorrow."

The opening scene portrayed a Board of Directors meeting. All the Directors were handsome and distinguished looking men in their forties or early fifties. They were discussing how they could best improve the lot of the unregistered. Thorne couldn't be bothered to follow what they were saying, but he could hear from the tone of their voices how concerned and caring they were.

Now that he was sitting he could feel the weight of the gun in his slimsuit pocket. He tried to ignore it but its presence would not be denied. He slid his hand into the pocket, feeling the grained surface of the weapon's grip, slipping his finger over the smooth metal of its trigger. He imagined what it would feel like to pull that trigger. He recalled the sharp explosion and that deadly flash of blue-white light. There was a part of him that wanted to see and hear that again, to release it at his will. Yet now that his initial rage at what Diana had revealed was dissipating, he admitted to himself he had no real intention of killing Coopersmith. He wasn't even sure the gun would fire again. Though he still planned to use it to scare the Director so thoroughly he would never terrorize another woman.

The scene on the holo shifted. A Guardener was talking to his daughter. Warning her that the streets were dangerous. Telling her they had reached a crucial time in the history of the City State when the entire Future Perfect was at stake. Thorne recognized the show as a repeat. It was the same program he'd tried to watch without sound, seeming eons ago, on the night he'd first met Josie.

He took this chance occurrence as further confirmation that he was embracing his destiny. He was exhibiting a classic schizophrenic symptom, attaching personal significance to external events that had no relation to him whatsoever. He had become convinced the world turned upon Richard Thorne.

"Where's Danny?" DeLyon's mother was looking at him aghast. "Who are you?"

"Don't you remember? I'm Danny's friend," Thorne reassured her. "He'll be back soon."

"But is it safe out there?" She pointed to the holo. "You heard what they said about the streets."

"Don't worry. He only went to Josie's for a few minutes. He'll be okay."

The woman's expression changed completely. "Josie comes to visit sometimes. And she always brings me a present! She's a dancer, you know, and an actress. A very talented girl. She's going to be on the holo someday. I just know it. I'll be sitting here...and there she'll be, big as life."

"Yes," Thorne said, "she's a wonderful...girl." And then, before he could bite his tongue. "I plan to make her my chosenmate." He was announcing his intentions to everyone except the two people who would be most affected by them, Josie and Diana.

Now the woman was frowning and shaking her finger at him. "Oh, no. You're going to have to wait. Josie's too young for that." Her face brightened again and she began to giggle. "Excuse me, young man, I must have forgotten my manners. I bet you'd like something to drink?"

"No thanks." Where was DeLyon? He glanced at his watch. A bare twenty minutes had passed.

She leaned toward him conspiratorially and raised one hand by the side of her face, cupping her mouth as she spoke to make sure no one could overhear. "It's not beer, you know," she whispered. "It's the real stuff!"

"No thanks. I'm fine." He had to keep a clear head for what was to follow, Thorne thought. He was forgetting that his head had not been clear for months, that confusion ruled his life by the day and the hour.

"Would you mind getting me some then?"

"Where is it?"

The woman shot up from the couch and headed for the microkitchen with more alacrity than he would have given her credit for. Thorne followed. The kitchen was in equal disarray to the room they had left. There were several bags of garbage piled next to the sink. One had spilled part of its contents onto the floor. DeLyon's mother was holding open a cupboard and pointing to the top shelf.

"It's up there. I can't reach it."

"Are you sure it's all right for you to have this?"

"Of course." She was smiling at him, almost flirtatious. "Danny gives it to me every night. It's like medicine. Only I'm not really sick."

As soon as Thorne took down the bottle, DeLyon's mother grabbed it away from him. She had a glass in her other hand. She pulled the cork out with her teeth, spit it into the sink, which was already full of dishes, and poured what Josie would have called four fingers.

"Take it easy!"

The woman threw her head back and downed more than a finger's worth in a single swallow. Her withered throat pulsed as the whiskey went down.

"That's better." She smiled at Thorne and blinked her eyes several times. "Much better! Thank you...young man!" Now she was definitely flirting with him.

He retrieved the bottle from her grasp, but DeLyon's mother stepped quickly away and held the glass out of his reach.

"Now, now," she said, "don't be a bad sport." She raised the glass, rocking it this way and that. "Unless you'd like to come and get some?"

Since he didn't feel like wrestling with the old woman, Thorne decided to let it go. Hopefully if she had enough to drink she'd settle down.

"You're missing your program," he told her.

After taking one look in the morass of the sink, Thorne put the bottle back without its cork. Perhaps the old woman was not so crazy after all, he thought. She knew enough to get what she wanted and hang onto it. Or maybe they were all crazy in some way or another. Every last one of them. Maybe the entire City was rife with madness and what he took for streets and buildings and parks and monuments were nothing more than the high walls and barred windows of an asylum.

A scream sounded from the living room.

Thorne found DeLyon's mother standing by the holo and pointing an accusing finger at it. "That's not my Stu," she shrieked. "My Stu doesn't look like that!" She was waving the glass around and had spilled half the whiskey on the floor.

The face of the actor who perennially played Jimson filled the holocube. He was surrounded by a motley assemblage of SDL followers who could only be described as rabble. Spittle flew from the man's lips as he shouted and waved his arms. "We have to destroy them!" he bellowed. "We have to kill the Directors. Kill the Guardeners. You will never be free until they are dead!"

Thorne was searching frantically for the holo remote but couldn't remember where he'd put it.

"Kill! Kill! Kill!" The fake Jimson's tirade rose in volume. The crowd took up the refrain. The man's fist beat the air and his long unkempt hair tumbled across his face.

"Make him stop," the old woman wailed plaintively. "Make him go away."

The conapt door opened and DeLyon entered carrying a folder. On his knees by the couch, Thorne at last found the controls and shut the holo off. In the sudden silence the echo of Jimson's battle cry reverberated through the small cluttered room. DeLyon's mother gulped down what remained of her drink in a single swallow before her son could take it away. She began coughing. There were tears running down her cheeks and whiskey dribbled from her mouth and onto her dress.

"What the hell is going on?" DeLyon glared at Thorne. "Didn't I tell you to keep an eye on her?"

Thorne sat in a chain cafe, sipping a cup of scalding coffee and leafing though the papers DeLyon had given him. The incident with his friend's mother should have impacted on him and altered his consciousness. He should have asked himself if the woman he had just met was a foreshadowing of what Josie would someday become. Crazy. Sick. Alcoholic. This was the genetic inheritance that brewed in Josie's veins. Blended with the rabid fanaticism and violence of Stuart Jimson.

Reason dictated a reexamination of the commitment he had made. Would he love Josie when her beauty faded, when she babbled on incessantly and her mood changed by the minute? When the "high ideals" she espoused failed her and she waited only for her next drink? There is no evidence that Thorne considered such possibilities. Like most of his cyberscan, the interlude with DeLyon's mother—belying the intensity of its retention—exists as one more isolated and discontinuous strand in his scattered projection.

Most of the folder was taken up with Coopersmith's history, his accomplishments and the awards he'd received.

Thorne didn't care about that. There were numerous photos of the Director, including several recent ones. He didn't look that different from the image Thorne had envisioned of him with his head upon an executioner's block. Except the actual Coopersmith was far older, practically an old man. That made what had transpired with Diana even more disgusting and outrageous. Thorne's skin crawled when he thought about it. Yet it was also going to make what he had in mind easier.

DeLyon had been thorough. The folder contained more than public records. His friend had managed to access secure information and break into Coopersmith's personal files, including the man's appointment book. The Director had two residences, a conapt in Lambda Heights and a house on the outskirts of Omicron. He lived in the City proper during the week and spent the weekends in Omicron with his family. Except for a business meeting at 1400 hours, most of the current day's office schedule was blank. In the evening, Coopersmith was due to dine at his club at 1800. Two hours later he had an appointment at the Halls of Expression.

Thorne called the Lambda residence from a public booth. The only answer was a recorded message. Coopersmith was still at the Halls or out somewhere else. When the Director arrived home, he planned to be there to greet him. Once again, circumstances seemed to have conspired in Thorne's downfall.

As the glideway rose into the hills of Lambda Heights the neighborhood changed rapidly. The buildings were spaced farther apart and there was more landscaping between them. Soon the landscaping was no longer artificial but consisted of actual trees and shrubs, some of them in bloom. This part of the City was old yet immaculately maintained. Islands of real grass abounded both in the median strip between the glide-ways and along the sides of buildings.

The streets were mostly deserted. Thorne had no business being here at this hour. If a passing Guardener Patrol stopped to question him, he'd have to come up with a convincing explanation for his presence. Yet the only crimes committed in Lambda Heights were occasional cases of domestic abuse. There was little reason to patrol this area and his passage remained unchallenged.

Thorne rode the glideway beyond Coopersmith's building, and then circled back in the other direction on foot, using the landscaping as cover. He was walking on real grass and there was no one to stop him.

The night was unseasonably cold. An icy wind swept down from farther up the hill. The Weathermen had never regained complete control since the storm of two weeks earlier. The wind pierced Thorne's slimsuit and light jacket, rippling them against his body. He felt chilled and feverish at the same time, exhilarated by the cold and burning with energy from within. All of his senses seemed immensely alive, his mind and body operating in overdrive.

The clouds were moving swiftly overhead and what stars he could see were blurred by the wind's passage. When the moon showed its face it was a nearly featureless white disk. All about him Thorne could hear the rustling of the branches and leaves. He could see the play of light and shadow on the ground at his feet as they were tossed this way and that.

What he was about to do felt as natural to him as this small segment of the natural world in which he now stood. Intoxicated by his own delusions, he was convinced he was asserting his true nature, realizing what was meant to be. He felt as if all that had transpired over the last several months was at last coming to fruition. Yet by now he was only on a

downhill plunge, a slave to compulsions he could no longer
control. Just as Thorne embraced the night he was embracing
the darkest urges within himself. He had no comprehension
of the force of these urges once released.

Beneath its surface surety and apparent singleness of
purpose, his mind was a complex chaos. He told himself once
again he had no intention of killing Coopersmith, but he
continued to fondle the gun in his pocket. He told himself
that once he freed Diana from Coopersmith, he would then
be free to leave Diana and claim Josie as his own. Yet he had
no sign from either woman this would be the case. This was
not a game of chess he was playing. Even seen in terms of
that game, he was far more a pawn than a player.

Thorne waited, a shadow among shadows, more feverish
by the moment despite the chill wind, his thoughts leaping
from his imminent confrontation with Coopersmith to far
future idylls with his slum lover, hatching one improbable
scenario after another in his imagination.

He watched as several couples and individuals passed
along the street, walking briskly in the cold to add their own
pace to that of the moving glideway. And then Thorne spotted a lone figure, approaching more slowly and already on
the glide's outer belt. As the figure passed beneath an overhead arc light, the countenance of his prey was revealed. Coopersmith looked even older than in his photograph. His
hands were shoved deeply into the pockets of his coat and he
moved like a man who was ready for sleep.

Thorne stepped from the shadows and onto the glideway a few paces behind the Director. With a few quick steps
he fell in beside him, matching his stride.

"Nice evening, thanks to the Weathermen" he said sar-
castically. "They've outdone themselves tonight."

Coopersmith gave him an incurious sidelong glance,
added a noncommittal grunt, and kept walking.

"Not as bad as last week though," Thorne went on. "They really fouled up then."

"No one's perfect," the Director mumbled.

"Say," Thorne said, "did you ever hear the one about the Weatherman, the Guardener, and the Architect at the Halls of Expression?"

Coopersmith's attention seemed to pick up. Thorne had correctly surmised from Diana's descriptions that the man would always be ready for some salacious humor.

"No...I don't think so."

"Well, the Weatherman wanted a woman who was like a balmy summer day."

They reached the door of the building. Thorne held it open for the Director. They entered a large lobby illuminated by overhead lighting. Ornate metal sculptures of bronze and steel adorned the walls. The ceiling was high and vaulted. Trees with silver leaves grew from evenly spaced planters.

"And the Guardener wanted a woman who was like a rose in full bloom."

Thorne leaned close to Coopersmith as they passed the sentry station in the lobby. The man seated at the station was watching something on a handheld holo. He barely glanced up as the two men swept past. Recognizing Coopersmith, he assumed they were together.

"And the architect wanted a woman who was built like..."

An empty lift awaited them and they entered, standing at opposite sides of the cylinder. Coopersmith punched a button on the wall panel. Thorne noticed that the lifts here were more luxurious and spacious. As the doors closed and it accelerated, its action was smoother.

"Go on," Coopersmith said, "built like what?"

Thorne took a step forward and stood with his legs apart.

"And the architect wanted a woman with freckles."

"What?" Coopersmith said.

"I want you to stay away from my chosenmate."

Coopersmith looked startled for the briefest moment, but he quickly regained his composure. "And who would that be?"

Thorne realized that Diana was probably not the only woman Coopersmith was intimidating into sexual relations. "It doesn't matter who she is. Just stay away from all of them!"

The man shrugged. His hands were still in his pockets and he was leaning back against the railing mounted on the walls of the lift. "I don't know what stories your chosenmate has been telling you, but I can assure you I've done nothing to her. Or anyone else's chosenmate for that matter. Why should I? A man in my position already has more single women throwing themselves at him than he knows what to do with," he asserted smugly.

As he stared at Coopersmith's pasty face with its arrogant expression, Thorne felt a torrent of hatred for the man rising within him. He wanted to wipe away that arrogance forever. He was not only defending Diana. Coopersmith had become an emblem for the entire City State and the unjust life he believed it imposed upon him.

"You son of a bitch!" Thorne exploded. "Bastard! Sick rapist!" He had of course been conditioned against profanity. At this point another violation as minor at this should hardly surprise us. He pulled the gun from his slimsuit pocket and leveled it at the Director's chest.

Coopersmith looked at it strangely for a moment, as if he didn't understand what it was, or at least couldn't believe it. Then Thorne saw fear blossoming in the Director's eyes. In the midst of his craziness he realized that if you acted crazy enough, you could frighten anyone. Although he was completely out of control, at the same time he felt as if another part of his being was watching this performance from a distance with a calm certainty, even pleasure. All of it was happening exactly as he had planned for it to happen.

"Now wait just a minute...," Coopersmith began. His hands were out of his pockets and he was holding them up in front of his chest, as if they could shield him from a bullet.

"I said," Thorne shouted, cutting him off, shaking the gun in his face, "stay away from her!" He swung with his free hand, slapping the Director hard on the side of his head.

"That's for threatening her career!"

Thorne felt a satisfying sting on the flesh of his palm as Coopersmith stumbled against the wall of the lift, grabbing the railing for support. Thorne swung again, backhanding the Director's other cheek and temple.

"That's for forcing her to couple with you."

Coopersmith gasped and fell to one knee. The lift slowed and the doors opened on his floor. He made an attempt to rise but Thorne grabbed him by the collar of his coat and hurled him back. He punched a button at random. The doors closed and they began to accelerate again.

Waving the gun wildly, Thorne closed his free hand into a fist and aimed it at the Director's face. Coopersmith finally reacted, ducking to one side and half coming to his feet as he charged against Thorne's body. The force of his weight carried both of them crashing against the opposite wall.

The next thing Thorne knew they were rolling on the floor of the lift and Coopersmith was grappling for the gun. His fingers closed in a viselike grip on Thorne's wrist and his weight pinned him down. Although the man was grunting and breathing heavily, he was surprisingly strong for his age.

The door whooshed open on another floor.

The Director suddenly released his hold on Thorne, but he made no attempt to rise. His arms and legs began to thrash wildly. A series of unintelligible cries escaped from his throat. Thorne shoved his twisting body to one side and scooted back against the wall of the lift.

Breathing heavily, he watched in horrid fascination as Coopersmith's struggles slowly ceased. The man's face was mottled and there was a thin line of blood trickling from his nose.

Thorne didn't know if Coopersmith was dead or merely unconscious, but realized there was no time to find out. Someone else could call the lift or come down the hall at any minute. He stood and shoved the gun back into his slimsuit. The doors of the lift began to close. He reached out and forced them open again. Grabbing the Director under his arms, he dragged his unresisting body into the empty corridor, and then returned to the lift.

Moments later, back in the ornate lobby of the building, his mind racing and his breath still short, Thorne hurried past the guard at the sentry station. The cold night welcomed him and claimed him as a creature of its own. The deed was done, the crime committed, its ultimate consequences inevitable.

We must admit the investigation was bungled. Though much of it was not our fault.

A couple returning home from a late dinner, residents of the building, discovered Coopersmith's body only minutes after Thorne had fled. They had ridden up in the same lift in which the confrontation had taken place. Rather than notifying the sentry on duty on the ground floor or calling MedAlert, they first tried to revive Coopersmith themselves. When Guardeners and medical help were finally summoned, they also took the same lift. By this time, the evidence of the crime scene had been thoroughly polluted. And if he had not been already, Coopersmith was thoroughly dead.

Although the direct cause of death was determined to be a massive heart attack, the circumstances were suspicious. What had brought on the attack remained unclear. Why was Coopersmith found on the thirtieth floor of the building when he lived on the twenty-fourth? The residents of the floor were questioned at length. None of them had seen or heard a thing. None admitted to knowing the Director personally.

A number of minor injuries were discovered on Coopersmith's body, bruises and scratches. Once we had tracked his activities for the evening, these were attributed to a sadomasochistic session he had engaged in with two Courtesans at the Halls of Expression.

The sentry on the ground floor reported that the Director had entered the building in the company of another man who had left shortly thereafter. He described the man as short and blonde and of medium build. He had confused Thorne with one of the actors in the holoplay he had been watching. He had never really seen him at all.

Without specific leads to follow, the investigation was shortly closed. The murder of Willem Coopersmith was officially recorded as a natural death until weeks later, when we placed Thorne under the cyberscan, emptied out his mind, and confirmed his guilt.

They heard the news on the morning holocast as they sat eating breakfast. The authorities were seeking a short blonde man for questioning, supposedly the last person to see Coopersmith alive.

Diana stared at her Chosenmate, her face drawn and blanched in the harsh morning light, her eyes wide in disbelief.

"What have you done?" Her voice was thick and the words rasped in her throat. She shook her head back and forth, her uncombed hair falling against her cheeks. "What did you do?"

"I didn't do anything," Thorne told her. He had lied to Diana so often by now it came naturally to him. "Do I look short and blonde to you? I would have done something, I wanted to do something, but I never had the chance. I couldn't find Coopersmith. You heard it yourself, he died of a heart attack."

"But where were you last night?" Diana was staring at him as if she had never seen him before. "Where did you go?"

"Never mind," Thorne said. "That's not important. The important thing is that you don't have to worry about Willem Coopersmith anymore. You're free of him forever." He stood up, his breakfast unfinished, barely touched. "I have to leave for work or I'll be late."

He could see the doubt on her face. He knew that she only half believed what he had told her if she believed any of it. Thorne walked out the door without another word. He didn't care what his chosenmate might think. As far as he was concerned, he no longer owed her a thing.

On the way to work Thorne picked up a news sheet at the local kiosk. Coopersmith's death had made the front page and a lengthy continuation on page nine. The article summarized the Director's life and his numerous achievements and awards. It ran on and on with praise and concluded by stating how much Coopersmith's talents would be missed. The man was portrayed as a patron saint of the City State.

Thorne had seen such displays before when a high City State official died. He knew it was only transitory. By tomorrow or the next day most everyone would have forgotten about Willem Coopersmith. Still, the canonization of the man irked him. It wasn't like that at all, Thorne thought. It was only a fragment of the truth and that made it a lie. Coopersmith had used his power and stature to molest Diana and who knew how many other women. He'd probably been doing it for years. And his death had been prosaic and mean. He had died in an altercation over another man's chosenmate. Thorne wondered how many other high officials led lives that were just as disreputable.

At any minute and every minute, for the next few days, Thorne expected armed Guardeners to storm the apartment or show up at his office and carry him off for incarceration and reconditioning. From everything he had learned from primary school onward, wasn't that exactly what he deserved? Coopersmith's actions may have been criminal, but they were nothing compared to his own. He had committed the ultimate crime against society, the murder of another human being. He tried to tell himself he wasn't responsible for the Director's death, but knew enough to admit that he was the direct cause, even if he hadn't stabbed the man, shot him with the gun, or pitched him off a high building.

The minutes became hours, the hours turned into a day, and the days conspired to a week...and nothing happened. And when nothing happened *to* Richard Thorne, something happened *within him*. In killing Coopersmith he had also killed a part of his old self and stripped away the last of his conditioning. He wrote in his notebook:

"Though I still live in the same building and work in the same office and walk the same streets, I have crossed the border into another land. Everything I have leaned since childhood, the truths that were drilled into me as absolutes, I now see as no more

139

than relative. They no longer apply to me and to be free of them is exhilarating. I now perceive the world with different eyes than ordinary men and it is a vision I cannot deny."

His megalomania had scaled new heights. He no longer thought of himself as Richard Thorne, Statistician, G-12. His consciousness was no longer divided and the transformation to the criminal deviant known as Rick Thorne was complete. He had become a sociopath, a man who would take what he wanted and do what he needed to survive with no concern for the welfare of others.

Although Thorne told Diana nothing, he told Josie everything. He expected his paramour to be shocked by the deviant act he had committed. Instead, in her own deviance, she was sympathetic.

"You didn't kill him," Josie said. She was sitting on the bed, her legs tucked under her. Thorne was pacing the oversized room. "The man died of a heart attack. It was an accident. Besides, you were only doing what any decent man would have done for his chosenmate. You were defending her against a monster. Sounds to me like he was someone who needed killing."

"But I don't want Diana as a chosenmate," Thorne stopped his pacing and turned to face her. "I don't love Diana." He paused significantly. "I love you. I want to be with you."

Although DeLyon's plan number one had come to fruition, although Thorne was not only ready but eager to leave Diana, Josie now rejected the idea completely.

"Love me?" She was looking away from him. She ran one hand down her leg, then began picking at the nubs on the worn bedspread. "There's no point in loving me. There's no future for us beyond what we have here. This is the limit of our world. And you'll tire of that sooner or later."

Thorne sat down next to her. He reached out and with the tips of his fingers against her cheek, forced her to turn to face him. "Don't you feel the same way? Don't you want us to be together?"

She wouldn't look up. She stared down at the bedspread and there were tears gathering at the corners of her eyes. She quickly wiped them away with the heel of one hand.

"You've been good to me," Josie said. "I'm very fond of you. But there's no point in talking about it. I can't enter your world, and you won't live in mine. It's just a fantasy. Why can't you just leave it at that? It's enough that you can be here as much as you are."

Rick's hand cradled the nape of her neck. He leaned forward and kissed her. He put his arms around her and her body fell into his embrace and returned it.

"Don't worry," he whispered. "We're going to be together. One way or another. I promise you that."

Thorne sat in a chain cafe, sipping a cup of coffee and eating a sandwich, mulling over his dilemma and his options. There were only a few tables occupied beside his own. Across from him a man already grossly overweight was chewing with great gusto. At the other end of the room, two teenage girls were trying to listen to one pair of earphones at the same time. Faint strains of tinny music escaped across the room.

As far as Thorne could determine, there were no laws against a Citizen mating with a non-Citizen. Though it would certainly be frowned upon. There was no way that he and Josie would ever be accepted for modern accommodations, which meant living in some decaying older conapt like the one DeLyon shared with his mother. He could also forget about further advancement at work. There were always certain social events attached to that and attendance with one's mate was mandatory. Diana had always shined more than he had on such occasions. Josie, if she even agreed to attend such affairs, would be more likely to detonate them.

None of this dissuaded Thorne. He had just killed a Senior Director, a highly respected member of the robed professions. And still he walked free. If that was possible, he reasoned that anything could be possible.

His first obstacle was of course Diana. If their mating was to be dissolved, they would need City State approval. They would be encouraged to seek counseling. Their final decision would have to be mutual. Or one of them would need sufficient grounds to leave the other. Thorne had no grounds beyond Diana's protracted affair with Coopersmith. Under the circumstances, that was not something he wanted to record in an official hearing.

He also knew Diana well enough to be aware that she would oppose anything he suggested. Particularly something that would change both of their lives forever.

The only thing to do was to become so unpleasant, so inadequate and indifferent, so intolerable as a chosenmate, that Diana would make the decision herself. It wouldn't be hard for him. Every time he looked at her, he invariably thought of Coopersmith. Even though she claimed none of her actions had been willing, that the Director had blackmailed her from the beginning, he couldn't get the image of the two of them together out of his mind. It made him shudder and feel cold all over. And the more he thought about it, the less he believed Diana's version of the events.

Thorne looked down. He realized he had eaten the entire sandwich without tasting a single bite. He had unconsciously crumpled the wrapper and was now tearing it methodically into smaller and smaller pieces. The pieces were scattered over the table, in his lap, on the floor. When he looked up he saw the fat man across aisle had stopped chewing and was staring at him. The two teenage girls were whispering back and forth, and giggling when they glanced in his direction. When they saw him looking back, they both got up and quickly left the restaurant.

As soon as she realized the shadow of Coopersmith no longer fell across her existence, Diana's recovery was a rapid one. She returned to work, welcoming the routine assignments that occupied her mind. She didn't want to think about the Director's death and whether or not her chosenmate had been involved. She wanted to forget Coopersmith and return to the life she had known before entering his office. And though she was for the most part successful in blocking out memories of the humiliation and terror she had suffered at the Director's hands, it soon became clear that the life she sought to return to no longer existed.

Diana took the first good look at her chosenmate that she had in months. She watched him coming through the door, sitting at the table, opening a cupboard, and she saw a different man than the one she had mated. Or at least one who thought he was different.

Thorne barely spoke to her or looked at her any more. In the mornings he would leave for work without their sharing breakfast together. Most evenings he would go out and not return until late. When she asked him where he had been, he told her he had been playing chess with his friend DeLyon.

"You don't have to always go out," Diana suggested. "You could invite him over and play chess here."

Her chosenmate didn't bother to answer her.

On the few nights Richard did stay home, he watched the holo or sat reading a book. Not a hand reader, but a book! She couldn't imagine where he had found such a thing.

143

Diana was no longer sure what Richard might do. Nor could she tell what she should say or do to regain control of their lives. So one night she decided to follow him.

Then there was the effect of Coopersmith's death upon De-Lyon, who suddenly became a stranger to Thorne, or at least acted like one. He would look away when they passed in the hall. There were no more daily games of chess in the concourse. DeLyon was eating his lunch elsewhere.

The single time Thorne cornered DeLyon at his desk in the midst of a busy office, his former friend spit out two sentences under his breath before becoming intensely involved with his computer screen.

"Stay away from me! And stay away from Josie!"

Though DeLyon was unaware of the particulars, he was convinced that Thorne had been somehow responsible for Coopersmith's death. Yet as Thorne knew, DeLyon was the last person who would be likely to report anything to the Guardeners. Hadn't he been involved himself by pointing the direction to Coopersmith with his own illegal computer?

Thorne shrugged and dismissed DeLyon from his life in the same way he planned to dismiss Diana. He told himself it was Josie alone that mattered. In truth, the only thing by this time that mattered to Rick Thorne was himself. His own perverted needs and desires.

Diana watched her chosenmate, a block ahead of her, disappear around a corner. She had planned to trail him to whatever destination he had in mind, but she could go no farther. Everything about the slum environment—the dirt, the smells, the vendors in the street with flies crawling on their food—sickened her. Worst of all, her esthetic sensibilities were appalled at how the buildings were thrown up at random, like puzzle pieces forced into place where they didn't fit. Diane turned and hurried back the way she had come until she was once again safe within the controlled environment of the City.

She still didn't know what her chosenmate was up to, but she had some sense of what the slum had to offer. Whatever it was, she knew it must be illegal. Illegal women, illegal drugs, illegal gambling, probably all three. Whatever it was, it could lead to no good. She had also learned that in a few weeks, perhaps sooner, the slum was scheduled for demolition. There would be no more illegal whatever-it-was in Delta Sector for her chosenmate to seek.

A lot could happen in two weeks. Diana didn't want to wait even that long. If she could get Richard to herself for a while, she was convinced she could seduce him all over again. Not only his body but his spirit and mind. That was when she decided to book the virtual vacation. According to what Heather had told her, anyone who knew anything was trying it. And the reports were absolutely fantastic.

Vacation

Certain decontaminated lands have been set aside as resort areas for those who have achieved Robed Status. In addition to superior accommodations and live entertainment, these vacation enclaves offer a variety of recreations in natural settings. Superior service to the City State naturally leads to superior rewards.

Even if their careers progressed rapidly, it would be many years before Diana and Richard would be granted such a privilege. Like most Citizens, they took their vacations at one of the Sector Recreation Centers. The Centers also offer excellent accommodations, a range of fine dining, entertainment, swimming, and various group activities. Though all of this takes place indoors and under one roof.

Many Citizens, even those with less critical natures than that of Richard Thorne, had faulted the Centers for their lack of variety and predictable routine. No matter which Center one chose, every vacation was much the same. There was no sense of adventure, no impression of leaving the everyday behind. It was in response to such open dissatisfactions that the virtual vacation was developed and released.

When Rick tried to leave their conapt for the evening, Diana stood in his way. She was leaning against the door with her arms behind her. Her hair was cut shorter and in a different style. Her eyeliner was precise and excessive.

"I've got a surprise for you!"

He looked her up and down without responding. She seemed hard to him, hard and wasted.

"Well...don't you want to know what it is?"

"All right," he sighed, "tell me."

"We're going on vacation this weekend."

Thorne frowned and shook his head. "Don't be ridiculous! I can't take a vacation now. There's too much to do at work. They'd never give me the time off." Work was no different than usual. What he couldn't see was spending time without seeing Josie.

"But it's only for the weekend," Diana assured him. "We leave on Friday night and we'll be back by Sunday night. It's the latest thing. It's not a real vacation, but it's more real than real...better than real! It's a virtual vacation. You must have seen the adverts on the holo. We can go anywhere we want. Look at these!"

Her hands came from behind her back. She was holding several colored brochures and smiling at him. He thought of her smiling at Coopersmith.

Thorne reluctantly took one of the brochures and began to leaf though it. Animated holographic images leaped out at him from each page. Sunlit white beaches, frothy waterfalls tumbling in emerald forests, blue lagoons with sailboats tacking back and forth, a panorama of brilliantly lit and landscaped city streets where handsome couples moved along the glideways.

More mindless entertainments, he thought by way of Josie, more distractions. He was about to toss the brochure to the floor and force his way past Diana when the idea came to him. A vacation could be the perfect answer. He could make their two days together so hellish, his behavior would be so truculent and outrageous, Diana would never want to see him again. She would be as eager as he was to dissolve their mating.

"All right," Thorne shrugged, "I'll give it a try."

"Wonderful!" Diana burbled. She put her arms around him and gave him a quick hug. She was acting the way she had when they were first together, he thought, before they were mated. "I've got another surprise for you, too...but that can wait until we reach our destination."

"I suppose you're already packed," Thorne said, chilled to the bone by her embrace.

"No," Diana said, "we don't have to pack a thing. Every-thing we need will be there waiting for us."

"But where exactly are we going?"

"Where else?" Diana said with satisfaction. "We're going to the Future Perfect."

Thorne had seen holo ads touting this new form of travel but never given them much attention. What Diana neglected to tell him was that although their trip would take two days objective time, it would seem much longer subjec-tively. She also failed to mention that besides offering a choice of destinations, virtual vacations were packaged in different emotional flavors.

There was the "Happy Family Vacation" for those who had decided to raise their own children. Some active singles opted for "Lone Wolf on the Prowl," while others found the more sedate "Solo Sabbatical" to their liking. If Diana had been taking the vacation with Heather, they could have cho-sen "Two Friends on a Lark." Since she was going with Rich-ard and seduction was her aim, she had settled on the "Chosenmates Love Holiday."

The room they entered was dimly lit. Soft vaporous music filtered from concealed speakers. The walls and ceiling offered a continuous holo of slowly moving colored abstracts that flowed to the rhythm of the music. There were two chairs awaiting them, side by side, both cushioned and with footrests raised. Beside each chair, on a small table, stood a frosted glass filled with pale green liquid. They had been told to relax, enjoy the beverage, and their vacation would begin shortly.

"This is delicious!" Diana said, already seated and sipping her drink. "You should try it."

Thorne stood with his hands jammed into his pockets, turned away from her, watching the moving patterns unfurl. They reminded him of clouds trailing across the sky in the aftermath of a storm. Ever since leaving their conapt he had been surly and uncommunicative. When Diana tried to take his hand on the tunnel train, he had disengaged it immediately and continued staring out the window at the gray nothingness rushing past.

"Really," Diana insisted, trying her best to ignore his behavior. "I've never tasted anything like it."

Thorne shook his head to clear it. He had been looking at the patterns too hard. They seemed to have a hypnotic effect.

He turned to the table and picked up the glass. He thought he could take a swallow, then spit it out and spray Diana in the process, exclaiming how foul it tasted. Yet as he raised the tall frosted glass to his lips an enticing odor filled his nostrils. He took a sip, then another. It was very cold, tart and sweet at the same time, even spicy, fruit flavored though he couldn't name the exact fruit. And it *was* delicious. If there was such a thing as the nectar of the gods, Thorne thought, this could be it. He took a deeper swallow and sat down.

Instead of leaning back he hunched forward, his legs on each side of the footrest, his elbows on his knees and his feet planted firmly on the floor. He made an elaborate pretense of looking at his watch. "What's taking so long? Are we going on this vacation or not?"

"It's only been a few minutes," Diana told him. "Just sit back and relax like they said. If you don't relax you won't enjoy yourself. That's what a vacation is for."

Thorne tried to think of some acid retort, but his heart wasn't in it. It had been a hectic day at work and now, despite himself, he *was* beginning to feel relaxed. After a few more swallows of the drink, he leaned back in the chair and put his feet up.

The tempo of the music and the moving abstracts began to slow down. The clouds elongated and began to change color. Thorne yawned. All the tensions of the past months drained from his body and a delicious weariness flooded his limbs. He felt as if he were floating. An immense sense of well-being enveloped his consciousness. By his side, Diana had already closed her eyes and was breathing evenly.

At the last instant before he toppled into the well of sleep, a bit of paranoia surfaced in Thorne's mind. This was all a trick. The Guardeners knew about his crimes. They knew everything and they were waiting outside the door. He would wake up incarcerated and primed for reconditioning.

The door opened and several white-coated medtechs entered. The music and holographic images had ceased. The room was now brightly lit. Diana and Richard were lifted from their chairs and placed on gurneys. The clothes were stripped from their insensate bodies and each was given a cursory physical, aimed chiefly at making sure they would remain unconscious. They were sprayed with disinfectants and attired in hospital gowns.

The gurneys were wheeled from the room.

Their virtual vacation to the Future Perfect was about to begin.

It was everything Diana had dreamed about as a young architecture student. She was gliding down the streets of the City transformed, with her chosenmate by her side. A hundred years in the future? A thousand years? Who could say? It was clear the goals of the State had been realized and the Future Perfect had become a reality.

The glideways were wider. The buildings were spaced farther apart and the natural landscaping that interspersed them was astonishing in its abundance and variety. The buildings themselves offered a compendium of the history of architecture. Gothic spires. Corinthian colonnades. Rectilinear Bahaus facades. Baroque ornamentations. Through the genius of design and placement, all these diverse elements fit together and complemented one another without the slightest conflict.

The sky above them was clear and filled with more stars than Diana had imagined existed. A rising full moon peeked between the gaps in the buildings. The night was balmy, just the right temperature, and a velvety breeze caressed their cheeks. Even the air of the City smelled different, fresher and cleaner.

Yet the greatest difference could be seen in the City's inhabitants. This was truly a world of beautiful people. The individuals, couples, and groups who passed them on the glideway looked uniformly healthy and serene. They did not leap from strip to strip, trying to cut one another off. There was no frantic rush to reach their destinations. They did not look away from others they passed, absorbed only with their own concerns, but smiled openly at those around them, smiles that radiated a calm assurance and contentment. And the dresses and tunics they wore were magnificent.

Diana felt momentarily self-conscious until she looked down at her own clothes. She was wearing a silken sarong in muted rainbow colors that fit her like a glove without constricting her movement in any way. Her chosenmate wore a tunic in a matching pattern. The way it emphasized his shoulders and tapered down his sides, it had clearly been tailored especially for him.

"It's all so fantastic," Diana exclaimed. "I can hardly believe it. Doesn't it make you feel wonderful?"

"Yes," Richard agreed, "it's wonderful. I'm so glad we came."

Her chosenmate slipped his arm around her waist and gave her a squeeze. Diana laughed and reciprocated in kind. They moved into an entertainment district, richer and more diverse than any they had known in real life. There was every kind of show imaginable, from plays to concerts, dances to artistic exhibitions to sporting events. Giant screens projected the scenes taking place within each theater or arena so that one could sample the fare before deciding to enter. Smaller screens outside restaurants offered a changing display of the dishes that each had to offer.

"Aren't you hungry?" Richard asked.

"I'm starving," she said. "Where shall we eat? There's so much to choose from."

"This one looks good." Her chosenmate took her arm and guided her as they stepped from the glideway.

Next thing she knew they were seated at a table amid luxuriant surroundings and a white-coated waiter was handing them oversized menus embossed with gilt.

The euphoria Thorne had felt before drifting off to sleep remained with him. He was moving along a glideway with

Diana by his side. A barrage of impressions rushed upon him, reducing his span of attention as his senses leaped from one to another.

They were passing through the streets of what looked to be a hypothetical city of the future, a radiant city where everything shined with newness as if it had just been born. The air was clear and fresh. Overhead, the sky offered a riot of stars.

Diana slipped her arm around his waist and pressed her body against his. Before he could summon the concentration to disengage himself and pull away, he was distracted by a giant holo screen where strange animals pranced and played musical instruments.

From the depths of his mind the voice of a man called Rick shouted: *None of this is real! Tell her that! Spoil it for her!*

A part of Thorne tried to fasten on that shout. Yet by the time it surfaced in his consciousness it was no more than a whisper that could be easily ignored. His thoughts were entrapped in the moment and the waves of euphoria continued to wash over him.

A series of restaurants stretched along the street on their left, each looking more sumptuous than the one before.

"Aren't you hungry?" Diana asked.

And suddenly he was. Ravenously hungry. He'd eaten shortly before leaving their conapt, but felt as if he had not eaten for days.

"Yes," he answered, "let's get something to eat. I'm starving."

Taking his hand, Diana pulled him along as she leaped from the glideway.

They didn't walk to the restaurant and enter. They didn't wait to be seated. As soon as they stepped off the glideway they were at a table with menus in their hands. A white-coated waiter hovered over them, awaiting their choices. The transition had been instantaneous, as if they were characters in a holodrama transported from Scene One to Scene Two.

Diana leaned back and looked around her. They were sitting in a corner booth that provided a view of the room and the other dinners. The restaurant wasn't crowded but it was crowded enough with the right kind of people so that you knew it had to be good. Crystal chandeliers hung from the ceiling and romantic music played in the background. The tablecloths were white linen. On each table there were fresh flowers and a lighted candle.

Diana ordered the braised lamb shank with mint sauce. Richard chose the filet mignon, medium rare. But there was more to it than that. Each entree came with a full course dinner. Oysters on the half shell. Onion soup coated with baked cheese. An endive salad with black olives, grape tomatoes, croutons, and crumbled egg yolks. Baby asparagus sautéed in a lemon butter sauce. The food was unbelievably delicious and the service was impeccable. Each time their wine glasses were half empty a waiter miraculously appeared to refill them.

They didn't talk much except to comment on the different dishes. There was no need for talk. It was enough to be together and in love. Her chosenmate was looking as handsome as she'd ever seen him—she'd noticed several women staring at him—and seemed to be enjoying himself as much as she was.

"Are you ready for dessert?" Richard asked.

"That was scrumptious," Diana exclaimed with a sigh, "but I have to watch my figure."

"You don't have to worry about that," he reminded her. "Have you forgotten already, darling? This is virtual food. There are absolutely no calories."

"What was I thinking?" Diana said, her face splitting into a wider grin than it held already. "It's all so real, I did forget. Do you think they have chocolate mousse? Or maybe some cheesecake?"

"I'm sure they have whatever your heart desires," Richard answered. He gazed at her longingly and reached across the table to caress her hand.

Thorne had once again become a man divided, virtually split in two. The personality and emotions the vacation overlaid upon his own were so far from the truth of his life and intent there could be no common ground between them. He was Richard Thorne, Statistician G-12, taking the vacation of a lifetime with his beloved and loving chosenmate. At the same time he was a criminal deviant who called himself Rick, a murderous sociopath entrapped in an intoxicating dream world he was determined to corrupt into a nightmare.

The dishes kept coming, one course after another. They were all mouth watering. If the pale green drink had been the nectar of the gods, Richard thought, the food he was consuming could easily be their ambrosia.

Meanwhile, Rick railed helplessly within his mind.

None of it is real. Gag on it. Spit it out. Make a scene. You've only got two days. Make her as miserable as possible! Make her hate you!

Richard was letting Diana do most of the talking. He wasn't sure he was capable of carrying on a coherent conversation. She prattled on about nothing in particular, praising the food and the service, making assorted small talk, suggesting that at some point they visit the City Circus. It didn't matter what she said. Each time he glanced at her he

155

couldn't help but realize how stunning she was. Diana looked younger and more radiant than he'd seen her in years.

Think of her with Coopersmith. Naked on her back. Or on her knees before him. His wrinkled hands exploring her body. Think of the ways she has controlled your life. Denigrating your true self.

She wore a golden gown of some satiny material. It left her shoulders and arms bare. Her lightly freckled flesh glowed in the candlelight. Richard had noticed several other men in the restaurant staring at her. Even a few of the women. To be there by her side made him feel like the luckiest man in the room, in the entire world. How could he help but love her as much as he did?

It's a pack of lies. You don't love Diana! You love Josie! She's the one that matters.

"I think that's the most wonderful dinner I've ever eaten," Diana sighed. "And best of all there's not a single calorie. It's virtual food." She patted her lean belly and sighed again. "Wonderful!" she repeated. "Now what shall we have for dessert?"

Wonderful. Wonderful. The City is wonderful. The streets are wonderful. Diana is the most wonderful of all! Everything is so very wonderful it's completely sickening. Wake up, you fool! None of it is real!

The beast that was Rick suddenly erupted successfully into Thorne's consciousness. He looked around the room and saw its charm and beauty and denied it. He looked at Diana and did the same. He overcame the happiness that filled his being with his own perverse compulsions.

Rick's fist slammed onto the table. The silver rattled and the wine glasses rocked.

"Dessert?" he shouted. "You mean there's more of this nonsense on the way? Let's try the denatured rat pudding.

How about some muddy gravel compote? I'm sure it will all taste like heaven warmed over!"

The other diners continued eating and chatting, oblivious to his outburst. Diana looked confused for a moment, but not in the least embarrassed. It made no sense. She should have been shocked by his behavior.

A white-coated waiter materialized at his elbow.

"Is there something the matter, sir? Whatever we can do to please you, all you have to do is let us know." He bobbed up and down solicitously as he spoke.

"Just relax, darling," Diana chimed in. She reached across the table and placed her palm on his closed fist. She gazed at him adoringly. "Why don't you have some peach cobbler? Isn't that one of your favorites?"

Then the blind euphoria hit him again like a tidal wave, overwhelming in its intensity, as if they were injecting a euphoric drug into his veins. What could he have been thinking, trying to spoil such a beautiful evening?

"I'm sorry," Richard said. "I don't know what came over me." He shook his head, trying to clear it. "Peach cobbler sounds just perfect," he sighed. "It sounds absolutely wonderful!"

"That's all right, dear," Diana said, patting his hand. "Just relax and let it happen. You know how much I love you."

With those words, Richard felt his own love for Diana welling up in his chest. He could also feel Rick raging within him, his anger tamped down by a crushing weight of mindless joy. Thorne wasn't sure he could survive two days of this and maintain his sanity.

Dessert was finished and they were sipping their coffee. Diana was tempted to have a third helping of chocolate mousse. Or try some different dessert. With food like this she could spend the entire vacation eating, except there was so much else she wanted to do.

"What shall we do next?" Richard asked, as if he had read her mind. "Would you like to go dancing at one of the arenas?"

"Oh, I'd love that," Diana said. "That's exactly what I'd like!"

No sooner had she spoken than her wish was granted. Richard was twirling her around a lavish ballroom. A live orchestra was played enchanting music. A giant silver ball turned and sparkled over their heads. Wherever they moved across the floor the other couples made way for their passage.

She had never danced like this before in her life, with such grace and style. This was what dancing was meant to be. She could feel the music in her bones, her very soul. They moved together as if they were lighter than air. And whatever cologne Richard was wearing was driving her crazy.

He had barely finished his peach cobbler, each bite melting in his mouth, when Diana suggested they go dancing. Richard had never liked dancing except for the times he'd danced with Josie. He had never been very good at it even then. Yet now the thought of holding Diana in his arms and whirling her around a dance floor was suddenly irresistible.

How could he refuse?

Cut to Scene Three. They were dancing.

That's how Thorne was starting to think of each abrupt segue. As if they were the successive scenes in a holoplay. And himself as an actor with no choice but to deliver the lines that were expected of him. His desire to spoil the vacation had momentarily vanished. There was no need to think about that anymore. Not with the music playing, his chosenmate in his arms, her eyes bright, her lovely face flushed, and whatever perfume she was wearing driving him crazy.

There was no question that Rick was both manic and criminally insane. Yet despite his delusions he could still function. He possessed all the intelligence of Richard Thorne coupled with a vicious and devious cunning. He soon realized that if he tried to fight the effects of the vacation, if he became angry and frantic, he subsequently experienced an ecstatic rush that overcame his resistance. So he began to ride with the high and bide his time, to separate himself from the constant pleasure he was feeling and try to grasp what was happening to him.

He was also beginning to suspect something else. Not only were the streets, the buildings, the food, the entire City and those inhabiting it an illusion, perhaps Diana was also. Whoever he was taking this vacation with, he was no longer sure it was his chosenmate.

She could have danced all night, only there was something she wanted far more. Again it was as if Richard could read her mind. As the music stopped, in the space between numbers, he crushed her to him in a fierce embrace. Right there in the middle of the dance floor, he kissed her full on the lips.

"I can't stand it any longer," he whispered. "I have to have you!"

"Oh, yes," Diana answered, breathless though not from the dancing. "Yes!" She had never wanted Richard so much, could not remember wanting any man the way she wanted him now.

The ballroom disappeared. They were in the spacious bedroom of a hotel suite high above the City. One entire wall was a plate glass window that offered a view of the thousand and one lights below. The moon in the eastern sky seemed very close, filling the unlighted room with soft and romantic illumination.

Diana was sitting on the bed, the largest bed she'd ever seen, wearing a filmy black negligee. Richard was beside her wearing absolutely nothing. He took her in his arms and kissed her again. He unfastened the negligee and slipped it from her shoulders with practiced ease. Then he began to make love to her. Gentle and passionate. Wild, tender, and fulfilling. He had become her consummate erotic dream.

"Let's go home," Diana whispered in his ear. "Let's make love." With one hand clasped to the nape of his neck she pulled him toward her. She kissed him full on the mouth, right there in the middle of the dance floor.

Skulking in the shadows of Thorne's awareness, Rick thought for the barest second that Diana was suggesting they end the vacation and return to their conapt. As the world about them changed again, he realized that was wishful thinking.

Scene Four. They were in the bedroom of a richly appointed hotel suite. One entire wall was glass. They were sitting on the edge of the bed. Before he could fully take in the surroundings, Diana was all over him. Ripping off his clothes, shedding her own. Touching him in ways she never had before, revealing an uninhibited sensuality that shocked and thrilled him. There was nothing for Richard to do but respond in wonder and appreciation with his own unbounded desire. Nothing for Rick to do but watch silently from a sheltered distance and ride with the high.

They were lying side by side, sipping the complimentary champagne that had been left for them in their hotel suite. Diana wanted to hold this moment in her consciousness forever. All the troubles and difficulties of life had slipped away. They were inconsequential. She felt satisfied and complete in a way she hadn't known was possible.

She had intended to save her surprise until near the end of the vacation, once she was sure she had regained control of her chosenmate. Yet everything was going so well, she could wait no longer.

"Remember I said I had another surprise for you," she began.

Richard turned toward her. "Yes, darling, what is it?"

She had planned to lead up to it gradually, to hint at the new project to which she'd been assigned and gauge Richard's reaction. Yet the evening had been so wonderfully overwhelming, she was having trouble organizing her thoughts. She'd lost track of how much wine she'd had at the restaurant, and now there was the champagne. Strange as it seemed, she was so happy she was having trouble thinking straight. So she just blurted it out.

"My promotion came through last week. They've made me a G-16."

There was a pause, as if Richard were digesting the information. "That's wonderful, darling!" he said at last. "You certainly deserve it!" He leaned over and kissed her on the shoulder and gave her a hug.

She had been worried how he would take the news since his own career remained stalled at G-12. But Richard seemed genuinely pleased for her, so she decided to charge ahead.

"And that's not all. It's supposed to be a secret, only a few people know, but I can tell you. They're finally getting rid of that slum. And I'm in charge of designing an entire block of new housing!"

There was another pause before he answered her, but when he did, it was exactly what she wanted to hear.

"That's wonderful. Slums are a blight on the entire City. They should get rid of all the slums. But let's not think about unpleasant things like that. Let's talk about how we're going to spend tomorrow."

Richard Thorne had just experienced one of the most memorable sexual encounters of his life. And judging from Diana's reaction, it had been just as special for her. He was totally relaxed, sipping champagne and drifting off into a pleasant haze. Rick chose that moment to force his way to the surface again. He turned toward Diana. Her face was only inches away from his. He decided the time for subterfuge was over.

"I don't love you," his voice suddenly boomed in the quiet room, louder than he had intended. "I love someone else. I want to dissolve our mating."

Diana didn't respond immediately. She took another sip of champagne. By the light of the moon through the plate glass window, Rick could see the same puzzled expression she had registered after his outburst in the restaurant.

"That's all right, dear," she finally said, reaching out and patting his hand. "Just relax and let it happen. You know how much I love you." She looked at him wide-eyed, totally adoring, as if she had not heard him at all.

Rick retreated, his mind reeling with the implications of Diana's response. It was identical to the one she had given him at dinner, a programmed response from a program whose parameters were not designed to deal with the situation. Whatever the specific mechanics of this vacation, he and Diana were not taking it together. The woman beside him was not his chosenmate, not even a real woman but a generated image, an artificial intelligence that had been equipped with a complex yet finite range of reactions. Its outward appearance and behavior were perhaps drawn from Diana's City State files. Or they could have been somehow extracted and projected from his memories. And then idealized.

He recalled how on a few of their past vacations they'd had arguments, how resentments and differences suppressed in everyday life had surfaced with leisure time, so that when they should have been enjoying themselves they were fighting instead. There was no danger of that here. There was only beauty and harmony and love, all of it fictitious and enforced. And then he thought of the real Diana, who must have been having a vacation similar to his own in the company of an attentive and totally loving surrogate of Richard Thorne. They were on vacation together yet they were taking separate vacations, totally alone, surrounded by mannequins, creatures that existed only in their minds.

There was no way he could ruin this vacation for Diana, no way he could make her hate him as he had planned. No way he could even speak to her until the vacation was over.

Breakfast was another feast, served to them on the terrace of a restaurant overlooking a white sand beach and a brilliant blue ocean.

Diana couldn't stop eating. She devoured two helpings of pancakes with strawberry syrup, a platter of scrambled eggs, bacon, ham, biscuits, three slices of melon, fried potatoes. Between bites she couldn't stop staring at her chosenmate. After last night, she wanted to consume him too.

"You must think I'm terrible," she blushed, patting her lips with a napkin, "stuffing myself like this."

"Never darling," Richard answered, reaching across the table and touching her hand. "Eat whatever you like. Just relax and let it all happen. You know how much I love you."

Richard was wearing a simple white short-sleeve pullover, open at the collar. His blue eyes were as brilliant as the color of the ocean. The breeze from over the water tousled his dark hair. Diana had never realized before that a man could be so beautiful.

"When you're finished," he added, "let's go down to the beach."

"Wherever you like," Diana answered. "As long as we're together."

Diana had been ensnared by her own intentions of seduction. If she'd read the detailed description of the "Chosenmates Love Holiday" she would have understood that it was a two-way street. The feelings it generated were mutual. The vacation was designed to reawaken and strengthen the love between chosenmates. To accomplish this, not only did it create an idealized Diana Logan and fill Richard Thorne with desire and devotion for her, it fashioned the perfect Richard Thorne for Diana Logan, the man of her dreams, dreams she had never been fully aware of until now.

How she could have lived with Richard for years, she wondered, and been so blind? How could she have not realized how fortunate she was to have him by her side? Diana vowed that when they returned home to their conapt and their everyday lives, she would be a better chosenmate than before. She would no longer question Richard or try to manipulate him. She would stop spending so much time worrying about her career. She would try in every way possible to become the woman he deserved to have.

The "Chosenmate Love Holiday" was having the exact effect on Diana that was intended in its creation.

Scene Five: Breakfast on the Terrace.

Richard had no memory of falling asleep. He did not recall waking up and taking a shower and getting dressed. One minute he was drifting in a pleasant haze, his chosenmate by his side. Next thing he knew they were eating breakfast overlooking a white sand beach and bright blue ocean.

The food was delicious and plentiful. Diana was so beautiful that she made his heart ache every time he glanced in her direction. There wasn't a cloud in sight and the azure sky looked limitless. He could smell a salt breeze from over the water. It would be hard to imagine a more perfect morning.

Then why, Richard asked himself, did he feel vaguely troubled?

An image of Josie flickered across his mind. A complete scene in freeze frame. She was bending over to water one of her illegal plants. Her top had ridden up several inches to reveal the smooth dark flesh of her back and hips. He reached out and touched her and she turned, smiling at him over her shoulder. He could hear her strange ancient music playing. He could see the books lining the shelves, the rocking chair moving back and forth, the oversized bed with its creaking metal frame.

Richard pushed the images away. There would be more than enough time to think about Josie after the vacation was over. What mattered most for now was being with Diana and sharing whatever new pleasures and delights the day held in store.

He wanted to go down to the ocean and walk along the sand and touch the water. He had never been on a real beach or seen a real ocean before. Then the disturbing thought struck him that this ocean and beach were not real either.

"Would you like to go down to the beach?" Diana asked as if she had read his mind.

"Yes," he answered, "that would be wonderful."

Though the prospect didn't seem quite as wonderful as it had moments before.

Scene Six: A Day at the Beach

The perceptions of Rick were beginning to bleed into the persona the vacation had created for Richard Thorne. The division between the two personalities was breaking down. Although Rick could not spoil Diana's vacation, he was succeeding in corrupting his own.

They were stretched out on a giant blue beach towel beneath a giant yellow beach umbrella. A few feet away, a gentle white-capped surf lapped the shore. They were both wearing red bathing suits, Diana's so abbreviated it left little to the imagination. Yet instead of looking at Diana's body, as delectable as it was, Richard was examining his own.

He was holding his wrist up to his face. He'd just discovered that if he looked too closely at his flesh, he couldn't see the pores. He knew there was nothing wrong with his vision. His eyesight had been corrected when he was a child and he'd never had any problems since.

He tried the same thing with the sand. From a distance it looked real enough. Yet if he looked close enough it lost focus and became a smooth unblemished surface. He could not make out the individual grains. Nor did it feel right when he picked it up and sifted it through his fingers. He wasn't exactly sure how sand should feel, but it seemed as if it should be rougher to the touch.

A white-coated waiter from the restaurant above them materialized at his elbow. Virtually materialized, Richard/Rick realized, out of thin air.

"Is there anything I can get you, sir? Would you like a drink? Or something else to eat? We can provide a full service menu right here on the beach."

"No...no thank you," Richard/Rick answered. "Not right now. I'm fine." Though he wasn't feeling fine at all.

The waiter vanished as abruptly as he had appeared.

"Is there something the matter, dear?" Diana asked, propping herself up on an elbow and turning to face him, one of her breasts dangerously close to escaping from its halter. Richard/Rick was aroused even though he didn't want to be.

"No," he told her. "Everything is...okay."

"Just okay?" she pouted.

Diana stood up and stepped off the towel. Digging one bare foot into the sand, she kicked a spray of it directly at him, laughing as she danced away toward the water.

"I bet you can't catch me," she taunted. "Bet you'll never catch me."

Before he knew what was happening, Richard was on his feet chasing after her. He caught her at the edge of the surf and they collapsed together onto the wet sand. His hands were on her arms. He was kissing her shoulders as the low waves broke across their bodies. Diana's halter had come loose, they were pressed against one another, and Richard felt rich with desire. His doubts of a moment before were swept away. If it weren't for the other people on the beach, he would have stripped off the rest of Diana's suit and made love to her right there.

To his horror and consternation, Rick found himself helplessly caught up in the moment. Having stumbled from his cynical and distant stance, he felt the same as Richard. With the warm sun on his back and the warmth of Diana's body squirming beneath him, with the cool waves breaking against his legs and sea birds screeching overhead, it was hard to believe that none of this was real. It was impossible not to want the woman he was holding.

The division between the two disparate personalities was breaking down in both directions. Just as Rick's negative perceptions were invading the vacation persona of Richard Thorne, the positive perceptions the vacation had generated were having their effect upon Rick. The vacation was acting as a kind of conditioning agent, just as it was intended to do. Not only was it attempting to turn Richard/Rick into a loving and devoted chosenmate, at a deeper level it was trying to cure his deviance, to imbue him with attitudes that would lead to a healthy and satisfying life as a productive Citizen.

Scene Seven: They skimmed across the deep blue sea in a small sailboat. Just the two of them. Richard had never been in any kind of boat before yet his hands knew instinctively what to do. Diana as his first mate was flawless at trimming the sails.

Scene Eleven: They ate another unbelievable dinner in a restaurant atop a high tower. Crab-stuffed mushrooms. Cucumber bisque. Tomato aspic. Veal scallopini. The decor was glass and metal. The room was circular and all the diners had window seats. While they were eating the floor slowly revolved. By the time they reached dessert, they had been exposed to a full three-hundred-and-sixty degree view of the City.

"Ingenious," Diana observed. "And very smart! Don't you agree?"

Of course he did. It was all very smart and very real. You could see it, touch it, taste it, and breathe it. If you didn't look too closely, if you didn't think about it too hard, you could easily forget that it was an illusion for hours at a time.

It was soon apparent to Rick that he had no choice where they would go next. Like any series of computer instructions, the vacation was executed in a set order. It was always Diana—the construct called Diana, he had to keep reminding himself—who proposed their next activity or destination. If he suggested something different, Diana would put him off. Or some distraction would arise for long enough so that his suggestion could be dismissed and they could proceed with the schedule.

Meanwhile the real Diana was moving through the same schedule with less conflict and more satisfaction. There were moments when a stray doubt would trail across her mind. She wondered why it was so hard to think clearly or to discuss anything other than the vacation. She realized at some level she wasn't quite herself, that she was acting and reacting spontaneously rather than with her usual forethought. Yet her newfound happiness overshadowed such concerns. Her chosenmate had returned to the man she wanted him to be and so much more. Despite what had happened between her and Coopersmith, regardless of what it was that had attracted Richard to the slum, things could now return to normal and their lives would proceed as planned. She was convinced of it.

Scene Fourteen: They rode on horseback through a verdant sun-dappled wilderness. Massive trees towered above them. Flowers of every color and description bloomed in profusion in the undergrowth that covered the forest floor. Each of their horses was a golden palomino with a streaming white mane. They stopped by a jewel-like lake, so clear they could see fish swimming in its depths. They picnicked by the side of a river and a covered bridge. Fresh fruit. A cold roast chicken. Assorted cheeses and small pentagonal crackers. A semi-dry white wine that had remained perfectly chilled although their picnic basket contained no cooling unit.

Scene Sixteen: They attended the City Circus in Founder's Square. Severin's Fountain was still there, half again as large as Thorne remembered it from real life, its murals now illuminated from within. The circus was many times more impressive than any they'd seen before. The clowns were hilarious. The lions and tigers were frighteningly ferocious until they started performing their tricks. Then they became

169

the picture of animal grace and intelligence. The jugglers and acrobats, with only virtual gravity to contend with, performed some truly amazing feats. The applause was thunderous from all sides.

One scene segued into another and another after that. It seemed to go on and on.

"I thought we were only staying two days," Richard/Rick asked. "Don't we have to be back at work?"

"It *is* only two-day's objective time," the virtual Diana explained. "but we're living in subjective time now. Isn't it wonderful?"

There was still an occasional outburst when what remained of the Rick persona surfaced. He knew the real Diana would be unaware of his actions, but was hoping in some way to short circuit the vacation and escape.

At one point he dumped a carafe of steaming coffee into the virtual Diana's lap.

"My, my, aren't we clumsy!" she scolded him.

He watched as she ineffectually blotted the front of her dress with a napkin. The coffee quickly evaporated. By the time he set the carafe back on the table, it was full again.

Another time while they were dancing he kept stomping on her feet. Diana put her arms tightly around him, lifted him off the floor, and finished the number carrying him several inches in the air. That same evening they won a dance contest and accepted a silver cup on the stage before an admiring and envious crowd.

Rick was pushing the limits of the virtual vacation to the point where its responses could no longer be rational or conform to reality. His outlandish actions could not have been foreseen by its programmers. A normal Citizen would never have conceived of them or acted them out.

Whenever the computers monitoring Thorne's real body detected turmoil or negative emotions, more euphoriants and relaxants were released into his system. The program continued to run and Richard/Rick moved through it in an increasingly ecstatic daze.

He was a prisoner in a kind of mindless paradise. There was apparently no way out of this vacation until the time Diana had signed up for had elapsed.

Scene Eighteen. Scene Twenty-Three. Scene Thirty. Scene Thirty-Six. Scene Forty.

Each night they returned to their spacious suite with its bottomless bottle of complimentary champagne and plate glass window from floor to ceiling. Each night there was their lovemaking, intense and satisfying. It was as if they were making love to the field of stars shining in the sky and the lights sparking in the streets below. Richard wanted to consume every inch of Diana. It no longer mattered whether she was real or not. If the Rick persona tried to resist, more drugs—euphoriants, sexual stimulants—were released into his system. And the virtual Diana would come after him with a seductive repertoire that could not be denied.

Scene Fifty-Three. Or was it only Forty-Eight. Richard/Rick had lost track some time ago. He wondered if the first act were over.

They were sitting on upholstered chairs in an open amphitheater watching a play. The night was balmy as it always was. Overhead, the moon was full. It was always full. Richard/Rick was smiling. He was always smiling. It was wonderful.

"What happens when it rains?" he asked Diana. "Won't the chairs get ruined?"

"It never rains here," she told him, "unless we want it to rain. Even then it would only be a virtual rain. It couldn't hurt the chairs."

"That's right," he said. "I forgot." He laughed.

"Now watch this," Diana said, gesturing toward the stage. "Pay attention. This is important."

The play was a political drama about how the Future Perfect had come into being. It had lots of characters and was rife with complex political intrigues. Richard/Rick was trying to pay attention because Diana wanted him to. Given the level of drugs in his bloodstream and mind, the play proved far too complicated to follow. He took his cues from Diana. When she nodded or applauded, he would do the same.

He didn't care about the play. It was more than enough to be sitting here on such a beautiful night with his chosen-mate by his side. Not only more than enough, it was wonderful. And so was Diana. He couldn't imagine what he'd do without her.

Devastation

First thing Diana was aware of on waking was the vaporous music, the same that had been playing when she'd fallen asleep. Now its tempo was slowly rising rather than falling. It was such lovely music. She hoped she would remember it always. She opened her eyes. A white-coated waiter was bending over her.

"How are you feeling?" he asked.

No, it wasn't a waiter. Looked more like a Doctor or medtech. Only too young for a Doctor. And he wasn't wearing a robe.

"I'm fine," Diana smiled. "How are you?" The euphoriants were still streaming through her system.

"I'm doing just fine." The young man smiled back and patted her hand. "Just close your eyes and relax. We need to run a few tests." Diana closed her eyes. "Then you can get up and get dressed."

Her eyes came open again.

She was lying on a gurney, wearing a hospital gown. To her left she saw Richard stretched out in similar fashion. He was still unconscious. There was another medtech bending over him. Diana realized the vacation was over.

"This one is really zipped," the second man said. "He's not coming around."

The tech by her side moved over to Richard's gurney. He peeled back one eyelid and checked his pulse. "Let's try a stim injector," he suggested.

He pawed through a lower shelf on the gurney and came up with a small metal tube. It emitted a flat buzz as he pressed it against Richard's upper arm.

By this time Diana was sitting up. "Is he all right?" she asked with growing alarm. "What's the matter?"

The tech returned to her side. "Don't worry. Everything's going to be fine. Now just lie down for a minute and relax." He placed his hands on her shoulders and began easing her back.

Richard's body shot upright. His hair was uncombed and standing out in every direction. His eyes were wide and wild. He looked like an escaped maniac and proceeded to play the part.

The first time he came awake he didn't know where he was. A waiter was standing over him. Another waiter had his hands on Diana's shoulders and she looked frightened. Someone was hurting his chosenmate!

Richard leaped and landed on the man's back. As the waiter staggered in one direction with Richard clinging to him, Diana's gurney careened in the opposite, leaving her behind. She managed to land on her feet but didn't stay there for long. She toppled backward and sat down hard on the floor. A single yelp escaped her throat.

The second waiter was on Richard's back, trying to pull him off the first.

"Get a sed! Get a sed!" the first waiter screamed, and gasped as Richard's forearm closed on his windpipe.

A moment later Richard heard a buzzing noise and felt a sharp sting on his arm. His grip on the waiter relaxed and he crumpled to his knees. He was nearly face to face with his chosenmate. Before he lost consciousness, he had time to realize how much he loved her. He leaned forward and lowered his head into her lap.

This wasn't the homecoming Diana had envisioned. She was sitting on one side of a desk in a dimly lit office. It was a rather large office by contemporary standards, yet after the vistas and spacious environments of the vacation it felt small and cramped. The man sitting on the opposite side of the desk, wearing the white robes of a Doctor, was explaining the situation to her.

"It's nothing that serious," he assured her. "Your chosenmate has merely had a negative reaction to some of the drugs we used to enhance your vacation experience. It's not that uncommon. Though we will have to keep him sedated and under observation for a few days."

An oversized nameplate on the desk identified the man in capital letters as "EDWARD EDMUNSON." Not Dr. Edmunson, and there were no degrees listed after his name. Diana, still in the aftermath of the virtual experience and readjusting to reality, was feeling confused and uncertain. "You are a Doctor, aren't you?" she asked anxiously, suddenly afraid that the fate of her beloved chosenmate was in the hands of some exalted medtech.

"Of course I am," Edmunson replied, firmly gripping the lapels of his white robe with both hands and sitting up straighter in his chair. "I'm a Doctor of Psychiatry and Medicine. G-18. What would make you think otherwise?"

"Oh, nothing," Diana mumbled. "I'm just feeling upset."

"Well, that's understandable, my dear. But I can assure you, there's really nothing to be upset about."

Edmunson was a distinguished-looking man in his late forties. He gave the impression of being the kind of man you could trust with your life. Slightly graying at the temples. A wide smooth forehead above straight dark brows, serious eyes, a strong and prominent nose. Diana realized she was looking at an expensive dermask.

"Why are you wearing a mask?" she asked.

"No particular reason," Dr. Edmunson shrugged. "I like to wear one. I guess it makes me feel more like a Doctor." Reaching across the desk, he placed a small pile of papers in front of her. "Now if you'll just sign these release forms we can begin..." he paused and glanced down at the open file before him, "...yes, Richard...we can begin Richard's treatment and he'll be home by your side before you know it."

The vacation had been so perfect, Diana thought, and now Richard had to spoil it. Though it wasn't really his fault. And she did love him, she really did. If only he didn't start acting strange and distant again. If only they could be on vacation all the time and live forever in the Future Perfect.

That evening, after a lonely trip home on the tunnel train, Diana called Heather and told her what had happened. Her friend reassured her as everyone else had.

"Don't worry about Richard," Heather told her. "He'll be his usual cranky self in a day to two. You can't get hurt on a virtual vacation. It's about as dangerous as a good night's sleep. Now tell me everything about it! What did you see? Is it really as wonderful as everyone says?"

Later that same evening, with nothing to do but worry, Diana decided to keep herself occupied by straightening up the conapt. That way it would be nice for Richard's return home. She'd never been particularly domestic in the past, but now she began to think that had been one of the problems with their mating. The man she loved surely deserved a little domesticity now and then.

She started with the kitchen, rearranging the contents of the cupboards and cooling unit, dumping food that had spoiled into the disposal. In the living room she came upon Richard's books piled next to his chair. Here was his strangeness confronting her. They were certainly an eyesore with their tattered covers and yellowed pages. For a moment she considered throwing them away. But no, she concluded, if her chosenmate wanted to read books he should be able to read books. What was the harm in it? Everyone had their little eccentricities. Yet they shouldn't sit out like this in the open where anyone could see them.

She gathered up the books and carried them to Richard's storage unit by the side of their bed. She tired to jam them onto a high shelf but they wouldn't fit. The storage unit was a jumbled mess, its contents spilling every which way, its floor covered with dirty clothes. So she started in on that.

Most of the clothes went in the laundry shoot, some straight to the disposal. Once she had the floor nearly clear she came upon an old pair of shoes that Richard hadn't worn in more than a year. They were completely out of style. As she was carrying them to the disposal she noticed that one was heavier than the other. That was when Diana discovered the gun.

She stared at it in disbelief.

It was lying on the floor where she had dropped it as soon as she realized what it was. She backed away from it slowly as if it were alive, a small dangerous animal that might pounce if she made the wrong move.

Her mind kept racing and snagging, searching for some reasonable explanation, any explanation she could fasten on as to why Richard would possess such a horrible thing. It must have something to do with his obsession for the past, she thought frantically, more of his eccentricity. That had to be it! Like the old coins he collected. Or his books. Or the boring historical documentaries he insisted on watching even though he often ranted about their inaccuracies. But there were limits to how eccentric one could be!

Diana knew she should take the gun to the nearest Guardener Station and tell them where she had found it. It was her clear duty as a Citizen. Yet that would spoil everything, their lives, their careers, and just when she and Richard had reaffirmed their mating and love for one another. At that point a bit of the old Diana, the pre-vacation Diana, began to surface.

She loved her chosenmate but she realized that like all men there would be times when he would need guidance and control. If she loved him too much, if she let him do whatever he wanted, there was no telling where it might lead.

Diana picked up the gun carefully, holding it as far from her body as possible. She found some old newssheets and working at arm's length wrapped it securely. Twenty minutes later she was back in the conapt after shoving the package deep into a public disposal unit. On the way there she had stopped twice and nearly changed direction, momentarily convinced she should go a Guardener Station instead. But she had denied her conditioning and persevered. She knew it would always bother her that she had not fulfilled her duty as a Citizen. Yet if you really loved someone as much as she loved Richard, certain sacrifices had to be made.

The second time Richard woke up he knew he was in a hospital room, though he wasn't sure how he had gotten there or what was the matter with him. Diana was sitting by his bedside looking concerned. When he tried to speak, his voice emerged as if from a great distance, cracked and unrecogniz-able, the words collapsing in his throat.

"He's awake!" Diana exclaimed.

"So he is."

A figure appeared on the other side of the bed. Distin-guished looking. Wearing the white robe of a Doctor. "Probably dehydrated after what we've been giving him. See if he wants some water."

Diana lifted Richard's head from the pillow and held a plastic cup with a straw to his lips. He sucked at it greedily. The water tasted bitter. His chosenmate didn't look right to him. As she leaned close, her freckles loomed like hills and craters. Some of them reminded him of the holos he'd seen of extinct volcanoes.

White Robes leaned over him and held up two fingers. "How many fingers am I holding up?" he asked in a voice of good cheer.

Richard started laughing uncontrollably. A hacking laugh from deep in his chest that sounded more like a cough. He had just noticed that White Robes was wearing a dermask. Someone he knew would have thought that was very funny. Someone who once said to him that those who wear robes are always wearing masks. He thought of a woman with short dark hair and large brown eyes and an inquisitive ex-pression on her face. A beautiful face. In that instant he knew something was terribly wrong.

"Where's Josie?" he croaked.

"Who's Josie?" White Robes asked Diana.

"We don't know anyone named Josie," Diana said.

Before he could correct her, Richard fell back asleep.

Dr. Edmunson caught up with Diana in the corridor.

"Now don't you worry about your Richard," he advised. "He's going to be just fine."

Diana stopped and turned to face him. "He'd better be," she said. Her voice was trembling. An image of the gun flashed through her mind. And who was Josie? "I don't know what I'd do without him, Doctor."

"Oh come, now, call me Edward. And believe me, you won't have to do without him. He's still a little high, still dissociative. That's all it is. He should start coming around just fine in the next day or two." Dr. Edmunson's face brightened and he smiled broadly at her, revealing two rows of perfectly even teeth. "Say," he went on, leaning close and placing one hand on Diana's shoulder, "it's almost time for lunch. Would you like to join me in my office? We could relax a bit and have a bite to eat sent up from the cafeteria. Or we could order out if you like. You could even take a little rest on the couch and then see your chosenmate again before you go home."

Diana stared at him. She couldn't conceive of what his face might look like underneath the dermask and she didn't care. Nor did she bother to answer him. Brushing Dr. Edmunson's hand roughly aside, she turned and began walking rapidly in the other direction. Diana didn't know where she was headed, but she knew for certain what she was walking away from.

Richard kept waking up and going back to sleep. Interspersed with a series of jumbled dreams, reality came filtering back to him piecemeal. He remembered the vacation and his plans to spoil it. He had a vague recollection of his wild ride in the recovery room. He realized he was still being drugged. Only now the drugs they were giving him were bringing him down rather than making him euphoric. More down than he wanted to be.

His dreams took on a deadening repetitive quality. He would invariably be at work, sitting in front of his terminal, trying to solve a problem that went on and on in an interminable series of intricate yet muddled steps that never quite made sense. Somewhere the chain of logic was awry. No matter how many times he pored over it, he couldn't find the flaw. Just as he thought he was about to grasp a solution, the screen of his monitor would start to flicker and Josie's face would appear on it. Her eyes were closed as if she were sleeping. Sometimes Sol Thatcher would be leaning over his shoulder and Richard would have to stand up quickly in front of the screen, trying to block Josie's image so Thatcher wouldn't see her. In the dream it was not so important that Thatcher not see Josie, but that he not see her sleeping. In another version, it was Coopersmith's face that appeared on the screen. His complexion was mottled and there was a thin line of blood trickling from his nose. His eyes were blank as stone but his lips kept moving. Although there was no sound, Richard could understand exactly what the man was saying. "Burning the midnight oil," Coopersmith mouthed over and over like a cycling propaganda holo. Then Thatcher would suddenly be there once again, sneaking up from behind, resting one large hand on Richard's shoulder. "Who's that?" he would ask, gesturing at the screen, clipping his sentences as if they were hedges. "Looks familiar. Looks bad for him. Bad for you."

Each time Richard woke from one of these nightmarish interludes, the reality he confronted struck him as harsh and abrasive. The light was far too bright and the surfaces of ordinary objects too sharply defined. The food they gave him tasted bitter and mealy.

Diana was often sitting by his bedside. Her face was gaunt, as if she had lost weight. There was a gray lifeless quality to her flesh and her eyes were feverishly bright, as if she were the one suffering from an illness. His chosenmate was only a pale reflection of the image he had just danced and dined and traveled with for however long it had been. Yet each time he looked at her he felt a love he didn't want or need and could not comprehend filling his heart and over-flowing.

"Shouldn't you be at the office?" he asked.

"I'm taking a few days off," she told him. "You're more important to me than work." She took his hand in both of hers. Her palms were cold and damp. "Don't worry. I called your office. They aren't expecting you in until next Monday. You'll have plenty of time to rest up."

Richard wasn't sure who he was anymore. He wasn't sure who Diana, with her adoring and possessive gaze, had become. It had been nearly a week since he had seen Josie. He couldn't imagine what she must be thinking. Or what he would say when he confronted her.

They released him on Thursday morning, at Diana's insistence and under her recognizance. He was still less than normal. Rather than returning from a vacation, Richard felt as if he were a convalescent recovering from a long illness. His arms and legs were weak. The slightest activity quickly exhausted him. Dr. Edmunson gave him some capsules to take and recommended continued bed rest for several days.

On the tunnel train home, Diana snuggled next to him and clung to his arm. He made no attempt to push her away.

"I'm so glad you're going to be all right," she said. "Next time they said it wouldn't be a problem. They could monitor you more carefully and make sure nothing bad happens. I can't wait until we can go again. We could try something historical next time if you like."

"But it's not real," Richard said, his voice still hoarse. "None of it was the least bit real."

"Who's to say what's real?" Diana countered. "It's real enough for me. I could live like that forever." She snuggled more closely and rested her cheek against his shoulder. "Don't tell me you didn't think it was wonderful."

Richard thought of the food, the panoramic vistas, the nights of unbelievable lovemaking in their hotel suite. He remembered skimming across the open waves and urging his mount up a steep incline with stunning greenery on all sides. He could still feel Diana's body, firm and willing beneath his hands, as they moved as one across the dance floor. He could smell the heady fragrance she had worn.

"It did have its moments," he was forced to admit, only half realizing he'd spoken aloud.

They returned to their conapt in silence, Diana helping him along and clinging to his side, Richard accepting her solicitous embrace. Diana's silence was one of satisfaction. Richard's was that of an ongoing emotional turmoil and exhaustion. He realized that nothing was resolved between them. Diana still didn't know about Josie. She still didn't know that he planned to dissolve their mating and leave her. After what she must have experienced on the vacation, it was no doubt the furthest thing from her mind.

The chaos of his own mind made him think of a battlefield tableau he'd seen at the Museum of Unnatural History. Trees uprooted. Vehicles overturned. Huge chunks of earth dislodged here and there. Bodies and body parts of the dead strewn across the ground. Only unlike that static tableau of some insane war out of the past, the carnage in his mind continued. Fresh troops kept arriving and the conflict raged on, with new corpses piled upon the old.

Every time Richard thought about Josie he wanted to rush to her apartment in the slum and be by her side. Only he still felt too weak and tired to rush anywhere. Every time he looked at Diana, he felt an unreasoning love for her that could not be denied. Despite the fact that she had been the one who had tricked him into the virtual vacation with its enforced emotions, those emotions remained in force.

Once she helped him undress and had him installed in bed, Diana began fussing over him.

"Can I get you something to eat or drink?" she asked.

Richard shook his head.

"I put your books right there." She pointed to the bedside table. "In case you want to read." She seemed very proud of herself.

Richard nodded.

"I really should go in to the office for a few hours. You know, the new project? But I can stay if you need me."

"Go ahead," Richard said. "I'm okay."

"Are you sure? I hate to leave you alone."

He nodded again.

"All right, darling. I'll pick us up something special for dinner." As he concentrated on not looking at her, Diana leaned forward and planted a wet kiss on his cheek. "Love you," she said. "I'll be back as soon as I can."

"Love you, too," he mumbled. He wanted to bite his tongue as soon as he'd spoken, even if it was the truth.

"Don't forget to take your pills," she reminded him. "I'll put them right here next to your books."

Who *was* this woman? She was not the old Diana that Richard knew from their years as chosenmates. She was not the radiant virtual Diana of the vacation.

Whoever she was, she hurried out the door leaving him to his private war.

Richard woke to the familiar walls of his conapt. He didn't remember falling asleep. He stood shakily and staggered to the bathroom, grasping the door frame as a wave of dizziness passed over him.

Back in bed, he looked at the bottle of capsules that Dr. Edmunson had given him. "Take two every four hours," the instructions read. More sedatives, he thought. That was probably what was making him feel tired and weak more than anything. He put them back on the bedside table. Less than a year ago he might have complained about a Doctor's orders, but would never have considered ignoring them.

He sat on the edge of the bed for several minutes, willing himself not to fall back asleep. He stood and made his way to the microkitchen. The cupboards were for the most part empty, but he found what he was looking for, a diet drink called SlimStim that Diana used to control her weight and maintain her energy. You were supposed to mix it with milk but there was only water. He downed the foul concoction half dissolved, grimacing at the taste, some kind of ersatz chocolate.

He sat on the couch in the living room. As soon as he felt better, he thought, he would get dressed and go to Josie's. If anyone could help him exorcise the conditioning of the vacation, it was Josie. Perhaps all he would have to do was see her again. He closed his eyes and framed her image in his mind. Her dark eyes and aquiline features. Her slender limbs. Diana's image appeared beside her. His chosenmate was wearing a yellow gown of some satiny material. It left her shoulders and arms bare. Behind the images of the two beautiful women, the scenes of the vacation played on in an unending stream.

He returned to consciousness a second time without remembering he'd fallen asleep. This time it was the conapt door closing that brought him awake. He was sitting on the couch and wearing a slimsuit. He could barely recall getting dressed.

"What are you doing up?" Diana scolded him. "You're supposed to be resting!"

She was carrying several large plastic bags which she deposited in the microkitchen. She had not only been to work, but to a salon and shopping. Her hair was frosted and her nails painted a reflective silver. She was wearing a dress he'd never seen before, also silver, what there was of it. Silver stockings and reflective shoes with large blocky heels completed her ensemble.

"Do you like it?" she asked, walking back and forth in front of him, turning and posing. Her nails and shoes flashed. Her hips swayed. She looked nearly as provocative as the virtual Diana.

"It's very nice," Richard answered. What else could he say? It was not only true, it was an understatement.

"Don't worry. I've got something for you, too!"

Diana went back to the microkitchen and began digging in one of the bags. When she returned, she was holding a small white box in one hand. She sat down on the couch next to him and held it out. The box was tied with a red ribbon.

"What's this for?" Richard asked.

"Because I love you. And because you were so very nice on vacation."

"That wasn't me," Richard blurted out. He was still coming awake.

"Don't be silly," Diana laughed. "I know my own chosenmate. Here. Aren't you going to open it?"

Richard took the box from her. He pulled the ribbon loose and lifted the lid. Inside, sealed in plastic and resting on a bed of dark red velvet, there was a slightly worn and highly polished silver coin. It was from a country known as the United States of America, once the most powerful nation in the world. One side of the coin depicted an emblem of the country, a stylized eagle holding two branches. Richard picked up the coin and turned it over. On the other side there was the profile of a bushy-haired man who had apparently once ruled that country. The coin was dated 1972.

At one time Richard had harbored a passion for collecting coins, viewing them as pieces of history that had survived into the present. Sometimes he would take them out of their cases and run his fingers across the letters and images on their surfaces, imagining all the places they might have traveled and the people who had touched them. Yet it had been many months since he'd looked at his collection or even thought about it. It was an expensive hobby—"a foolish indulgence" Diana had once called it—and all of Richard's spare credits had gone to support Josie.

"Do you like it?" Diana prompted.

"Yes, of course. Thank you. It's fine. But can we afford all of this?" He held the coin up in one hand and gestured to Diana with the other.

"Oh, we're a little overextended right now, with the vacation and all, but with the extra credits from my promotion, we'll be all right. One thing I learned from the vacation is that we need to worry less about tomorrow and learn to enjoy ourselves more today."

"What promotion?" Richard asked. He realized she'd mentioned something about a new project before leaving for work. His mind was beginning to function again.

"Don't you remember, darling? I told you all about that on vacation, that first night in bed. I can't believe you've forgotten."

"That wasn't me," Richard repeated, this time aware of what he was saying. He was beginning to feel awake for the first time in days. Not alert, but at least awake. The only clouds passing across his mind were the kind that trailed after a storm.

Diana looked at him with a quizzical expression, eyebrows poised. "Why do you keep saying that? Are you feeling all right? Maybe you should go back to bed and rest for a little while."

"We need to talk," Richard said. "We need to talk about the vacation."

"I know," Diana said. "There are so many things to remember we'll be talking about it for years. But first I'm going to make dinner for us. I think it's one of your favorites. At least I hope it is."

Diana hadn't cooked for them since the first year of their mating. This charade had to stop, Richard thought. The more she said and did, the more she fixed him with her gaze of possessive adoration, the more thoroughly he felt entrapped in a contrived connubial bliss. Worst of all, the contrivance was so convincing he could learn to enjoy it. Not unlike the virtual vacation.

Richard Thorne's choices were clear. He could remain with Diana, his chosenmate, a woman who clearly loved him and whom he now loved in return, or abandon her for a woman who took his money in return for sexual favors and had never admitted loving him at all. He could choose a secure and rewarding life with Diana or the uncertainty of whatever life he could hope to have with Josie Jimson. Richard knew that Diana's feelings for him had been conditioned by the vacation, just as his own feelings for her. He also knew that all of us are products of our conditioning from birth to death. What difference could it make if the conditioning was circumstantial or by intent? The results were the same. At least they should have been.

Once again the persona of Richard Thorne eludes us. The sociopath had vanished and was now being superseded by another stage in his development and disintegration. Here the scattered strands of his projection grow even more disparate and discontinuous, some of them no more than isolated points of light that can be linked to no reference whatsoever.

As Diana rose to go to the kitchen, Richard grabbed her by the wrist and pulled her back onto the couch. She fell against him awkwardly and their shoulders bumped together.

"Ow!" Diana cried. "You hurt me! Why are you acting this way? Did you take your pills?"

Richard released her wrist but ignored her questions.

"I'm sorry," he told her. And he was. "But you have to know the vacation wasn't real."

"We've been through that already. I told you what I thought. Why do you have to tear everything down? Why do you have to spoil everything? We were so happy together on vacation."

"You're right," Richard said, "happier than we've ever been. But we weren't together! That wasn't me. You were with an idealized computer construct of me and I was with one of you. It was all a sham, an illusion to make chosen-mates love one another."

"That's nonsense!" Diana wasn't looking at him. "I don't believe you! Why do you have to say such terrible things?" Her body was bent forward on the couch, her elbows resting on her thighs. "It's just more of your craziness." She turned her head and glanced at him for a second. "Next you're going to tell me that we didn't even go on vacation."

"Just listen," he said. "Please listen to me. There's more I have to tell you."

"No, I don't want to hear it!" Diana threw her hands up in front of her face and her nails flashed. "There's something still wrong with your mind." She began shaking her head back and forth. "Dr. Edmunson was right. I brought you home too soon!"

Richard couldn't help himself. He reached out and put his hand on her shoulder, to try to comfort her in some way.

"Don't touch me!" Diana hissed.

In the next instant, as he was pulling his hand away, she reached out and grabbed it in both of hers.

"I'm sorry! I didn't mean that." Her mouth opened and closed awkwardly several times before the next sentence came out. "You do love me, don't you?"

"I love you," Richard told her, "I really do, but it's not enough. I love someone else more."

Diana's face twisted as if it were made of putty. Her artfully applied makeup looked grotesque. She flung his hand from her grasp and stood up, taking several quick steps away from him. She was holding her arms at her sides with fists clenched.

Richard thought she might run out of the room, perhaps leave the conapt all together. Instead she slowly straightened her shoulders and turned to face him. The adoration had left her eyes. The possessiveness remained. His confession had forced the old Diana back to the surface. At last he could recognize her as the chosenmate he knew. The conditioning of the vacation was momentarily stripped away.

"You think you can hide things from me?" Diana said. "You think I don't know where you've been going at night, about that slum bitch you were carrying on with? Josie's her name, right? Well, you can bet she's gone by now. Her and all of her filthy kind. Gone forever."

"Gone?" Richard was suddenly on his feet in front of her. He nearly fell back onto the couch as a wave of vertigo swept over him, but managed to maintain his balance. Diana's unexplained knowledge of his transgressions was incidental to the second blow she had just delivered. "What do you mean, gone?"

"I already told you, you fool, when we were on vacation. That slum is being leveled. It's being demolished even as we speak."

"But what about the people who live there?"

"How should I know? They probably shipped them to a work farm or factory or a slum in some other sector. Who cares? They aren't even Citizens. One thing is for sure, you'll never see your little bitch again." Diana laughed harshly. "I'm all you've got so you better get used to loving *me and no one else*! I can have you sent back to the hospital any time I want. Just like that!" She snapped her fingers in front of his face. "All I have to do is tell Dr. Edmunson you're acting crazy again."

How could he love this woman when he didn't even like her? Even if he did love her, he realized that he hated her in greater measure. Richard shoved his chosenmate aside and headed for the door. He was walking unevenly, and the walls of the conapt were pitching back and forth, but he was walking.

"Where do you think you're going? Come back here, you fool! Come back here right now or you're going to be very sorry!"

The infamous Riots of '37 were a result of the proposed slum clearance of '37. The clearance had been a touted media event, heralded as a further advance into the Future Perfect. It gave Stuart Jimson and his SDL followers the fodder they needed to foster an armed resistance. It was a mistake we would not make again. We learned from the Riots of '37 that when you are going to clear a slum and relocate its population, you do so quickly and quietly, with a minimum of publicity and a high degree of efficiency. Once the goal is accomplished, it can then be touted as a success in the media.

The previous Sunday morning, while Richard and Diana lived their virtual dreams, when most people were likely to be home and in bed, armored Guardeners had entered the slum in cadres of twenty. Moving methodically from building to building, room to room, they rousted the inhabitants.

The slum dwellers were herded into the streets. They were subsequently transported to a relocation center where their cases could be dealt with individually. Resistance was minimal and no Guardeners were seriously injured.

In the course of this operation Josie's illegal plants were discovered, and of course, the computer terminal, which in turn led us to Daniel DeLyon.

From blocks away Thorne could see the dust cloud of the demolition expanding in the air. As he came closer it grew wider and higher in the sky, blotting out the late afternoon sun and throwing a broad shadow on the streets below.

At his usual entrance to the slum his passage was blocked by a large orange barricade that stretched across the street and walkway. Thorne backtracked and circled the perimeter of the wreckage, trying to find another entrance, but he could see that it was hopeless. There were barricades everywhere. Most of what remained within the slum was already in ruins and the destruction continued.

He watched in a thrall of despair and fascination as a huge spiked wrecking ball delivered its blows. Each time it struck, another section of building collapsed. In an avalanche of noise, entire rooms and their furnishings cascaded down to join the debris in the street below. Chips of plaster flew into the air and rained in all directions. Thorne had a vision of Josie's books buried in the rubble, never to be read again. The wrecking ball should have had a face, he thought, a grinning malevolent face with rotting teeth and an insane expression in its eyes.

Spotting an orange-suited worker not far behind one of the barricades, Thorne waved at the man and tried to call out to him, cupping his hands around his mouth to be heard over the noise of the wreckage.

"Where are the people? Where did they take the people?"

The man couldn't hear him. He merely smiled, shook his head, and pointed to one ear.

On the jagged fragment of a broken wall, protruding from the debris around it, a bit of slum dweller graffiti had temporarily survived the devastation, a scrap of doggerel that echoed an earlier inscription and brought a rash of memories streaming back to him.

Are the Dead Lands hot with rads?
Is the City any better?
When the Guardeners slash and burn,
Which will kill you deader?

Thorne had a vision of armored Guardeners entering the slum, gathering up its inhabitants and herding them along the streets as if they were cattle, slaughtering all those who resisted.

No, his mind screamed, Josie couldn't be dead!

A sob broke from his throat. His head was aching and he was feeling physically sick. He began to tremble. Thorne bent over, coughing violently. He tried to retch into the street, but nothing came up but a little saliva and a foul chocolate taste from the back of his throat.

Once the tremors had left his body, he turned away from the debris of the slum and began walking in a new direction. If anyone knew where Josie was, it would be her brother, Daniel DeLyon. It was already late in the afternoon and DeLyon should be home from work soon. If he wasn't, Josie's mother might remember him and let him into their apartment. Perhaps Josie herself would have taken refuge there.

He knocked on the door and then pounded, but there was no answer. He leaned against the wall and was about to sit down on the dirty hall carpet to wait for someone to come home when a door across the hall cracked open. The chain was still on it, but he could see the vertical segment of a face. A pale gray eye rimmed with wrinkles peered out at him.

"There's no one home," the woman told him. "They're gone. The Guardeners came and took them away. You should have heard the screaming. You would have thought the world was coming to an end."

Thorne cried out, hoarse and incoherent, and slid down the wall into a sitting position. The woman quickly slammed the door shut. He heard several locks clicking into place.

Back on the street he began to wander aimlessly and was soon lost. His steps continued to move at random as his mind raged inwardly. There was nothing to smash, no one he could strike out at. There was the City all about him, in every direction, block upon weary block, building after building, imperious and indifferent. It had swallowed Josie without a trace, stolen her away from him with no thought for either of them.

He could go to the closest Guardener Headquarters and ask to see the records of where Josie had been relocated and they would laugh in his face. What business did he have with any of their records? He could try searching through other slums and slum remnants. There must have been dozens scattered throughout the various sectors. He didn't know where they were or how to begin to find them...and Josie probably wasn't in any of them. He recalled the novels he'd read where lone individuals had confronted and overthrown entire societies and he realized how ridiculous they were.

The final stages of Richard Thorne's disintegration now laid claim to him. He lost his last hold on reality and the world he inhabited became one of his own tortured imagination.

The workday ended and crowds of commuters filled the glideways and walkways. Thorne's vacant stare and faltering gait drew little attention. He was just another iota among the millions, one more insignificant individual whose life had nothing to do with theirs. He tried not to look at the faces streaming past him. Each time he did they became grotesque exaggerations. Some appeared like fiercely snarling animals. Some had no features at all, just two eyes glaring from a blank wall of rounded flesh. Others were elongated or compressed caricatures with noses or chins grossly out of proportion. Some were pocked with pustules and running sores, as if the Plague Years had returned.

When he looked up, the buildings of the City that rose about him took on cartoon fluidity, leaning this way and that, threatening to topple into the street at any moment. Shifting patterns writhed across their facades. Similar patterns rippled across the backs of the passing pedestrians and the streets or glideways beneath his feet. Thorne staggered on and tried to concentrate on his own moving feet, his dark shoes plodding forward in a faltering rhythm one step after another.

The dinner hour came and passed and the sky darkened and still he walked on, oblivious to the fact that he hadn't eaten and that night had fallen. Unaware the he was often backtracking and moving in circles.

The entertainment districts blossomed with light and he made his way along their colorful thoroughfares, his senses further barraged by the changing signs and music. He began to think he was still on vacation, that he was surrounded by images without any real substance, projections that existed only in the mind of a computer. He stared at the marquees uncomprehendingly and wondered why the virtual Diana was not by his side, telling him where they should go and what they should do next.

Then he saw Josie!

She was sitting with a man at an outdoor cafe. She had somehow escaped the devastation in the slum. He rushed toward her, nearly losing his balance, catching his fall at the last instant on the back of the man's chair and the edge of the table. The plates and glasses rattled.

Josie glanced up at him with a startled expression. He noticed immediately there was something wrong with her eyes. Their vibrancy was gone. They seemed lackluster and vacant. What had they done to her? There was something wrong with her face, too.

"Can we help you?" Her companion had half risen from his chair in a defensive posture.

It wasn't Josie at all, merely a woman wearing a dermask that superficially resembled her. Thorne felt a wrenching in his stomach as he stumbled back into the festive crowds.

"Probably drunk," he heard the man comment as he wandered off.

It was late by the time he found himself back on his own block in front of his building. Somehow his steps had carried him there by instinct. He dreaded seeing Diana but had nowhere else to go. He rode the lift up, half expecting that when the doors opened he would be confronted by a phalanx of Guardeners waiting to take him away. But there was only the same featureless hallway.

It was when he opened the door to his conapt that he found the Guardeners. There were four of them. The three who were standing wore armor, their bulky presence dominating the small room. The fourth Guardener was in his emerald robes, sitting on the couch next to Diana.

His chosenmate glanced up briefly when Thorne entered the room, then refused to look at him again. She had been crying and the silver eye makeup had run down her cheeks. Her hair was in complete disarray. Diana was hugging her body, her legs drawn up and pressed together. She looked as if she wanted to curl into a fetal ball.

"I'm glad you've returned," the robed Guardener on the couch said. "It saves us the trouble of having to track you down."

For a moment Thorne didn't recognize the man who had spoken. Sol Thatcher's entire demeanor had changed. He no longer spoke in clipped sentences. His posture and movements were rigid rather than lackadaisical. His once flabby cheeks and chin now had a hard solidity about them. It was as if someone had taken the old Thatcher and baked him in a kiln. "You are going to have to come with us," he said, "either willingly or by force. You are under arrest for suspicion in the death of Willem Coopersmith."

Thatcher stood up and crossed the room to face Thorne. He was the larger man, yet they were close to equal in height and their eyes met at the same level. To Thorne's deranged perceptions, Thatcher appeared to be towering over him.

"It was your so-called friend DeLyon who gave you away. I've been after that man for months, waiting for him to slip up. I can usually spot aberrants on sight, but I must admit you had me fooled. I never suspected you. I didn't think you had it in you." Thorne remembered it was the same thing Josie had once said to him, after he'd taken the gun away from the thief in the alley.

"I don't like to be fooled," Thatcher went on. "so I'm taking a special interest in your case." He glanced sideways at

Diana. "I'm afraid you'll have to come too, Citizen Logan, at least until we get to the bottom of this affair."

It was the last thing Richard Thorne heard before the devastation of his life overcame him and he crumpled to the floor at Thatcher's feet.

Confession

Science is the bedrock upon which we have fostered the modern City State and transcended the nightmare known as history. Rational thought is the colophon that defines our existence as unique and preserves us from the errors of our ancestors. Yet despite the knowledge we have accumulated and the advanced methodologies at our disposal, there are times when our science has failed us. This report, in an attempt to gain understandings that lie beyond the sphere of the rational, has departed radically from the accepted approach to problems in human behavior.

Our goal has by no means been a definitive analysis but rather the forging of another tool to aid in the conditioning and reconditioning processes. Although we have abandoned traditional structure and our path may seem circuitous, our posture overly dramatic, there is a point to such excess. Diligence has never been forsaken. Like winnowers of the psyche, we have selected the evidence carefully from the mass of data before us.

We must beg the Directors' forbearance....

But no, that's not right. Not right at all.

The Directors will never see this report. It will be disposed of by underlings long before it reaches their exalted purview. It will be filed for a future reference that will most likely never transpire. Or perhaps it will be erased, shredded and burned, summarily dismissed as subversive propaganda.

In truth, there is no "we" behind these pages other than a fictitious authorial one. It is long past time to abandon this anonymous persona that purports to represent the voice of an omniscient State, a state I am no longer deemed qualified to represent. There is no "we" behind these pages, only the singular "I."

Sol Thatcher.

And like the aberrants I have spent my life attempting to expose and cure, I now have been judged one of their kind for the crime I have committed. I have also been judged too old for reconditioning and too respected to be incarcerated except under the house arrest I now endure. I write these words in the forced retirement a beneficent state has delivered upon me. I suffer the sanctum and solitude of a disgraceful conclusion to a distinguished career. In the official document relieving me of my duties as a Guardener, they had the audacity to call me obsessive and incompetent. I will readily admit to my obsession, an obsession for the truth. Yet I can assure you, I am not incompetent!

As I fill these pages I sit in the study of my conapt in Lambda Heights, not far from where Willem Coopersmith met his violent death. My walls are lined with books, some of which once belonged to Josie Jimson and corrupted Richard Thorne. Now I too have read these books and read them again, and no doubt become corrupted myself. The purity of the vision I once held is lost and I find myself adrift in a sea of ambivalence.

But I must deny the triumph of such disintegration. I must reconstruct the scattered strands of Richard Thorne's web, the cause and effect behind the life he lived. I must find a way to order and relate what I have learned, or suspect I have learned, even if all I can gather are the segments of a larger puzzle that remains beyond my comprehension, that some other more astute investigator may one day solve.

There is nothing else left for me to do.

The fact that I persist in what has been dubbed my obsession and folly regarding this case may cause my reputation to be further vilified. If this document—report, account, novel, travail, call it what you will—does surface and is read in certain quarters, there will be those who will no doubt try to lodge additional charges against me. So be it. My life is already in ruins. My robes have been stripped away. The respect I once held among my colleagues is shattered beyond repair. My chosenmate of thirty years has left me and successfully filed for dissolution of our union. My children, with respectable lives of their own, choose not to visit or to acknowledge their father's disgrace. My friends, such as they were, I see no longer.

My sentence has been pronounced and carried out, both in a legal sense and a very personal one. Additional charges against me can have little effect upon the life I now lead.

Have no doubts. From the time I donned the robes of my profession, my intentions have always upheld the values of the City State. They do so no less in the preceding pages and those that follow. If there are times within this text when I have allow the expression of opinions and perspectives that are antithetical to conventional knowledge and beliefs, there is a point to such apparent heresy. I can assure you that I am no Stuart Jimson exhorting the masses to revolt.

So you can see, in some ways this document is mine as much as it is Richard Thorne's, and it is my crime that must be addressed as well as his, my confession that will be delivered as well as his. Yet before I can confess and resolve my own story, I must resolve the stories of those who contributed to my downfall.

So let me continue, stripped of all pretense. Or perhaps only with a different set of pretensions. All I can offer you are words and more words. As they accumulate and adhere to one another, as they form phrases and sentences and paragraphs, they strive to create a semblance of reality and draw order from chaos, meaning from the meaninglessness that threatens to overwhelm me. Even if they are successful in that artifice, a semblance they will remain, no different from the pretensions of a holodrama or a virtual vacation.

I cannot promise you truth absolute and definitive. I *can* swear to pursue that elusive goal in whatever way seems most appropriate, to relate and interpret the facts of the case as I perceive them. Do not judge me too harshly. There is truth to be revealed in the course of all human endeavor.

Incarceration

The flowers of spring were blossoming in parks and concourses throughout the City, a multicolored riot of roses,
poppies, jonquils, lilies, camellias, nasturtiums, and more.
Each day the air was filled with the rich scents of their in-
termingling fragrances. In those blocks once blighted by the
slum remnant, construction was well underway on the new
condominium complexes. Throughout City Center, in building after building, dedicated Citizens continued to spend the
workday striving toward the Future Perfect. During their
lunch hours they enjoyed the perfect weather, basking in the
sun on the public concourses. Each night they filled the entertainment districts with life, passing to and fro along the
glideways amidst the ever changing lights and entertainments. Severin's Fountain had been refurbished and enlarged,
its murals shining more brilliant than ever before. The City
Circus was once again performing in the park beyond Founder's Square.

Richard Thorne, locked within his small windowless
cell in the towering edifice of Delta Conditioning Center,
remained in a world apart, oblivious to all. He had once mistakenly thought of his virtual vacation as a kind of incarcera-

tion. Now he was discovering what real incarceration was like. Now he would have time aplenty—without illegal drugs, forbidden books, without Josie's perverse companionship and sexual favors—to contemplate his crimes.

The cases of the other participants in his tragedy had already been resolved and disposed of. Yet the problem of Thorne's resolution and disposition remained. And for the first time in my long and successful career, I was at a loss as to how to proceed. For you cannot recondition an aberrant until you first understand the factors that have fostered their deviance. And despite the sophisticated tools at my disposal, despite my utmost diligence, the puzzle of what fostered Richard Thorne's aberrance remained unresolved.

Once set in motion, the chain of events that led us to the arrest of Thorne for the murder of Willem Coopersmith had been a clear and direct one.

Due to an astute young Guardener—G-7 but subsequently promoted at my behest—who spotted the illegal terminal during the mass rousting of the slum denizens, Josie Jimson was segregated from the other evacuees and transported to Delta Conditioning. The terminal, and her illegal books and drugs, were confiscated.

Not surprisingly, Josie refused to divulge the origins of the terminal. She retreated into a sullen silence punctuated by hostile stares and would not cooperate with the investigation in any way. Yet a check of her background and birth records soon revealed the logical culprit. Our conclusion was later confirmed by Daniel DeLyon's cyberscan and by DNA testing of dead skin cells extracted from the terminal's keyboard.

DeLyon's arrest followed within hours the arrest of his sister. Their mother was relocated to a Senior Retirement Center where she should have been placed years ago. Unfortunately, she developed a bronchial infection that developed into pneumonia and she succumbed several weeks later. De-Lyon was taken into custody and housed at the Delta Conditioning Center a few cells away from Josie.

In response to the trauma of his arrest, DeLyon's behavior stood in marked contrast to that of his sister. He became agitated rather than withdrawn. He paced back and forth in his narrow cell. He rubbed the back of his neck and ran his hands through his thinning hair, clenched and unclenched his fists. He sat down on his cot only to stand seconds later and begin pacing once more. He now wore the baggy gray prison garb issued to all detainees. They had given him a size or two too large for him and he cut a ridiculous figure has he moved back and forth with only his fingers poking forth from the sleeves and his cuffs trailing the floor.

Outwardly, he acted as if he was more than eager to cooperate with us. He would periodically pause in his manic back and forth with arms raised and extended, and direct a plaintive monologue to the walls and the ceilings of his enclosure.

"I know you're there! I know you're watching me, that you can hear me. I'm telling you I've done nothing wrong. I am a registered Citizen, a Professional. My loyalty to the City State has never been questioned. Whatever the problem is, I will try to help you in any way I can. Just give me a chance to explain."

Even through the surveillance monitor I could see the fear that haunted his eyes. I could read the guilt in his facial expressions and body language as clearly as lines of text upon a screen. His extended dual existence had now come to an end, and neither of his split personalities could save him from what was to follow.

"How long has he been going on like that?" I asked the guard in charge.

"On and off for hours. Every since they brought him in. He keeps asking about his mother."

"Give him 30 ccs of Ameratal, intramuscularly," I said, "wait forty minutes, and then I'll see him in Room Three."

Whenever possible I hold all of my interviews with prisoners and detainees in Interrogation Room Three in the middle of the afternoon. I am not a superstitious man, far from it, but there can be a special quality to the light in that room—dare I call it spiritual in this age of enlightenment?—that I discovered quite by accident many years ago.

I was interrogating an illegal marketer who dealt in stolen and bogus medical supplies. Occasional civil unrest still existed at that time. An isolated terrorist group dynamited an electrical tower, cutting power to all of Delta Sector and parts of Gamma, while the interview was in progress. And for the first time I noticed the light streaming through the high marbled windows with their reinforcement of steel crosshatching. Beneath the overhead fluorescents that where now extinguished the room had been so bright that each object was bathed in a microscopic clarity. Now there were shadows in the room. The light, falling at an angle from the west, was chalky, even milky, mottled with varied buds of light that shifted almost imperceptibly across the floor, the pale green walls, the face of the man I was interviewing, with the sun's movement.

And nearly as suddenly, as the interrogation progressed, the resistance of the man broke down and he began telling me everything I wanted to know...as if he was a penitent seeking absolution and I was his confessor. From the information he provided, an entire ring of illegal marketers was uncovered and I received a commendation and promotion shortly thereafter.

Naturally, I tried to recreate the same conditions in other interrogations rooms and times of day by turning off the overhead lights. Yet it was only in Interrogation Room Three, in the middle of the afternoon, that I ever managed to recreate the phenomenon. And when I did, when the light was right, the effect upon the subject being interviewed was always noticeable and often profound.

I've never been able to determine the exact weather conditions needed to prevail for that ethereal light to stream through the high windows and work its magic. It does not suit a man of my stature to go running outside the building in the middle of an interrogation. I suspect it must be some exact mix of sun and clouds that only occurs by chance or providence that even the Weathermen could not recreate at will.

As it turned out, with DeLyon's interview, neither the weather nor the man was cooperating that day. When I killed the overheads the room merely filled with an unrelieved dimness, and I was forced to turn them back on. Though in DeLyon's awkward and futile attempt to bargain for his freedom, he did provide one salient bit of information that eventually led to Thorne's arrest.

By the time they ushered DeLyon into the room, the injection had begun to take effect. He was still agitated, but considerably less so than before. He glanced nervously about the bare green walls before collapsing into a chair on the opposite side of the table that separated us.

An armed guard remained on duty, standing several paces behind DeLyon. I also left the clear plastic shielding in place between us. One could never be too careful when dealing with aberrants. In my youth I had been less than cautious and still have a pencil-thick scar along one side of my neck as a souvenir.

"Citizen Thatcher," he began, before I could ask him anything. "What are *you* doing here?" Couldn't he see I was wearing the robes of a Guardener? "It's good to see a familiar face," he lied. "Please tell me what they've done with my mother? Is she all right?"

"Your mother is fine and receiving excellent care," I informed him. "Far better than you ever provided for her. But we are not here to talk about your mother. This interview concerns a computer terminal that you stole from Delta Standards Control. We want to know why you took it and what purposes you have put it to."

"But I don't know anything about it," DeLyon insisted. "What would I want with a terminal? What could I possibly do with one?"

"Then we can assume it is your sister, Josie, who is solely responsible for its possession."

DeLyon's head snapped up and his eyes widened. "No, Josie knows nothing about it!" His pupils were dilated and he blinked several times as if trying to focus. "Josie hasn't done a thing. She's completely innocent!"

"Then you admit the terminal is yours?"

DeLyon hesitated. He ran one hand along his cheek and rubbed his jaw. "The terminal...," he began, "...well, that's really nothing—I can explain that—it's nothing at all compared to what I have to tell you. I know of a far more serious crime, a *real crime.*" He paused for a second, as if gathering his thoughts, and then delivered what he must have thought was his gambit. "I can tell you...about a murder...the murder of an important man!"

At first I took it for merely more of his chicanery. "And what murder would that be?" I asked.

He leaned toward me, nearly touching the shielding, cupping one hand to the side of his mouth as if were imparting a secret and feared it would be overheard. Wasn't he aware that our every word was being recorded?

"The murder," he said in a near whisper, "of Willem Coopersmith."

Still, I did not take him seriously. "Willem Coopersmith was not murdered. He died of natural causes, a heart attack. Or so our reports concluded."

"No, you're wrong. Believe me! The man was murdered as sure as you and I are sitting here."

"And what makes you so sure of that?"

"I just know," DeLyon said. "I know for certain, the man was murdered."

"And who do you claim committed this murder? What evidence do you have?"

Once more DeLyon hesitated. "Well...if we could work out something about the terminal...it's really nothing...I didn't hurt a soul...then I could tell you about the murder. I would be willing to tell you everything I know."

I nearly laughed in his face. Even if he had valid information to give us about a murder, did he seriously believe the City State made bargains with aberrants, that it would tolerate one criminal activity in exchange for information about another? We had a much surer method of determining if DeLyon had anything to tell us and whether or not it was true.

"This interview is over," I said, nodding to the guard to return DeLyon to his cell.

"Does that mean I can leave," DeLyon said, "that I can go home now?"

"You're not going anywhere, Citizen," I told him, "until we find out exactly what it is you've done and what you know. And not until the nature of your aberrance has been determined and subsequently rectified."

"Wait!" DeLyon cried out, rising from his chair, his hands pressed against the plastic shielding. "You have to give me a chance! I'm telling you that I can explain everything!"

As the guard restrained him, I turned my back and left the room.

That evening, before returning to my conapt in Lambda Heights, I signed the orders for the scans of Daniel DeLyon and his silent uncooperative sister, both of which I planned to personally supervise.

Those accused of crimes in centuries past were judged by a variety of methods, none of them sure and few of them rational. In primitive eras—that is to say the bulk of human history—those under suspicion were often forced to endure physical ordeals based on superstition in an attempt to defend themselves. They would be required to retrieve a stone from a pot of boiling water, or walk across burning coals, the extent of their injuries and how fast they healed determining guilt or innocence. Those suspected of witchcraft, another superstitious absurdity that prevailed for centuries, were often thrown into a lake or river. If they floated, they were condemned as a witch. If they sank, they were judged to be innocent. Death being the end result in either case for these poor souls accused of a crime that did not even exist.

In more advanced and enlightened societies, complex legal systems evolved to determine guilt or innocence, lengthy trials presided over by judges wearing black robes, with advocates who argued for or against the accused. The fate of those being tried was decided by a jury, a group of their so-called peers, who discussed the case and took a vote after evidence was presented and arguments made. Whether those under suspicion were condemned to incarceration and sometimes death, or set free to return to society, was often determined more by debate and rhetoric, the forensic skills of those defending and prosecuting, than by any rational criteria.

Corrupt judges, bribed juries, individual prejudices and misconceptions, further corrupted the system. Religious and ethnic minorities, outsiders, anyone held in disregard by the society as a whole, seldom received a fair trial. In many instances, individuals who physically resembled those actually guilty of the crime were incarcerated and even executed because they had been mistakenly identified in eyewitness testimony. Every novice Guardener learns that conscious memory cannot be trusted on its own.

The City State has thankfully replaced such haphazard and harmful systems of justice by a far more certain one, Cybernetic Behavioral Analysis, the cyberscan.

We welcome the day when the scan can be applied to all Citizens on a regular basis, when the potential for aberrant behavior can be nipped in the bud before its blossoms flower and release their poisonous pollens into the air. For now, the cyberscan remains a costly and laborious process that can only be employed after the fact, once crimes have been committed and aberrance has been detected, not only to elicit information and determine guilt, but more importantly, to establish means for rehabilitating and conditioning the guilty parties.

Even if I understood them fully, I would not reveal the technical details of the cyberscan here. Not only are they classified, such incidentals are not relevant to this document or its conclusions. Enough to say that although the physical aspects of the procedure differ, the cyberscan employs a technology akin to that of the virtual vacation. Both processes came into existence as by-products of behavioral and reconditioning research. The cyberscan, rather than filling the mind with an ideal vacation scenario, records the memories that a mind already contains. And the subject must remain conscious during its execution.

There is an ancient saying, origins unknown, about one's entire life flashing through one's mind in the moment before death. No one can know this for sure, but it is exactly what happens with the scan. Only it does not take a moment, but several hours. The time required is dependent on the age of the subject, the willingness to cooperate, and to what extent conscious memories conflict with those encoded in the subconscious.

The individual being examined experiences a vastly accelerated montage of his past life, with its attendant emotions relived at that same accelerated pace. The joys and sorrows of existence rush past before the mind's eye, moments of triumph and shame, all the truths that ego's memory have denied or glossed over are briefly revealed, most of it passing by too quickly to comprehend at the time. The average subject emerges from the experience as from an intense and disturbing dream. Whatever unpleasant truths are revealed are for the most part quickly submerged into the subconscious again. Though there are often residual effects over the next several days as some forgotten memories resurface. And in some cases the scan can be a traumatic experience for those who refuse to cooperate, who attempt to close their minds and obstruct the process. This proved to be the case with Daniel DeLyon.

DeLyon approached the cyberscan as if he were a man about to be executed. Despite the fact he had been administered a mild euphoric to facilitate the process, he had to be firmly held by two guards and forced into the scanning chamber.

He continued to resist throughout the process, so that a scan that should have taken only three hours took nearly six. As the session progressed, one could hear him shouting unintelligibly through the chamber walls. He emerged extremely disoriented, mumbling a strange litany of gibberish and unable to stand on his own. In his struggles he had broken one of the restraints and injured himself by thrashing about in the chamber. Confronting the truths of his life and history had proven too much for the man to bear. Or perhaps it was the knowledge that his duplicities were now revealed for all to see.

Later that day, after DeLyon had been transferred to our hospital ward and examined, I spoke with the attending physician, a bright-eyed and bushy-haired Dr. Fox, who was newly promoted to Delta Conditioning. Though he looked young enough to be my son, he was already a G-17. There must have been a robe or two somewhere in his family to have achieved so high a ranking at his age.

"He reawakened an old childhood injury," the man informed me. "In his youth he fractured the tibia in the joint of his left knee. It never received proper medical treatment at the time and healed incorrectly. He grew up in a slum, you know. We don't even have records of when or how it happened."

Of course I knew DeLyon grew up in a slum! Didn't the man realize who I was?

"We also suspect," Fox went on, "there may have been some functional damage to the brain, but we won't know for sure for a few days. He's still mostly incoherent right now."

The scan of Josie Jimson proved to be a different matter entirely. As noted above, Josie was a woman who was proud of her aberrations. She harbored not only an unreasonable contempt for the City State, drilled into her by her radical father, but clung firmly to the paranoid misconception that the City State only intended to harm her. Even in the baggy gray jumpsuit, hair messed and falling loosely about her face, partially sedated and entering the scanning chamber, there was a blind arrogance about the woman that seemed unquenchable. I could see it in her dark unblinking eyes and sense it in the cast of her features.

And oddly enough, rather than complicating the cyberscan, it was this arrogance, approaching a kind of egomania, that carried her through smoothly. There was no shouting on her part, no thrashing about. Except for the whir of the processing machines an uncanny silence prevailed throughout her session. After examining her scan in detail at a later date, I concluded that whatever unpleasant truths about her life were revealed as her conscious memories confronted the sordid realities, the mistakes and hypocrisies of her past, she rejected them from the start. She held firmly to the belief that such realizations were merely lies that the City State was attempting to plant in her mind.

After three hours, the woman emerged from the chamber, clearly exhausted yet apparently unshaken by the experience. Sullen and silent as ever, she was returned to her cell.

The results of the scans of Josie Jimson and Daniel DeLyon revealed both DeLyon's bipartite flower configuration and the classic aberrant configuration of his sister's rebellious nature. There was no need to examine them in greater detail at that time. Instead, I merely performed a global search of the results for the stolen terminal, and of course, for Willem Coopersmith, and I soon had the information I was after.

Once he had committed the rather daring act of stealing the terminal, smuggling it piece by piece out of Delta Standards Control and reassembling it in his sister's apartment, DeLyon had been extremely cautious in its use. Except in the single instance of seeking out Coppersmith's whereabouts for Richard Thorne, he had not invaded confidential government files. Nor had he attempted to alter important records or documents. All of DeLyon's transgressions had to do with his own passion for gambling, and though considerable in sum, each was minor enough on its own so that it was unlikely to be noticed.

Like many Citizens who gambled compulsively, a behavioral flaw we have not yet been able to root out of our populace, DeLyon made most of his wagers at public betting machines, usually on fireball games and other sporting events. Unlike the average Citizen, he did not play one or two favorite machines, but many different ones, even traveling to other sectors to place his bets. They were always relatively small bets, none that would attract anyone's attention. DeLyon would then use the stolen terminal to access the betting files after the fact, once the wager was won or lost, not deleting his losses or attempting to place winning bets retroactively, but altering the amounts he had wagered, raising it a little each time he won and lowering it when he lost.

His resultant illegal winnings, over a period of several years, became considerable. Some of these credits went to support his mother and helping to support his sister. Most, it appeared, he had squandered on excessive indulgences at the Halls of Expression, a collection of expensive dermasks, and gambling in less certain ways, where he could not manipulate the results, such as card and dice games in the slum.

The global searches on Coopersmith revealed both DeLyon's account of Richard Thorne's manic attempt to find the man on the night of his death, and Josie's perceptions of what Richard had told her happened that night. The evidence was hearsay, still circumstantial, but more than enough to arrest Thorne and detain Diana for questioning.

The case was progressing rapidly and I was pleased with the results. Our failure to determine that Coopersmith's death had been a murder was clearly a black mark against our department. Fortunately, I had only been peripherally involved in that investigation. Now that I was directly involved in uncovering the truth of the matter, it would no doubt result in a significant credit for me, and perhaps my promotion to G-22, which I admittedly felt was overdue.

My next logical step was to interview and scan Richard Thorne, which at that time proved impossible. After Thorne collapsed at the time of his arrest, he remained unconscious for nearly a day. I again had to deal with the young Dr. Fox, who insisted that Thorne was in no condition to undergo either an interrogation or the rigors of a cyberscan. According to Fox, he was suffering from extreme exhaustion and dehydration. And although we had no clear understanding of the reasons at that time, he was still recovering from the virtual vacation, which had affected him in such negative fashion. Fox recommended bed rest, fluids, and continued observation to determine the nature of his mental trauma. I didn't like this delay, or Fox for that matter, but there was nothing I could do about it.

Richard Thorne spent his first week in incarceration in our hospital ward, at first completely unconscious, and then for several days in a semi-delirium, drifting in and out of consciousness. There was little for me to do but move on to the resolution of the cases of the other miscreants involved in this sad affair.

When the guard ushered Diana Logan into Interrogation Room Three, I confronted a woman who looked thoroughly beaten. She no longer wore the silver dress, but like Daniel DeLyon and Josie Jimson, the gray jumpsuit issued to all detainees. She had been disinfected and showered like the others and her silver hair fell limply about her face. Her features looked drawn and tired, her eyes red and swollen from crying.

Diana sat in the straight-backed chair with her shoulders hunched forward and at first wouldn't look at me. She had folded her hands on the table in front of her, and closed them together as if she were trying to hide the silver nails. At the same time she kept rubbing them against one another and staring at them. I saw at once that she was a Citizen desperately in need of help.

It was midafternoon. I signaled the guard to kill the overheads—he was aware of my little eccentricity—and once he did, the light pouring in from the high windows seemed very right.

"Do you know why you are here?" I began.

She nodded, and then she spoke, her voice hoarse and so low I had to lean forward to hear her.

"It's not my fault," she said. "I never told Richard to kill anyone. I just wanted us to leave...to go to another sector and get away from him."

"By 'him' do you mean Willem Coopersmith?"

She nodded again, but still she would not look up. "He wouldn't leave me alone. He took advantage of me. He did terrible things."

"Why didn't you report him?"

She paused for a moment, and then spoke in a rush.

"Because no one would have believed me! I was only a G-15. He was a Director, one of the most powerful men in the entire sector. Would you have believed me?"

"Do you think your chosenmate murdered Willem Coopersmith?"

She shook her head roughly from side to side and the silver hair swung back and forth in loose clumpings. "I don't know what he did!" She was clearly growing more distraught with each question I asked.

"Do you love your chosenmate?"

"Yes," she said, finally looking up with a shocked disbelieving expression. "I do love him...still...but I don't want to love him! Not anymore!" And with that she broke into tears and threw her hands over her face.

I lowered the plastic shielding and reached across the table. Taking both of her wrists, I gently yet firmly lowered them. The attending guard gave me a strange look.

Sobbing uncontrollably, Diana let her face fall forward against her arms. Her hair brushed my wrists and the cuffs of my robe. The guard shifted position as if he were about to take a step forward. One hard look from me and he resumed his place against the wall. What business was it of his? He probably wasn't even a G-10.

"Don't worry, my dear," I told her, "it's going to be all right." I shifted my grip until I was holding both of her hands in mine. I gave them a reassuring squeeze. I could smell the lingering odor of the disinfectant, harsh yet sweet upon her flesh. "We're not going to hurt you. Just tell me everything from the beginning. And take your time."

The light from above was working its magic and of course she did. It all came spilling out of her in an emotional rush. How Willem Coopersmith had promised her a promotion in return for sexual favors. How Thorne had flown into a rage and left their conapt despite her protests on the night of Coppersmith's death. How she had later found his gun and in spite of her duty and better judgment as a Citizen, disposed of it to protect her Chosenmate.

A scan of Diana the next morning revealed the irregular stalk of her configuration, graphically illustrating her past misdeeds, and the loosely spread blossom of the flower, indicating the possibility for more transgressions in the future. Though her crimes were slight compared to the others, and I did feel a certain sympathy for the woman, I concluded I had encountered one more aberrant who would have to be dealt with accordingly.

The case of Josie Jimson was the quickest and most easily resolved, for I concluded that conditioning would be a wasted effort. Admittedly, I disliked the woman from the moment I saw her and examined her files. She represented so much of the dissolute and diseased past that I had spent my life trying to eradicate. Yet I have always prided myself in my objectivity when dealing with aberrants, choosing the best course for each one and for the City State, regardless of my personal feelings. I can assure you, my intense dislike of the woman had nothing to do with my decision.

I had seen her kind before, slum dwellers all, and had even mistakenly attempted forced conditioning on a few in my idealistic youth. Some resisted so completely I had to abandon the attempt. And there was one who at first appeared to comply, enough to be released into society and confirmed as a Citizen, only to later explode into destructive madness. I had learned my lesson long ago. Josie Jimson had no skills to offer the City State, only trouble and aggravation.

The disposition of Josie's case was nothing special. I applied the same criteria that had been applied to most of the others who had been gathered up in the sweep of the slum. And I reached the same conclusion. Josie would be sent to an agricultural commune, where it was hoped that through the ancient therapy of working with plants and the soil in an agrarian setting that a healing of her wayward soul might take place.

Of course she would first be offered the opportunity for voluntary conditioning, just as she had when she had once tried to become a Citizen and her personality profiles registered well outside the normal range. I felt certain she would refuse now as she had then. Depending on her behavior and progress at the commune, she would periodically be offered this opportunity again. Yet even if she opted for voluntary conditioning at some future date, her case would be someone else's problem, no longer mine.

I saw her one last time as a guard ushered her into the lift, her hands cuffed behind her back, to transport her to the holding center from which the other slum dwellers were already being relocated. She glanced my way for just a second. I could see that the hostility in her eyes was beginning to break down. It was now laced with fear and an uncertainty about her future. It was possible that someday she would accept conditioning and become a well-adjusted Citizen. Regardless, I knew I had made the right decision.

Diana Logan and her case were far more to my liking. Her life had departed so radically from the path she had hoped it would follow, her emotional state was so devastated and her mental processes so confused, it was hard not to feel sorry for the woman.

Unlike Josie, Diana had been a productive member of society, a Citizen who had already undergone primary conditioning as part of her education. Her architectural skills had been of value to the City State in the past and could be again. If she had never known Richard Thorne, if she had not met Willem Coopersmith, her potential aberrance might have remained dormant throughout her entire life. Yet now that it had surfaced, a reconditioning to remove her aberrant tendencies and make sure they did not recur was clearly the course to follow. There was a worthwhile life here to be salvaged, and I intended to make sure that it was.

The success of any conditioning depends to a large extent on whether or not the subject cooperates. In voluntary reconditioning, for those Citizens who become aware of their own shortcomings and apply for the process, we use a standard template that reinforces primary conditioning and channels negative individualism into productive or benign paths. For someone afflicted with an overeating problem, we would suppress the compulsion to eat and replace it with another one suited to their disposition, a compulsion for dancing or watching fireball games or dedicating one's spare time to serving the State in a useful volunteer capacity, such as cleaning up the trash that often mars the borders of the glideways.

Criminal reconditioning can be more problematic, since criminals are often the last to confront their flaws, no matter how grave, and most often unwilling to cooperate in their correction. It also takes a more complex course than most normal adjustments by addressing all of the behavioral factors which have led to the commission of the crime, and subsequently creating a new persona for the individual in which such negative elements have been altered or eliminated. Diana Logan was a woman frantic with regret, eager to cooperate with us in any way she could. She was also more than ready to leave the disaster of her old life behind and be given a chance at a new one.

Sequestering myself in my office and telling my assistant I did not want to be disturbed, to hold all calls and refuse all visitors unless the matter was urgent, I sat down before the projection of Diana's flower configuration with its widely spaced cone of disparate lines. I concentrated on the contents of the brightest nodes and I began to play with them. Through trial and error, and my own experience in curing aberrants, I began to adjust her personal makeup, and to change her values, emotions, and needs.

First, I took the edge off her ambition and lowered her personal expectations. Her dreams of someday achieving the robed status of a City Planner were unrealistic in any case.

Although she was quite accomplished at the basic skills of design, she lacked the creative talent to ever achieve such a goal.

I reduced her libido and her sexual confidence to well below average, and curtailed her aggressiveness in that area to the point where it was practically non-existent. In the past Diana had used her sex as a weapon to manipulate men. It was not only her freckles that had attracted Willem Coopersmith to her, but the way she dressed and behaved. That would no longer be the case. In the future, the demeanor Diana would project would be reserved, demure, even shy.

Her memory of the events that had led to her downfall would not be effaced entirely, but a cloud would be placed across it. This would become a part of her past that she viewed as extremely unpleasant, that she wanted to leave behind and never think about again. This would include her love for Richard Thorne. On that count, I merely needed to follow Diana's own wish that she did not want to love him anymore. I reinforced all of her negative feelings about her Chosenmate and de-emphasized the positive ones. Just as the virtual vacation had strengthened her love for Richard, her reconditioning would not only weaken it but reverse the feeling. If she thought about the man again at all, it would be with a marked distaste. She would wonder how she had ever loved him in the first place.

Finally, in addition to reinforcing her primary conditioning, I imbued her with an overwhelming compulsion to report sexual harassment or illegal weapons, or any other violation of City State law that she encountered. When I applied all the projected changes to the configuration of her scan, the spokes of her flower figure regrouped almost perfectly to the unblemished cone of an ideal Citizen. Two or three sessions in a reconditioning chamber would be all that it should take. And now that I had created the perfect personal template for her, the techs could handle the task without my assistance.

Once her conditioning was complete, Diana Logan would spend a short period of recuperation in some state facility. She would then be given a different last name and relocated to a different sector. Although she would be allowed to remain an architect, she would be downgraded to a G-12, for her crimes could not go unpunished.

I glanced at the clock and realized that more than two and a half hours had passed. However, it had been time well spent. This was the most satisfying and rewarding aspect of my work, curing aberrants and returning them to society as productive well-adjusted Citizens.

That left DeLyon, who was still recovering in the hospital ward. When I talked to Dr. Fox again, in his rather cluttered office, I was not pleased with what he had to say to me or the manner in which he said it.

"We've set the knee joint properly and put a cast on it," he stated, flipping through the file on his desk. "But his mind is a different matter altogether. There has definitely been some damage."

"What kind of damage?"

"Neurological, of course. His records indicate that before you scanned him his intelligence was not far from genius. We tested him again today, and now he is barely above normal. There also appears to be some impairment of motor function in his left arm and hand. And his speech is noticeably slurred. Though the X-rays don't reveal it, I am convinced he suffered a series of very minor strokes. He could improve considerably over time, but I doubt he will ever be the person he once was."

"How can you be sure he's not faking? The man is full of tricks, as duplicitous as they come."

Fox shook his head. "Well, the knee injury is certainly not faked, and I have no reason to believe his mental problems are. We can't be certain unless he is scanned again, and as the Doctor in charge of his welfare as a Citizen, I cannot allow that to happen."

"Why not?" I demanded. There was an arrogance about Fox that I found intolerable. He was so young and so full of himself and his presumed expertise.

"DeLyon already had an extreme fear of the scanning process, which was only heightened by his experience. All I had to do was mention another scan to him and he began to tremble. If he is dissembling, then he is a consummate actor. If he is scanned again, and resists as he did the first time, there is the possibility of turning him into a vegetable. Then he'll be of no use to himself and a burden to the City State." Fox closed the file and slapped his palm against it. "I've looked at the recording of his session," he continued, "and in my opinion, it was mishandled. The scan should have been stopped the moment he started screaming. And you should have monitored his vital signs more carefully. There were times when his pulse and blood pressure were off the charts!"

The man was challenging my ability as a Guardener, my competence, even though I was twice his age and possessed more than twice his experience. I have never been incompetent and I scoffed at his assertion. "If I stopped scanning every subject when they started to make a little fuss, we wouldn't be able to process half the aberrants we do. DeLyon should be afraid. Fear on the part of the subject is a requisite element of a successful reconditioning. I'm not interested in a second scan for DeLyon. All I want to know is when we can recondition him?"

"I'm afraid that's also out of the question. Not with the reconditioning chamber. It's too similar to the scan, and as I'm sure you know, can be an even more arduous experience for those who resist. I'm recommending that DeLyon's aberrance be handled with more traditional methods. Stimulus-response conditioning and the implantation of a neuro-chemical regulator.

"We're not equipped to do that here. We abandoned those methods years ago because they are not as effective."

"I'm well aware of that, Citizen Thatcher. That's why I've ordered a transfer of the patient to the Conditioning Center in Beta Sector where those methods are still available. I believe that in DeLyon's case, they will prove effective enough. At the very least, they will not destroy his mind further."

By this time I was ready to explode, but maintaining the demeanor of a Professional, I controlled my anger. I was also feeling slightly lightheaded, almost dizzy, but I was not going to take one of my pills in front of Fox.

Of course I'd had problems before with Doctors who were trying to coddle aberrants in the name of their health. What Guardener in my position hasn't? I could call DeLyon's case before a Review Board and challenge Fox's decision. Doubtless I would have won as I usually had in the past in such confrontations. I was a G-21 and Fox, despite what connections he might have, was only a G-17. For a moment, I considered doing just that. Yet my promotion to G-22 was already overdue, perhaps imminent, and I didn't need another controversy on my record to confuse the matter. I am an assertive man when it comes to treating aberrants, and there had already been too many conflicts with Doctors and other Guardeners in the past. And last year there had been an unfortunate episode with a female detainee. I was cleared without prejudice of all charges in that case and it was expunged from my record, though it remained recent enough so that I could still feel the chill of its shadow.

DeLyon's possession of the terminal was a significant crime, yet considering the damage he could have caused, the ways in which he had used it were trivial. He was no would-be revolutionary like his crazed stepfather Stuart Jimson, just a selfish little man pursuing his own personal interests. Even if DeLyon was faking, even if his aberrance persisted or surfaced again after reconditioning, he was unlikely to pose a significant threat to the City State. I could now wash my hands of him just as I had done with his recalcitrant sister. Let whatever happened with DeLyon be Fox's problem, not mine.

It was Richard Thorne that I was after. He was the hub upon which this small circle of deviance turned. And his crime, the taking of another human life, was the most serious of all. Thus his confession and successful reconditioning would garner the most credit of all.

"Well, Doctor Fox," I said, "I do not agree with either your contentions or your conclusions. However, since you are now officially in charge of this aberrant, I will not object to your decision. However, I do plan to file a formal opinion to absolve myself of all responsibility in this case."

Fox nodded curtly. "That is your privilege, Citizen. File whatever you like!" He stood up. "Now if you'll excuse me, I have other duties and patients to attend to."

The bald insolence of the man was hard to believe.

I planned to have my revenge on Dr. Fox at some future date, once my promotion was secure. I wasn't sure exactly how, but the opportunity would no doubt eventually arise and I would enjoy making the most of it.

A week had passed since I had arrested Richard Thorne. Even the cautious and irksome Dr. Fox at last relented and admitted that the long overdue resolution of Willem Coopersmith's death must be postponed no longer. However, the procedures were delayed once again by an encounter that took place in the hospital corridor. I was not present, but I viewed the recording of the incident later.

DeLyon's transfer to Beta had come through and he was leaving the hospital ward at the same time that Thorne was being transported from the hospital ward to a cell. Each man was accompanied by a guard. Thorne's hands were cuffed behind his back, standard procedure when prisoners are in non-secure areas. DeLyon was on crutches, his leg in a cast. He had not been cuffed. The guard in charge was later reprimanded. He should have secured a wheelchair for transport, cuffed DeLyon, and carried the crutches. You don't give an aberrant a potential weapon and leave his hands free to use it.

The paths of the two men crossed and they confronted one another. Thorne's reaction appeared negligible, his expression nearly as blank as if he did not recognize his former friend. In contrast, DeLyon began shouting the moment he saw Thorne. Or rather he let out a single unintelligible roar and charged at him. Despite the fact that he was on crutches and supposedly suffering loss of motor control, before either guard could restrain him, he lunged forward on one crutch while raising the other and swinging it forcefully against the side of Thorne's head. Both men collapsed onto the floor of the corridor. Thorne, a purple hematoma spreading across his temple, was taken to the emergency room, and then returned to his hospital bed for observation.

It was not until the following Monday afternoon that Thorne entered Interrogation Room Three. I signaled the guard accompanying him to turn the fluorescents off...and today the light seemed very right. A milky illumination poured though the high windows and filled the room with its ethereal presence.

Though Thorne looked less disheveled and bewildered than when I had arrested him at his conapt, he now appeared as a ghost of the programmer I had known and never suspected of aberrance at Delta Standards Control. He was paler and thinner. He moved slowly across the room and sat in the chair opposite me with exaggerated care. His odd blue eyes, his sole distinctive feature, had faded to a bluish gray and for once no longer seemed out of place in his now angular face. The bruise from where DeLyon had struck him had bloomed like an ugly purple flower along his left temple and cheek. He looked as if the life had been drained out of him, like a man who had been emptied of feeling and most thought.

The light was right that day, I swear it was, ethereal and spiritual as I could ask, yet for the first time its magic seemed to have no emotional impact. Although Thorne readily admitted guilt to all that he was accused of, his confession entailed no sense of atonement or regret for the crimes he had committed against humanity and the City State. He exhibited a uniform indifference throughout the interrogation. He would sometimes look at me, but just as often his eyes wandered about the bare walls of the room. I felt that if I had lowered the plastic shielding, put a gun to the man's head and threatened to pull the trigger, he would not have blinked.

"Do you know why you are here?"

There was a substantial pause, and for a moment I didn't think he was going to answer me.

"You brought me here," he finally said. His voice was low and weak, without inflection.

"Did you kill Willem Coopersmith?"

The pause again, not as if he were framing an answer, but as if it took a moment for the question to percolate through his abstracted consciousness.

"You know I did. Why ask me?"

"Why did you kill Willem Coopersmith?"

There was no pause this time. "He needed killing."

And so it went. Speaking mostly in monosyllables, Thorne admitted to possession of the gun, the visits to an illegal prostitute, the consumption of illegal drugs and the possession of illegal books. I began to feel that he would confess to anything I accused him of, whether or not he was guilty, and exhibit no repentance whatsoever. There were moments when I thought I detected a flash of sarcasm in his faded eyes and attenuated expression? Was the man baiting me? Perhaps aping the terse style of speech I had adopted for my role at Delta Standards Control? There was no way I could be sure.

Of course the goal of this initial interrogation, like most, was not so much to elicit information—the cyberscan would perform that function—but to establish our authority over the subject and determine what kind of an aberrant we were dealing with, one who saw the error in his ways and would cooperate in our attempts to cure him, or one who continued to embrace his deviations and would attempt to resist. From Thorne's demeanor I was not sure he would do either. I was not convinced that he fully realized that the course of his life was now dependent on our decisions, on my decisions. Or if he did, it made no difference to him.

I admit I found the experience unnerving, most of all because the light had failed me in a way it never had before. It had lost its emotive content. Still, it was necessary to move on. I scheduled Thorne's scan for the following morning.

Unlike DeLyon, Thorne did not resist our attempts to scan him. Unlike Diana, he showed no willingness to cooperate. Unlike his departed paramour Josie, he was not sullen nor did he appear paranoid. As with his interrogation, both before he entered the scanning chamber and when he emerged more than three hours later, he appeared to exhibit no emotions whatsoever. He looked like a man who had lost everything except his life and no longer cared if even that remained.

It was only several days later, when I saw Thorne again, that I realize the scan and whatever it had revealed had affected him, that his chameleon personality was not through with its changes yet.

That afternoon, anticipating a swift resolution to the case despite the disturbing interview, I sat down in my office to examine the results of Thorne's scan.

When I first projected it into the holo cube and saw the strange configuration of his stalk and flower, or what I could only characterize as a lack of configuration, I suspected the equipment had malfunctioned. I contacted the techs, who assured me the system was working perfectly and there were no irregularities. The scans performed on other prisoners both before and after Thorne produced standard aberrant configurations. And indeed, when I slipped on the headset and initiated a cursory check of Thorne's memories and perceptions, I found that I could access them without difficulty.

Because Richard Thorne had committed the severest crime of all, the murder of another human being, along with a host of lesser offenses, his reconditioning would be the most severe and intense of all. I had looked forward to the challenge of creating a new persona for him that would embody none of the deviance and flaws that had nurtured his aberrance...but where should I begin? There were no bright nodes to fasten upon. There was no stalk, no widely disparate flower to reconfigure. There was no apparent cause and effect, only what appeared as well of blind chaos, filled with a random explosion of colored lines and dots.

It had been years since I had been forced to examine a scan in any great depth. Global searches would invariably provide whatever specific information I needed. Aberrants come in a limited number of types, all of which I had encountered and treated in more than a quarter century as a Guardener. I could recondition them without a detailed examination of their entire lives by concentrating on the significant nodes, working from experience, and by trial and error adjustments to their configurations. As I had accomplished admirably with Diana Logan.

Abandoning the useless projection, I began to sift through the particulars of Thorne's life in more depth, in search of the links that the cyberscan had failed to delineate. During my training and in my early days as a Guardener the scan had not reached the level of sophistication it has today. We could not rely on it alone and had to complement its results with hands-on methods of analysis. I reawakened those near forgotten skills and tackled the task before me.

I also ordered a second scan to be performed the following Friday morning. This would give me time to assess the results and calibrate the scan differently than the standard parameters. As soon as a flower figure emerged, the specifics of his reconditioning would become apparent.

There was nothing extraordinary about Thorne's genetic makeup or early life. He was an only child. His father had been an accountant for a City State manufacturing concern, his mother a secondary school teacher. Both had moderately successful careers, rising to G-16 and G-15 respectively, and no record of aberrance. Like most children, Thorne had been raised in a State crèche, returning home on holidays and occasional weekends. His parents had dissolved their union by mutual agreement when he was sixteen. He'd held no significant emotional attachment for either, nor they apparently for him. A few years into adulthood he had lost touch with both his parents.

I began making selections at random through Thorne's later youth and early adulthood. He appeared to be such a normal man, minor personality flaws and all, I could find no evidence of the severe aberrance that was to follow. I continued to search through his later years and his relationship with Diana. My absorption was so complete that it was not until my chosenmate called to remind me of a dinner engagement that I reluctantly removed my headset and shut down the system for the day.

Over the next few days I had other duties and cases, but I spent my spare moments exploring further fragments of Thorne's life, pursuing the elements that would unlock the origins of his aberrance.

By Thursday afternoon I decided the second scan would be calibrated with special reference to his interest in and fanciful misconceptions of history, his relationship with Josie Jimson, and the illegal books to which she had exposed him. These appeared to be such logical choices, I was puzzled why the first scan had failed to single them out.

On Thursday afternoon I also called the Properties Department and put in a requisition, ordering the books that had been confiscated at Josie's sent to my conapt in Lambda Heights. My motives were twofold, one of them admittedly a bit selfish. I thought that further study of these texts might illuminate the case, but also hoped to add them to my personal library, which has grown to well over a thousand volumes through the years due to similar confiscations. Once I successfully resolved the case, it would be highly unlikely I would ever be asked to return them.

When Thorne entered the scanning room on Friday morning, I realized I should have first conducted another interview with him. The moment I saw the man it was clear the previous scan had affected him more markedly than I had expected. It had taken a few days for its impact to register on his distracted awareness. Now he was no longer impassive. Whatever insights he had gained had wrought significant changes in him once again. Though they were far from the ones I would have predicted.

If Richard Thorne was nothing else, he was a wild card. Now he carried himself differently—no longer with the exaggerated invalid-like care he had exhibited a few days before—and his seeming indifference to all around him had vanished. His formerly emotionless eyes had come to life again in a peculiar and frightening way.

He was still as pale and thin. The bruise on his temple remained, though it was smaller and had faded to a mottled brownish-yellow. And the gray had vanished from his eyes. They were completely blue again, even a dark blue, and the look he gave me and everyone in the room I can only describe as one of defiance and contempt.

If anything, the first scan should have made Thorne more aware of his self-delusions and failings. He should have been contrite, perhaps anxious, even frightened. He should have been less sure of himself and more willing to cooperate with us. Instead, he seemed imbued with a confidence that had no merit in reality. From the eyes and the expression on his face, one might conclude that he viewed all of us as both misguided and inferior. I recalled seeing such a look of superior contempt once before in the eyes of an aberrant under treatment, yet at that time I couldn't place who it was or when.

What new kind of madness was this that had fastened itself upon him? I wondered if I was I now confronting Richard or Rick—for I had already become aware of this artificial distinction of identities in my examination of his first scan—or some hybrid personality fused from the two? Was I engaged in the pursuit of a shifting maze of identities that would never settle into one mold long enough to cure? I can tell you I didn't like the look of this latest incarnation of Thorne at all. His case had already become too confusing and troublesome. Whatever career advantage I had hoped to gain from it seemed to be quickly evaporating.

Much to my relief, the second scan went smoothly enough, except that Thorne was no longer silent as he had been before. This session was punctuated with incoherent cries that echoed through the scanning chamber and penetrated to the room beyond.

Back in my office I projected the new results into the holo cube...only to discover that although they were different than those of the first scan, they were just as nonsensical. The chaos of Thorne's projection remained in full force. There was no visible stalk, no flower, only a chaotic explosion of colored lines and dots. The nodes were there all right, the ones I had created with my calibration, yet they remained useless, for none linked significantly to any other or to the death of Coopersmith. It made no sense at all, and once again I found myself without means or method to launch a successful reconditioning.

There was nothing to do except conduct a more thorough examination of the details of Thorne's descent into aberrance, to fashion a still more accurate calibration that would cause his configuration to emerge as it should have in the first place, as it did in the cases of other aberrants.

Frustrated yet determined, with the headset clamped over my eyes and ears, I devoted my consciousness and intellect to the task. Rather than skipping here and there through

Thorne's life, I began to explore entire segments of his existence. I relived the early days of his mating with Diana and learned of his disillusionment as he discovered she was not the woman he thought. I sampled his flights of historical fancy and the scenarios through which he attempted to live them at the Halls of Expression. I walked by his side in his early explorations of the slum environment and suffered the frustrations he felt.

It was a tedious and time-consuming process, not to mention exhausting. When I finally emerged from its depths, tired and hungry, the sun was setting beyond the high towers of the City, etching them in dark relief upon the fading sky. I stood by my window and watched the last rays dissolve against the night. And still I was no closer to a solution.

That weekend I had the conapt to myself. My chosenmate was off on another of her virtual vacations, as often was the case these days. She couldn't get enough of this new fad, and I had no complaints on that count. I have always enjoyed and valued my solitude. Yet rather than pursuing one of my many interests, or whiling the time away watching some pleasing nonsense on the holo, I found myself brooding over the case. I suddenly realized that far more than a commendation and promotion, I craved a solution to the stubborn enigma of Richard Thorne. I would not let the man defeat me.

I activated my home terminal and accessed the files at Delta Conditioning. I called up not only Thorne's scan but those of Josie, DeLyon, and Diana Logan, to compare and contrast their perceptions with his.

That fateful and revelatory weekend, hunched in front my console, oblivious to the world around me, I became immersed in the projections that flowed across the screen of my mind. My absorption was so complete I felt that for minutes—no, hours at a time—I *became* Richard Thorne, and for briefer periods, Diana Logan, Josie Jimson and Daniel De-Lyon. I could not lead their entire lives, but I could experience entire scenes from them in complete and often frightening detail.

While my chosenmate lounged on an imaginary beach or enjoyed an imaginary feast or sailed an ocean that existed only as an electronic simulation, I inhabited a far less savory environment. I wandered the decaying streets of the slum remnant in search of an imagined adventure. I drank stale beer, watched a game of dice, encountered Daniel DeLyon and welcomed his friendship. I climbed a rickety fire escape and entered a room from out of the past. Despite my personal distaste for Josie, I suffered love's illusion in Thorne's physical and emotional infatuation with her. I experienced the instantaneous birth and rapid maturation of Rick as a distinct individual. Could calling someone a different name change them into a person they had never been, a person there was no indication they would ever become? I consumed illegal drugs and read illegal books and my thoughts and emotions were distorted by both. I perceived Willem Coopersmith through the eyes of Diana Logan. I hungered for a promotion and I learned to hate and fear Coopersmith for the beast he was. I was appalled at what I endured at his hands and reached the point where I could endure it no longer. I stood in a rain-drenched alley and wrenched an archaic firearm from a would-be mugger. I discovered that Josie, although she never admitted it, even to herself, was infatuated with Thorne from the start, in love with Thorne as he was with her. She had stopped seeing her other clients long before he asked her. I experienced Daniel DeLyon's unquestioning devotion to his mother and sister, and contrasted those feelings to my own tenuous familial ties with startling dissatisfaction. I rode the glideway into the luxurious environs of Lambda

Heights, as I did myself each evening on my way home from work, and this time I felt the night come alive around me in a way it never had before. I confronted Coopersmith and vented my rage, wrestled the man to the floor and watched him die. I planned and plotted how I would leave Diana and begin a new life beside my slum lover. I vicariously relived the confusion and trauma of Thorne's virtual vacation. Devastated in kind by the devastation of the slum and the disappearance of Josie, I walked the streets for hours, disoriented and desolate. And as I tracked back and forth across this jumbled landscape of cause and effect, of intertwining calculations and interactions, of aberrance and intoxication, unfamiliar emotions welled up inside me.

I would emerge from these excursions like some subterranean diver coming up for air, momentarily unable to recognize the walls of my study. And when I did, I would be struck by a sudden claustrophobia, as if those walls were closing in upon me, as if the perverse vistas I had viewed were somehow less confining than those of my own life. I would feel lightheaded for a moment and would have to take a pill before submerging myself again.

I confess that I became obsessed with solving this case, of wrenching order from its chaos, just as Thorne was obsessed with Josie, as DeLyon was obsessed with his games and gambling, and Coopersmith with his passion for freckles. As Richard Thorne was incarcerated in his prison cell I became incarcerated in the life he had led. And somewhere during this protracted descent into a world of aberrants, more thorough than any I had ever known before, my objectivity crumbled and my corruption began.

For a reason I could not fathom, since we were nothing alike except for our common passion for history, I began to feel an unwelcome identity with Thorne. I began to sympathize with him—no, empathize—with not only Thorne's plight but the plights of those around him. Beyond being cases to be processed and resolved, they emerged as individuals with peculiarities and traits, needs and desires. Much to my chagrin and confusion, I saw them as human beings as well as aberrant types.

Those scans are no longer available to me in my forced retirement and seclusion. Yet from my memories of those intense hours, flawed as memory may be, I have forged and extrapolated the report, discourse, explanation, you now have before you. If you are even there. If you can hear me. If you are bothering to listen. If you have not already condemned my voice to oblivion.

By Sunday evening I was convinced that I was onto something. The calibration I planned for the next scan would be the most complex and comprehensive of my career, employing all of my knowledge and skill, embodying all the significant elements and interactions I had perceived. I would be doing most of the work of the cyberscan for it. All it would have to do was connect the dots.

I hardly slept at all on Saturday night, and on Sunday night my sleep was fitful. Just as the personas of Thorne, Josie, DeLyon and Diana had consumed my waking hours, they now began to haunt my dreams, dreams which soon took on the flavor of nightmares even more bizarre and disconnected than the realities that had inspired them. In one particularly frightening segment I became Willem Coopersmith, inflicting my own sexual fantasies on both Diana and Josie. In another, the rungs of the fire escape I was climbing fell away beneath my feet and I found myself plummeting endlessly through a dark tunnel. Then I was floating over the City as if I were weightless. While beneath me, all of Delta Sector was in flames and all about me the sky speckled with flying particles of ash.

When I awakened to hear my chosenmate arriving home, the clock on the beside table told me it was after three. I closed my eyes and lay motionless, feigning sleep. Without speaking to me, she retired to her own bed.

On Monday morning I called in sick. I needed a day to recuperate and assimilate all that I had learned. I also put in the order for the third and what I was convinced would be the conclusive scan of Richard Thorne, which would take place on Wednesday. I would spend Tuesday at the office, reviewing and refining my calculations. For now, I would put my other cases on hold.

Late Monday morning Josie's books were delivered to the conapt. There were several crates, over three hundred volumes in all salvaged from her collection, most of them novels, most illegal or unclassified. I would need more shelves to hold them all. Many of these books I had never read or even heard of before, and there were dozens more where I had read only expurgated versions that had been censored before being transcribed to the system annals.

I began to pore over these texts for some additional clues, any clue, to help resolve the puzzle of Richard Thorne. And to my dismay, to this very day, I still return to them constantly in search of some understanding that has escaped me.

There is something I have not told you. Alas, there is much I have not told you, so much that I will never be able to tell you no matter how long I ramble on....

Did I ever tell you I once wanted to become an actor? Oh, yes, I had definite aspirations in my youth for a theatrical career in holodramas. I performed in a number of plays in secondary school and even rewrote some of my dialogue. I have a natural talent for mimicry, for assuming fictitious roles. It has served me well in my professional career as a

Guardener. I can be the terse and slack-jawed Sol Thatcher of Delta Standards Control, the garrulous and affable Thatcher who can elicit information from Citizens and slum dwellers alike without them realizing how much they are revealing until it is too late. I can be the brooding and fiery radical, thoroughly schooled in anti-State cant, who once infiltrated and exposed a terrorist cell leading to the arrest and reconditioning of more than a dozen aberrants. And of course, I can be the commanding and self-assured Sol Thatcher of my daily life and work.

I have always thought my flair for dramatic interpretation was closely related to another of my extraordinary talents, the ability of being able to read people merely by their facial expressions and body language, to spot potential aberrants before their aberration becomes manifest. I can recall one memorable occasion when....

No, that's not right. That's not what I meant to tell you, not what I need to tell you, what I should perhaps not be telling you at all. Still this one thing must be told to complete our tale and explain the actions that have led to my disgrace and forced retirement.

Richard Thorne's case, with its incomprehensible flower configuration, its missing chain of cause and effect, is a rare occurrence...very rare...*but it is far from unique*. Men such as Thorne are known as incurables and they are dealt with accordingly. Let me explain....

Having read long into the evening, I arrived at the office late on Tuesday to find a summons to appear in Director Wilkerson's office. I suspected I knew what Wilkerson wanted to see me about. I'd been running a little behind my quota of cures for the last two quarters. There had been too much field work, and several cases had proven more difficult to resolve than they first appeared. It was nothing I couldn't correct. And the successful resolution of Thorne's case, a capital murder case, would outweigh any shortages elsewhere.

Wilkerson had been in charge of Delta Conditioning for nearly a decade. Although he had been only a few years my senior in Guardener Training, due to several notable cases that had fallen his way, his career had advanced more rapidly than mine. Though I admit I felt a degree of understandable envy for the man, I also admired his talents, his sharp insight into aberrants and his proven ability to cure them. Yet I had always sensed something cold and removed about Wilkerson. Perhaps it was merely due to his physical appearance, which was tall and cadaverous, a look accentuated by a sharply receding hairline. Although the man had given me any number of commendations and signed my last three promotions, I could never be sure whether he liked me or not. I never felt as if I could make a personal connection with him.

Wilkerson kept me waiting in his outer office for at least fifteen minutes before seeing me. It was part of the game of authority, of demonstrating one's power over underlings. I did the same thing to lower-ranking Guardeners when they were waiting to see me. Normally I would have passed the time admiring Wilkerson's latest personal assistant. None of them seemed to last more than a few months and they were always young and quite attractive. I was too absorbed with finalizing my calibrations for the forthcoming scan to give her much notice. I kept running the causal factors through my head, wondering how much relative weight I should attach to each element.

When I finally entered Wilkerson's office, he briefly looked up from his monitor. "Oh, yes, Thatcher. This should only take a minute. I'll right be with you. Take a seat."

Apparently the waiting game was to go on a little longer.

Once I was seated I glanced around the room. I was always a bit taken aback by its size and austerity. My office is considered spacious by most standards, but Wilkerson's could have easily accommodated four of mine with room to spare. And of course the view of the City from his picture window was breathtaking. Yet there were no holographs on the walls, and most of the room remained empty. Other than his desk, which occupied the center of the floor, and a small cabinet behind it, nothing except a single couch, and a few tables and lamps, had been shoved at random against one wall. And near the opposite wall there was a covered billiard table left over from the last Director. I had never seen it uncovered since Wilkerson took office, and I doubt he ever played the game. As well as his acumen in dealing with aberrants, the Director was known for his economy. He had consistently brought the department in under budget year after year. He'd probably concluded it was less expensive to leave the table where it was than have it removed.

After several minutes, Wilkerson swiveled his monitor to the side and ran one palm across his nearly empty scalp. It had been some time since I had seen him up close, and he was now almost as bald as I was.

"Yes," he began, "let's get right to the point. This concerns the Thorne case. You've already scanned the man twice with the same useless results. Why in Severin's name have you requested a third scan? Can't you see that you are dealing with an incurable?"

"Well, sir, I'm not sure about that. I've been working on a different calibration than I used in the second scan. A very sophisticated one. I believe it will allow me to define Thorne's configuration properly."

"Nonsense!" Wilkerson retorted. "We know from experience that a third scan is generally a waste of time and manpower. This Thorne is only a G-12. And he is responsible for the death a Senior Director, a man who helped design this very building! He doesn't deserve a third scan. You need to resolve this case and move on. There are plenty of aberrants that can be cured swiftly and effectively without wasting more time on this one."

"But Thorne is a Citizen. What if he demands a reconditioning?"

"Citizen's rights only extend so far, and they do not apply to incurables. I'm sure you know the established protocol in matters such as this. I shouldn't have to spell it out for you of all people. I believe you assisted quite admirably in a similar case in your youth."

"What?"

"On come now, Thatcher, don't tell me you've forgotten about Stuart Jimson."

I glanced down at the polished wood surface of Wilkerson's desk, and then it all came flooding back to me, the event my conscious mind had buried so deeply and thoroughly and locked away in one corner of my past, an event I had repressed so completely and for so many years that I never thought about it anymore, almost as if I had reconditioned myself not to remember.

It happened nearly twenty years ago. I was a G-14 at the time, only a few outstanding cases to my credit, though I had already established myself as one of the brighter young stars of the department. An older Guardener by the name of Brach had taken me under his wing. I was his protégé. I greatly looked up to him in the way only youth can admire a mentor they seek to emulate.

My shift was nearly over when I was called to Brach's office. A slender athletic man in his fifties, always impeccably dressed, Brach seemed uncomfortable that day, not his usual self. For the first time I could recall, a note of hesitation had crept into his voice.

"There is a special task...extremely important...that needs to be accomplished without delay...and I have chosen you to help me carry it out. Tell me, Thatcher, do you know what incurables are?"

Of course I had heard rumors. I was never sure how much stock to put in them. There were always rumors of one kind of another circulating in the department.

"I think so, sir."

"Well, incurables are exactly what their name implies. They are individuals who...cannot be cured of their aberrance...who will remain a threat to others and the welfare of the City State no matter what we do with them."

"Yes, sir, that's what I've heard."

"And do you know...how we must deal with incurables?"

Again, there had been rumors. But they were impossible to substantiate and hard to believe, particularly for someone who had been indoctrinated with the conventional wisdom of the City State, values I had sworn to uphold as part of my oath of duty as a Guardener. The defining maxim of our service was to balance the welfare of all individuals with the welfare of the State, determining the best for both.

"I'm not sure, sir."

"Well...," Brach cleared his throat. "they must be eliminated. It's unfortunate but necessary...for the greater good of all. Come with me, Thatcher."

Brach did not speak again until we were descending in the lift. His arms were crossed on his chest and we were standing side by side. He was watching the numbers change on the panel over the door and did not look in my direction.

"I want you to understand, Thatcher, that you are merely an instrument of the State in this action. You are operating under my authority...and I am assuming full responsibility."

I was uncertain what to say. Was this some kind of test Brach was putting me through? Or was he seriously suggesting that we were going to take a human life in the name of the City State? Were all of the rumors about incurables and how they were dealt with true? It ran contrary to everything I had learned and believed. I recalled what Brach had once told me while demonstrating a novel choke hold on a prisoner. "They don't teach you everything you need to know in Guardener Training School!"

The lift descended beyond the first floor and the lobby to the basement level. I had never been in the basement of the building before. There had been no reason. As far as I knew it was for storage.

When the doors of the lift slid open we stepped forth into darkness. Brach flipped a switch to the side of the doors and the large room before us filled with a dim illumination. We had entered an extended warehouse area. The green walls were dirty and badly in need of paint, the floor bare cement. The ceiling was higher than I expected, and overhead you could see exposed heating ducts and water pipes. The room was filled with abandoned furniture and equipment. Rows of chairs stacked haphazardly atop one another. Desks piled three tiers high. Banks of discarded computer terminals and other objects I could not identify, draped in dusty plastic tarps. All of it scattered across the floor and shrouded in dimness, with only a few overhead lights burning. And more than a few burnt out. Brach led the way as we threaded our path through this diverse maze of darkness and abridged light, our tenuous shadows rippling, appearing and disappearing with our movement.

When we reached a closed steel door on the farther side of the room, Brach produced a key from the pocket of his robe and inserted it into the lock. This door was from another era. All the locks I'd ever seen in the building were electronic. Before he turned the key, Brach spoke. "Let's get this over with as quickly as possible. Steady, man, no hesitation." He was facing the door and I was several steps behind him. I couldn't be sure if he was talking to me or himself. Or both of us.

The door swung inward and I was assaulted by an unpleasant draft of air, dank and brackish, as if something organic was decaying in the space beyond. Brach held the door and motioned for me to enter. When he released it, it swung shut of its own accord with a heavy metallic clanking that reverberated off the floor and walls.

Brach turned to the right and we advanced down a corridor. The ceiling was lower here though the lighting was no better. We passed several closed doors and then a scanning room. I could see the scanning chamber through the observation window. There were no techs present and the device was open and empty.

At the end of the corridor we turned left and the odor grew more pronounced. We had entered an old cellblock, constructed before the days when video and audio surveillance were provided for all cells. These were simple chambers, ten by ten, with one wall open except for the vertical bars that contained each prisoner yet did not conceal him from view. We passed two such cells, both unoccupied, one with its door ajar. Brach stopped in front of the third cell and again motioned me forward.

Inside there was a small dark man sitting on a cot, staring at the floor. His elbows were on his knees, his head resting in his hands. He looked up at us briefly, and then resumed his surveillance of the floor beneath his feet. Even in the dim light I recognized him at once. He had been on our Most Wanted List for weeks.

It was the fall of '37. The riots were winding down, but there were still some isolated pockets of resistance. A number of Guardeners had been killed and dozens more injured as a result of the violence Stuart Jimson had initiated. The number of slum dwellers who had died was far greater. Although he had disappeared shortly after the first riots erupted, Jimson had been charged as an accomplice in the deaths. I assumed he was still at large and had no idea we had already taken him into custody.

Stuart Jimson was also a man I had been taught to hate, and I had learned my lessons well. All righteous Citizens who supported the City State and the Future Perfect despised the man and all he stood for, whether they knew what he looked like or not. He was a throwback to the imperfect past, a symbol of the divisiveness and the destructive chaos of history we all sought to abandon.

You must understand. I was young and impressionable at the time. My career as a Guardener was the most important thing in the world to me. I was eager to impress the powers-that-be. If it had not been Stuart Jimson in that cell, if my idol Brach had not been giving the orders, I'm not sure I would have been able to proceed with what followed.

Brach undid the sash of his robe, unsnapped his holster, and drew his weapon. He nodded at me to do the same and I followed suit. He took a step forward, edging the barrel of his gun between the prison bars and taking aim at Jimson. Again I followed his lead, thumbing off the safety.

"Steady, man," Brach repeated. "On the count of three."

Jimson looked up again, directly at Brach, and at that moment he must have realized what was about to happen to him. I expected him to panic, to charge the bars or retreat to the far wall of the small cell. Instead he just sat there staring.

"One."

I admit I was afraid, as close to panic as I had ever been in my life. I thought about what Brach had told me about incurables, how their deaths were unfortunate but necessary for the greater good of all. I concentrated on how much I hated Jimson, on all the deaths and suffering his rabblerousing had caused.

"Two."

Jimson turned his head to look at me.

Rather than ignoring him as I should have, I made the mistake of meeting his gaze. Instead of the fear I expected to find in his eyes, there was only defiance and contempt, utter contempt...for me, for Brach, for the City State and all of the world we represented. At the last instant before I fired, my hand wavered.

"Three."

If you have ever seen a Guardener discharge his sidearm, you know that there is not much to see or hear. Unlike the firearms of old, like the one Richard Thorne had taken from the thief in the alley, they do not function by means of a hammer striking an explosive charge that propels the bullet from the chamber, but from the release of compressed gas. There is no flash of light, no loud noise, just a sudden whoosh of air and almost simultaneously, if you are close enough to the target, the sound of the projectile striking. I had fired my weapon many times in training, yet practice targets were all I had ever known. I had never aimed my gun at another human being, let alone tried to kill one.

My hand had wavered at the last instant, but my shot proved true enough. I had aimed for Jimson's head and instead the bullet struck him full in the face. I could hear the sickening thud as it pierced his flesh, shattering cartilage and bone. He collapsed onto the floor of the cell, but he did not die easily. His body thrashed back and forth in convulsions. He cried out several times, clearly in severe pain, spattering blood across the floor and even onto the cot and walls.

With that sickening thud still echoing in my mind, I suddenly realized that only one bullet had struck Jimson. Only one shot had been fired. I turned to Brach.

He was holding his gun in his open palm and looking at it in disbelief. "Imagine that," he said, shaking his head. "I forgot to release the safety."

He looked down at Jimson, who by now had stopped moving. His final convulsion had left him lying on his side, his knees drawn up and his body curled into itself. He was mostly turned away from us, so that we could thankfully only see a part of his ruined face. Yet it was far too easy to imagine the rest.

"You should have aimed higher," Brach told me, "for the forehead. Faster and less messy. But well done nonetheless, Thatcher. Well done! You should consider yourself a hero of the City State."

I felt as if I were going to be sick. I bent over, hands on my knees, one still holding my weapon. I gagged several times and retched onto the bare cement floor.

"Steady, man," Brach said for the third time that day.

He came up behind me and placed one hand on my shoulder and another on my back. I straightened, taking a step away from him and shaking off his touch.

"Our work is done here," Brach said. "Someone else will handle the...uh...disposal. It's already been arranged."

I received a promotion the very next week, one that I had not been expecting until the following year. Yet from that day on I was no longer Brach's protégé. He seemed to actively avoid me, and when we passed in the halls I might as well have been invisible. He would look the other way or right through me as if I was not there. A few months later, Brach suddenly and inexplicably transferred to Sigma Conditioning Center. I have never seen or heard from him since.

"Thatcher, are you all right?"

Only seconds? Several moments? Half a lifetime? I didn't know for how long I had been staring at Director Wilkerson's desk without speaking while this repressed episode from my past had surfaced and torn through my mind. I glanced up at the Director's cadaverous face and domed forehead and then looked away.

"Yes," I told him, "I'm fine."

Though I was not feeling fine. My hands were trembling and I lowered them against my thighs to keep them still.

"I was thinking," I suggested, "that perhaps we could send Thorne to an agricultural or manufacturing commune."

Wilkerson dismissed the notion with a wave of his hand. "You know better than that. Or at least you should. Incurables are incurables. No matter where we put him—unless we lock him up in solitary confinement for the rest of his life!—he will prove to be nothing but trouble for us. I have already countermanded your order for a third scan. You know what needs to be done and I expect you to get on with it. This man deserves what's coming to him. If you no longer have the stomach for the act...well...find some young Guardener to assist you. It will do him good. Teach him what's what in the real world rather than that nonsense they fill them up with in training."

"Yes, sir, I'll take care of it." There was nothing else I could say.

"You know the routine. Take the man down to the old cellblock in the basement. We don't need to broadcast this to the entire department. Let me know when the task is completed," Wilkerson added, "and I'll arrange for the removal of the body and the deletion of the man's records. That will be all, Thatcher."

Wilkerson swiveled his monitor back into position and resumed looking at the screen. It was as if I had already left his office. I began to rise, but my legs felt weak. With my palms on the arms of the chair, I hoisted myself upright.

"Oh," Wilkerson said, without looking up, "one more thing. I almost forgot. I received a complaint from some Doctor named Fox. Claims you overdid it with one of the other aberrants in this case. Caused some brain damage. For Severin's sake, Thatcher, do try to be more careful! We don't need the Doctors up in arms again."

"I will, sir, I will."

I don't recall walking to the door or passing through the outer office. I must have done so for I found myself in the hallway leaning against the wall. Digging in the pocket of my robe, I fumbled out my pill bottle. It was almost empty and I would need a refill soon. I was still unsteady and as I opened the bottle it leaped from my grasp, spilling the handful of pills that remained onto the carpet. I tried to bend down to retrieve them. It was no good. Vertigo seized me and I almost fell before I leaned back and steadied myself against the wall.

As I stood there attempting to slow my breathing and regain a semblance of control, with the world about me spinning, the walls of the corridor buckling up and down, a young Guardener passing down the hall came to my aid.

"Are you all right, Citizen Thatcher? Can I help you?"

"Yes...please." I nodded toward the pills on the carpet.

He bent down and picked them up one by one, deposited them in the bottle and handed it to me. I took two in my palm and quickly swallowed them.

"Thank you...I'll be all right now.

"Are you sure?"

"Yes," I said, "just give me a moment."

I didn't know the man by name, but his face was familiar. I had seen him in the department before. Should he be the one I would pick to help me with Thorne? I decided then and there that he was as good as any other.

Most Guardeners never encounter a single incurable in their entire careers. I now had the grave misfortune of having encountered two.

Back in my office I took a cursory look through my other cases but found it impossible to concentrate. The repressed incident with Jimson, now that it had been reawakened, kept playing and replaying through my mind. I could recall the rank odor of those basement cells. I could hear the thud of the bullet as it destroyed Jimson's face, hear him scream in pain, see the spray of blood that dappled the cell as his dying body twisted this way and that. I remembered with painful clarity that look of defiance and contempt that had filled his eyes in the moment before his death, the same look I had seen in Richard Thorne's eyes only a few days before.

I riled at the trick Brach had played on me, if it had been a trick. Had Brach failed to release the safety on his weapon because he didn't have the courage to pull the trigger? Or had it been a legitimate mistake? Perhaps he was just as panicked as I was? I would never know for sure. Regardless of the truth, Brach had placed the weight of Jimson's death solely upon me.

The unwelcome identity I felt with Richard Thorne was now no longer a mystery. Though the circumstances were different, though I acted in the name of the City State and was only an instrument, though I had been absolved before the fact and later promoted, I had taken a human life just as Thorne had. We were both murderers.

I left work early that day, telling myself I would resolve the matter with Thorne first thing in the morning. I didn't head straight home. Rather than catching the tunnel train to Lambda Heights, I went directly to the Halls of Expression in Delta Sector.

Several months had passed since I had last visited the Halls. Of course they still had my preferences on file, and the setup I requested most often was available. I was not the only patron of the Halls who wanted their session to begin in the simulation of an interrogation room.

The Courtesan was one I had been with several times before. She knew how to act and exactly what I wanted. She could feign a confession for any crime I accused her of and even creatively begin manufacturing others. She could appear frightened and properly contrite when I instructed her on the proper duties of a Citizen and threatened her with deportation to a work farm. Yet when we retired to the bedchamber, I could not complete the act. At least not in the normal fashion. Afterward I felt some relief of the tension in my body, but my mind remained in turmoil.

When I finally arrived home I thought about talking to my chosenmate, telling her everything, but that was not something we did anymore. We hadn't talked seriously for years. Our mating had evolved to a routine that worked for both of us, a trivial routine, its terrain and boundaries well set. She took no real interest in my work nor I in hers. And what could she tell me except to carry on as Wilkerson had instructed me to do?

I spent several hours pretending to watch the holo with her. I don't even remember what shows were on. Claiming exhaustion from a hard day, I retired to the bedroom early. I took a sleeping tablet, which after some tossing and turning, granted me the release of a few hours of thoughtless oblivion.

When I woke the conapt was dark and quiet. I could hear the soft snores of my chosenmate in her bed across the room. The clock on the nightstand read just after one.

As I lay there in the dark, slowly coming to my senses, the events of the day past and the memory of Jimson beginning to churn again in my mind, I understood and accepted what I had to do and how it could be accomplished. I would have to do it entirely by myself. And I was convinced that if I didn't act that very night, I would lose my nerve forever. I dressed hurriedly in the dark and left the conapt.

The tunnel trains come and go all night, but earlier that evening there had been a destruct incident at one of the stations. Some lunatic had run along the platform and shoved half a dozen people in front of an oncoming train before leaping to his own death. My train was rerouted through Beta Sector and it was well past two by the time I reached Delta Conditioning.

When I entered the building, the guard at the front desk looked at me strangely. I realized that I hadn't shaved or even combed my hair. What little hair I have left was still standing up in all directions from sleep. I brushed it down as best as I could with my hands.

On the way up in the lift I took the bottle from my robe pocket and downed the last three pills. I didn't need any dizzy spells right then.

"Bring me prisoner forty-seven," I told the guard manning the cellblock station.

I didn't know the man and he apparently didn't know me. He looked at me strangely. I was tired of guards looking at me strangely. What was I, some kind of freak? And what were they? Nothing but would-be Guardeners, the lot of them. Only a few would ever achieve that status, and far fewer would accomplish what I have.

"That's a bit irregular at this time of night," he said. "The prisoners are all asleep. Lockdown was hours ago."

"I am Sol Thatcher." I showed him my ID. Surely the man had heard of me even if he didn't know me by sight. "Are you refusing a direct order from me?"

"Well...no, sir...it's just that I'm the only one on duty and I'm not supposed to leave my post except in emergencies. If you'll just let me check first."

I leaned forward and read his name tag. "All right, Snowden, if you want to wake up one of your superiors from a sound sleep at 2:30 in the morning to confirm the orders of a G-21, be my guest."

He hesitated. And wisely so.

"I'll watch your post while you are gone. And I accept full responsibility."

"I'll have to reset all the alarms," he told me. "It's going to take a little while."

"Then I suggest you get started."

I paced up and down while I waited, trying to maintain my nerve and my purpose. I thought about Brach. If he were still alive he would be an old man by now, living in some Senior Retirement Center. I thought about Wilkerson and the cavalier way in which he treated me, insulted me. I wondered how many times Jimson had been scanned before he was deemed incurable. I wondered if he had ever been scanned at all. I again saw him dying on the floor of his prison cell. I saw Coopersmith thrashing back and forth, dying on the floor of the lift as I backed away from him. I shoved the gun into my slimsuit and dragged his body into the hallway.

No, that wasn't me! That was Thorne.

And then all at once my thoughts cleared and it all un-folded for me. I knew who I was and where I was and what I was about to do. I suddenly felt very calm, calmer and more clear-headed and sure of myself than I had been for months. Perhaps more than any time since. The pills had taken effect and I knew I would not fail, could not fail. I knew that any-thing was possible if I willed it so.

It was past three by the time the guard returned with Thorne in tow. His hands were cuffed behind his back and he looked as if he'd been roused from sleep, his hair standing up as mine had. I didn't look at him too closely. I didn't care whether the last scan had changed him again or not. I no longer cared whether he was Richard or Rick, whether he hated me or feared me, whether he could be cured of his ab-errance or not. It no longer made any difference.

I took him by one arm and forcibly propelled him down the hall to the lifts. He stumbled once and I pulled him up-right. Then he spoke to me for the first time since his inter-rogation.

"Where are you taking me?" he asked.

So he cared about his life again. It now made a differ-ence to him what was going to happen. I didn't answer. He would know soon enough.

When the doors of the lift opened on the basement level, I shoved Thorne into the darkness beyond and followed. I flipped a switch by the side of the lift and my eyes blinked several times in the sudden brightness.

This was the same warehouse Brach and I had once en-tered together, yet it was no longer the same. It had been completely renovated over the years. The walls were no longer dirty or in need of paint. The overhead pipes were no longer exposed. The ceiling was covered with acoustic tiles and lines of burning fluorescents that left no shadows any-where. Stretching into the distance, the discarded furniture and equipment were stacked neatly on pallets arranged in vertical and horizontal rows. Yet there was one element of decay they had not been able to renovate or remove, one that was beginning to spread. I was sure I could smell it, faint yet distinctive, dank and brackish. That foul odor of death from the old cellblock, from beyond the steel door, now permeated this room to taint the air around us. And sooner or later it would penetrate to the floors above.

I undid the sash of my robe, unsnapped the holster, drew my weapon and leveled it at Thorne.

"Turn around," I ordered.

He was fully awake now and those blue eyes that didn't belong in his countenance blazed their contempt at me. He didn't move. "If you are going to shoot me," he said, "you can do it to my face."

"That's what they want me to do," I told him. "They want me to kill you because you cannot be cured." When had the City State become a "they" for me rather than a "we?" When had I started to think like an aberrant?

"Cured? I'm not sick. You are the ones who are sick. Your entire world is sick and it will eventually die of its own disease." Now he was beginning to sound like Stuart Jimson.

"What if you could escape from this world?" I asked. "What if you could leave it all behind?"

"Leave?"

"Yes, leave the City forever."

"You mean go to the Dead Lands?"

"Yes," I agreed, "the Dead Lands. But how can you be sure? Are the Dead Lands really dead?"

That threw him as I knew it would. He shook his head in puzzlement and his eyes were no longer blazing at me. He had shocked me often enough with his behavior. Now it was my turn to shock him.

"You can't go wearing those cuffs. Now turn around."

I could see that he still didn't trust me, but he slowly turned away. I approached and swiped my card across the sensor lock. The plastic cuffs came free from his wrists and fell almost soundlessly to the floor. I quickly backed away, still holding the gun on him.

"Where is Josie?" he asked as he faced me again. "What have you done with her?"

"She's all right," I told him. "She's being relocated to an agricultural commune, a work farm."

"Where?"

"I have no idea. There are hundreds of them. You'll never find her."

Switching the gun from one hand to another, I struggled out of my robe and tossed it at his feet. "Put that on. No one is going to question you if you are wearing that. There are identification papers and credits inside." My identification papers, my credits.

He looked at me strangely—just as everyone has looked at me strangely ever since—but he picked up the robe and slipped it on. He was thinner than I was, but it fit him well enough. It fell to his ankles and would hide the prison grays if he were careful.

I could feel a muscle pulsing in my left arm and a burning sensation in my chest. Perhaps three pills at once had been too much for me. Perhaps the entire day, the entire situation, was too much. But I refused to give Thorne any sign of my discomfort.

"How do I leave?" he asked. "How do I get to the Dead Lands?"

"Look in the left pocket," I told him. "But not now."

I had scribbled down the directions for him while I was on the tunnel train. It was not nearly as hard to leave the City as most people thought, not if you were wearing a robe and had papers. The lift still stood open behind us. I nodded toward it.

"Give me the gun," he said.

The pain in my chest was spreading and there was a humming noise in my ears. It sounded as if every word either of us spoke was now echoing off the walls, winding its way magnified through the pallets of stacked furniture and equipment. I feared someone on the floors above would hear us and report a disturbance.

I shook my head, as much to clear it as to deny Thorne's request. "If I give you the gun you might have to use it. There's been enough of that already."

"But why," he asked, "why are you doing this? Why don't you just kill me like they want you to?"

I had to think about that for a second before responding.

"Because I'm not through with you yet," I said. It seemed to make perfect sense to me at the time, and in a way it still does.

Thorne looked puzzled once again, but he said nothing more. At that moment, I realized he had not defeated me after all. Not completely. On at least one count the score was even. For Thorne was now as confused about who I was as I had always been about him.

As he entered the lift, an ancient word I had learned from some ancient text slipped into my mind, a benison for one departing on a long and difficult journey.

"Godspeed," I told him as the doors slid shut and I saw him for the last time. I'm not sure whether he heard me or not.

So yes, I admit it. I am the guilty party and no other.

I set Richard Thorne, incurable aberrant and murderer, free. I conceived his escape and I made it possible. I assume full responsibility for the act that was committed and I accept its consequences.

But I ask you, what else was there for me to do except carry out the order of his execution and leave him lying on the floor in his own blood?

I still had Stuart Jimson's blood on my hands. That was surely enough for one lifetime.

Some workmen entering the warehouse found me unconscious in the morning. I was taken to the hospital ward and spent several days there recuperating. As almost seemed inevitable, Dr. Fox was my administering physician. His diagnosis was a mild heart attack brought on by hypertension and emotional exhaustion. He has prescribed a whole new regimen of pills for me to take at regular intervals, morning, noon, and night. The vertigo and lightheadedness are gone for now.

I discovered that Fox was not really such a bad sort after all once I got to know him. We played a few games of chess. We even talked as colleagues rather than adversaries. He's a bright young man and will no doubt go far. There might even be a Directorship in his future.

Of course there was a formal enquiry into Thorne's escape. It was quickly resolved for I told them everything they wanted to know. I fully confessed my guilt just as I have in these pages.

I suppose I could have planned it differently. I could have given Thorne the gun, had him strike me, claimed later that the handcuffs had not been properly secured and he had slipped them off. Yet it all seemed so pointless at the time and still does. For even if I'd only been reprimanded for negligence and received a demotion, I knew that I could no longer go on the way I had.

The life I am now consigned to is not a bad one.

I have my books and my solitude. There is always the holo to watch, more than a hundred different channels. They did not strip me of my G-21 rating and the retirement benefits that includes. Of all people, it was Director Wilkerson who stood up for me. He said, and I quote verbatim from the transcript: "Although his health and judgment have now failed him, this man has given his life to the service of the City State and he deserves to be rewarded in kind."

The supplies I need to survive are delivered to me once each week from a list I provide. I am even allowed an occasional visit from a Courtesan of the Halls. I can escape from everyday reality often enough while the reality of the City State goes on without me.

My life is not a bad one except for one thing. More than the loss of friends and family, more than the respect I once commanded and the authority I held, I regret the loss of my certainty, the faith that has sustained me through the years. For I no longer believe in the glorious ascension to the paradise of a Future Perfect. And even on the off chance it may someday be achieved, what could it mean to me? I no longer believe in the sanctity of the City State, for I have realized that like all states that have preceded us through history, we are rife with our own blind spots, our own hypocrisies and corruptions, our own societal madness. And in place of the faith I have abandoned, and that has abandoned me, all I have discovered is an obsession with a case and the lives of those involved that I may ponder forever without resolution.

Were the crimes committed intersecting ripples in a pool or did one ripple spreading outward initiate the rest? If Richard Thorne had mated with a different woman, would he still have visited the slum? If Josie had not fallen in love with Richard, would she still have tried to change him? If Diana Logan had been born without freckles, would her career as an architect have progressed as planned? Was Daniel DeLyon really brain damaged or only acting? Did Brach fail to fire his weapon on purpose? Does Willem Coopersmith now burn in some fiery pit of Hell for the crimes he was never punished for during his life? Will Stuart Jimson one day be revered as a martyr for the cause of freedom? Will I ever see or speak with my children again?

The world I inhabit is one of shifting illusions and transitory ideas, where cause and effect become endlessly entangled. Each moment holds its own conclusions and none of them is definitive. And most frightening of all, I sometimes suspect that we may all be both Guardeners and aberrants at heart, unpredictable, stray creatures of fine or foul circumstance.

Enough of introspection and doubt. My story is over. For I will surely die alone in the state of disgrace I now endure. There will be no reconditioning, no absolution and redemption, for me.

Yet if my story has ended, perhaps Richard Thorne's has another act or two to play. Perhaps his chameleon personality is still changing. To my knowledge he was never apprehended. He either escaped to the Dead Lands or he remains in hiding under a new identity in some slum remnant. In either case, he is beyond my reach. I will never know what he found.

And what of the subsequent lives of the supporting players in this drama and discourse? As to their futures I can only speculate. After all I have been through, you must allow me that.

Speculation

It was Sunday afternoon and Daniel Devins was at the fireball arena in Sigma Sector just as he was every other day of the week. Only today, rather than sitting in his ticket booth watching the game on a portable holo, he had a first-class seat in the clubhouse with the elite.

He was wearing a new dermask and slimsuit, and the Stalwarts, his favorite team, were playing the Valiants. It was the fourth quarter and the Stalwarts were leading by two points. Devins had made a substantial bet on the Stalwarts, and although the game was still close, he was having trouble concentrating on the field. He was having one of his bad days, when scattered memories from his past rose up to haunt him and he couldn't put them to rest.

Devins knew he couldn't think as well as he once had, but he was convinced he could still outsmart most people. For that was exactly what he'd done with the Guardeners who'd reconditioned him, not only pretending he was slower than he was but convincing them they had succeeded more thoroughly than they had. After his conditioning, they stripped him of his G-12 rating and his last name, transferred him to Sigma Sector, and released him into an unskilled labor pool as a G-5. They told him that he could return for future testing, and if his tests improved, he might someday be allowed to work with statistics again. Devins had no desire to work with statistics again, no plans to return to government service. He applied for a job at the fireball stadium and they hired him.

A sudden roar went up from the crowd around him and his eyes and thoughts went back to the playing field. Carmichal of the Stalwarts had broken free from the pack and was headed toward the Valiants' goal. The ball was barely glowing. He scored easily and the Stalwarts now led by three points with only minutes to go.

Devins wasn't surprised. He had been almost certain the Stalwarts would win. He not only worked at the fireball stadium, he practically lived there, and had gotten to know all the coaches and most of the players. They liked him and called him Danny. He had learned how to tell when a team was up for a win and when it was not. He kept track of which key players were suffering injuries. Best of all, he often got wind of it when a fix was on. Of course it was illegal to fix the games, but they did it anyway. It wasn't illegal that counted, but whether or not you could get away with it.

The first time he'd tried to place a bet, he'd been violently ill. Yet he kept going back again and again until whatever nonsense they had filled his mind with had been thoroughly dissipated and he had unconditioned their conditioning. Then, once he'd accumulated enough money, he found the right slum doctor and had the implant they had placed below the surface of his neck neutralized. It was supposed to release drugs into his system for the rest of his life that would make him a better Citizen. He didn't want to become a better Citizen. He thought most good Citizens were fools.

Just before the final buzzer sounded, the Stalwarts scored again. Devins had purchased a graduated ticket—the greater the point spread, the more money he won or lost—and today he had won more than he'd expected. Still he was not feeling his usual jubilation.

He remained seated as the stands about him gradually emptied, and he found himself thinking about his mother and sister. As always when such thoughts filled his head, they were accompanied by a sense of disquietude and emptiness. What bothered him was not only that some of his memories were missing, but that there should have been more sorrow than he felt, and it should have been deeper and sharper. Devins wanted his grief and they had taken it away from him. He wasn't sure how to uncondition that.

Sometimes he thought about Richard Thorne. He was sorry he'd ever met the man. Still there were times when he missed him. No one at the fireball stadium could play chess worth a damn. Not that he was all that good himself anymore, but he felt if only he could find someone decent to play with, it would all come back to him.

He waited until the clubhouse was nearly empty before limping downstairs to collect his winnings. The knee had never healed properly after the second break and it often bothered him when the weather was damp.

The man behind the betting window smiled and shook his head as he handed over the payoff. "Here you are again! I don't know how you do it, Danny. Sure wish I had your luck."

Devins smiled back and tapped the side of his head with one finger. "All it takes is a little smarts," he said, as he pocketed his winnings.

The woman had left several messages on her answering service, but Diana Winston saw no reason to return them. Of course she vaguely remembered the woman from her other life, but she wanted nothing to do with that anymore, didn't even want to think about it. It was over and done with and that was for the best. She couldn't even imagine how the woman had managed to track her down in Omicron Sector now that they'd given her a different last name. But the woman had kept calling and calling, leaving one message after another, and when Diana never responded, she had the presumption to turn up at her conapt.

It was already late in the evening when the door chime sounded. Diana had no idea who it might be. She had few visitors, and never anyone who would arrive unannounced at this hour. When she opened the door she found herself confronting a garish blonde woman dressed entirely in red. Diana stared at her blankly.

"It's me, Heather, don't you recognize me? Aren't you going to invite me in?"

"Well...I was just about to get ready for bed," Diana said. She didn't really want to let the woman in, but it was no longer in her nature to be impolite. Hopefully she would not stay long. Diana stepped back and opened the door wider.

"Ready for bed!" the woman exclaimed as she swept past her and waltzed into the apartment as if she owned it. "It's way too early for bed! The night is still young." Stopping in the center of the floor, she looked around. "Well, it's not much compared to what you had with Richard, but I guess it will do for now."

"Please don't mention that man to me ever again," Diana said, standing by the hallway to the door.

The woman gave her an odd look. Without being asked, she took a seat on the couch. "You know, I had one hell of a time finding you," she said, crossing her legs. Her red skirt rode more than halfway up her thighs. She wore blocky red heels that must have been at least three inches high. Diana recalled that she had once dressed in this absurd and ostentatious fashion and it made her blush to think about it.

"I've really missed you," the woman said. "I kept wondering what ever happened to good old Diana...and well...of course I knew about some of it...it was on the holo and all, about Coopersmith...who would have ever thought Richard had it in him? Oops! I'm sorry!" She raised her fingertips to her lips for a mere second before chattering on. "Well, anyway, I just had to see my best girlfriend again...and it wasn't that easy, but finally I managed to pull a few of the right strings...and here I am."

Diana didn't like the sound of that. About pulling the right strings.

"What are you doing way over there?" the woman said. "Come here and let me have a good look at you."

Diana took a few reluctant steps farther into the room. The woman looked her up and down in the light. Her face fell and her mouth dropped.

"I don't want to be mean, dear, but you look awful. They must have really washed you good."

"I don't want to talk about that," Diana said. "And I do have to go to bed soon," she added as firmly as she could. Despite what the woman thought, she knew she looked just fine. At least she wasn't decked out like some painted Courtesan from the Halls of Expression. Why wouldn't the woman just leave her alone? What could she possibly want?

"Calm down, dear, I'm sorry. It was just a bit of a shock. Come here and sit down next to me." She patted the couch by her side. "I'll show you what a little makeup can do, in case you've forgotten. And then we can do something about your hair. That style doesn't suit you at all. Come on, it will be fun. Maybe we can go out together after. You can show me some of the sights of Omicron."

"No, that's quite impossible, I have to get up early and go to work tomorrow," Diana insisted, taking another step toward the couch without realizing it. Despite her outlandish appearance and behavior, there was something so lively about the woman. She seemed to radiate a vitality and warmth.

"Well, aren't you going to at least offer me a little something before you send me away into the night?" she asked, pouting and tilting her head to one side.

"I don't have anything to offer...except coffee or tea." Diana thought she knew what the woman was suggesting and she didn't like the idea.

"Well, guess what, I do! Come on, let's get high together, just like in the old days."

The woman pulled something from the beaded red purse by her side, a small white cylinder. She withdrew another larger cylinder, a shiny red plastic one that matched her outfit. When she struck the red cylinder with her thumb, it produced a tiny flame. Holding the flame to one end of the white cylinder, she leaned forward, put the other end in her mouth and appeared to pull on it. A thin trail of smoke rose into the room as the white cylinder caught fire and began to smolder.

"What are you doing?" Diana asked with alarm. "Stop it!"

The woman exhaled loudly and more smoke appeared, billowing about her face. "It's called Mary Jane," she smiled. "It's the latest thing and everyone's doing it. Come on, sit here!" She patted the couch next to her again. "You should try it. It's really great fun!"

It was too much for Diana to bear. "No, I don't want to try it! Just get out of here," she shouted. "Just leave me alone. I *never ever* want to see you again!"

The woman's face fell farther than the first time.

"Well...if that's the way you feel about it!" She looked around for a moment, and then snuffed the burning cylinder out on the glass coffee table. "There," she said, nodding toward it. "In case you ever change your mind and decide to live a little. And you don't need to bother showing me out. I can see the door from here." For some reason Diana could not comprehend, she looked as if she were about to cry.

After the woman strode out of the apartment as swiftly as she had waltzed into it, slamming the door behind her, Diana breathed a sigh of relief. She paced back and forth in the small room, fidgeting, regaining her composure. Then she sat down on the couch at the opposite end from where the woman had been sitting. Without thinking about it, she reached over and felt the other cushion. It was still warm and she pulled her hand away.

She picked up the crumpled white cylinder. She sniffed it and made a face. It smelled just terrible! Burnt and sweet at the same time. Why would anyone want to breathe smoke?

Rising and crossing to the microkitchen, she dropped the cylinder into a plastic bag and sealed it. She returned with a damp sponge and wiped the glass coffee table clean. She rinsed out the sponge and dried her hands. Then she called the local Guardener Station and reported the woman for possession of what was no doubt an illegal drug.

As she prepared for bed, Diana thought about how good that had made her feel, and how much she looked forward to going to the Station the next day, turning the illegal drug over and explaining everything.

Before retiring, she took her regular sleeping tablet. Now she could get a decent night's rest and be ready for work in the morning.

The sun dominated her world completely. As it moved from one flat horizon to the other, it seemed to be searing the sky in half. She crouched amid the dirt, the plants, the evenly spaced rows, hunched and moving forward. The other men and women scattered about her did the same. In every direction the perfectly level fields seemed to stretch on forever, the thin horizon broken here and there by clusters of the low blocky buildings in which they lived. They moved from one building to another depending on which field they were sowing or harvesting.

How long had she been here...months?...years? Time had little meaning when every day was much the same. Her hands, once beautiful, had at first blistered and then grown hard and callused. Her hair was stringy and dry. Her back and legs ached, an ache so constant, so daily, it had become an accepted part of existence. Like the searing sun. Like the sentries that watched her every move from her first waking breath in the morning to the exhausted sighs that carried her into sleep at night.

The sentries stood before them and behind them and around them. Blank-faced men in khaki. Burnt out brutish men whose conditioning had somehow misfired. They were another irrelevancy. Sentries? When there was no escape, nowhere to run beyond the world that had sent and sentenced them here except into the Dead Lands.

She barely knew any longer what it was that she picked and stuffed into the sack that she dragged by her side. It no longer mattered. She knew they must have machines to do this work. They had machines for everything else. This was her punishment for being herself, for refusing to submit to their laws and their ways.

They had taken away her books, her music and her plants. They had taken away her lover and her life. She no longer had a name, only a number that she was expected to know and respond to as if it were a name. They had offered to condition her, to wash her mind clean and to fill it up again with their lies, to make her a different person, one suited to the needs of the State. At first they had asked her every month. How many times had she refused? Enough so they now had stopped asking her at all. They had written her off completely. The stubbornness in her would not die and she knew it would be the death of her. She would not become some other person of their creation. Yet now they had succeeded in turning her into a different person anyway.

Late in the evenings, before an exhausted sleep claimed her in the crowded dormitory, the thought of death sometimes opened before her like a cool well of rest, a place where they could punish her no longer. Yet there were other nights when memories of her past life carried her into the brief safety and shelter of dreams. And then morning would come again too soon and she would rise with the others and repeat the deadening routine.

She was glancing up, wiping the sweat from her brow, when it happened. Swiftly. Almost in complete silence.

She saw them beyond the ragged ring of guards. They seem to sprout out of the earth like the plants all about them. Wild men, bearded savages. Dark and half-naked. They wore only the tattered remnants of clothes or furs that looked like the skin of animals. A few carried guns. Most were armed with thick sticks and crude axes and long knives.

These intruders moved with a surety she had never seen before. The slow-witted sentries, despite their superior weapons, did not have a chance. They fell nearly as a man without a single shot being fired, without a cry of warning sounded.

The intruders then regrouped at one end of the field, moving with a precision that belied their savage appearance. A giant of a man, bearded and with a dark visage, stepped forth from the group and approached the workers, still

271

crouched in the fields, half expecting that they would be the next victims of these savage apparitions.

"Come with us!" the man shouted. "Join us. Free your-selves from this slavery and leave it behind forever!"

With one long heavily muscled arm he pointed across the flat fields in the direction of the Dead Lands, which apparently were not so dead after all.

A few of the workers were standing now, staring dumbly into the distance. Josie stood too. Bewildered. Then another man separated himself from the group at the end of the field and began coming toward them, directly toward her.

At first she didn't recognize him. His hair was longer, hanging about his shoulders. The lines of his face were more deeply etched. From a distance it was the eyes that she knew first, their strange blue contradiction against his dark complexion and hair. How could she have ever thought that his face lacked character? If it once had, that was no longer the case.

Forgetting the pain in her legs, she began running toward him. Out of the corners of her vision, she could see that others were also rising from the fields to follow.

Dr. Edward Edmunson was home from another long day at the Virtual Vacation Center. The work wasn't hard, mostly routine, except when some client inexplicably resisted the pleasures the vacation had to offer. The hours were long because they always seemed to be a bit understaffed these days. And granted, as of late, despite the constant refinements they were making to each scenario, there seemed to be more incidents of those who did not adjust well to the pleasures of the vacation or to confronting reality in its aftermath.

Edmunson had eaten a tasteless salad at a chain café, and then, shunning the glideways, had chosen to walk home to his luxury bachelor conapt. He'd been feeling a bit logy as of late, and he thought the exercise might do him good. Single, and with a G-19 rating, he could afford excellent accommodations. He had spent his life dedicated to his work and it had paid off. His apartment was not only a new one for him, he was its first occupant. As he passed down the immaculate streets with their tasteful landscaping and changing pastel illuminations, he found it hard to believe that only months before a slum had blighted this entire area.

Now, standing in front of his bathroom mirror, Edmunson peeled off his dermask for the night and carefully applied it to its holder so that it would not lose shape. He then washed his face thoroughly from top to bottom with a soap he had bought on the medical black market. Although it was said to have special curative properties, he never expected it to help much. It was a ritual for him, something to try to believe in.

Edmunson didn't have to look at his unmasked face in the mirror and he seldom did. He'd seen the grotesquerie of himself, the scars from the destruct incident, often enough to know them by heart. Fourteen people had been killed and he'd been lucky to escape with his life, even with the injuries he'd sustained. The three corrective surgeries had mended his arm, and leg, and broken ribs. They rarely bothered him anymore. But his face was still far too disfigured so that anyone would trust him as a Doctor unless he was wearing a mask.

Bruce Boston is the author of forty-five books and chapbooks, including the novel *Stained Glass Rain* and the best-of fiction collection *Masque of Dreams*. His work has appeared in hundreds of publications and received a number of awards, most notably, a Pushcart Prize, the Bram Stoker Award, the *Asimov's* Readers' Award, the Rhysling Award and the Grand Master Award of the Science Fiction Poetry Association. He lives in Ocala, Florida with his wife, writer-artist Marge Simon. Visit his website at http://bruceboston.com/.